Susan Hudson Chellis was raised in the Lowcountry of South Carolina. She attended Bishop England High School and then graduated from the MUSC School of Allied Health. After working for a Charleston surgeon, she received a scholarship and attended The College of Charleston. She married her husband, Stephen, and moved to Summerville, SC. Susan's previous novel, *The Kitchen Table*, took place in Charleston, SC, or the Holy City as referred to by the locals. Her latest book, *The Four Poster Bed*, takes place in Ireland and England. While travelling with her grandparents, when she was eighteen, she fell in love with Ireland. She loved listening to her grandmother's tales about her country of birth and hopes that her readers will do the same.

Susan Hudson Chellis

The Four-Poster Bed

AUSTIN MACAULEY PUBLISHERS™
LONDON • CAMBRIDGE • NEW YORK • SHARJAH

Ordering Information:
Quantity sales: special discounts are available on quantity purchases by corporations, associations, and others. For details, contact the publisher at the address below.

Publisher's Cataloging-in-Publication data
Hudson Chellis, Susan
The Four-Poster Bed

ISBN 9781647502522 (Paperback)
ISBN 9781647502515 (Hardback)
ISBN 9781647502539 (ePub e-book)

Library of Congress Control Number: 2020908967

www.austinmacauley.com/us

First Published (2020)
Austin Macauley Publishers LLC
40 Wall Street, 28th Floor
New York, NY 10005
USA

mail-usa@austinmacauley.com
+1 (646) 5125767

Chapter 1

It seemed like the screams went on all night, at first being far apart and then closer and closer until they were continuous. Brady put his head on the kitchen table and put his hand over his ears. His heart pounded so that he could hear it pounding in his head and then, the screaming suddenly stopped. He heard the baby cry; finally, his child was here. Maureen's pain started last night at around ten and continued all the next day. Her cousin, Claire, came down as soon as she received word that Maureen was in labor. Brady was up all night, waiting for the sound of his child's cries and when they finally came, he could not stand the excitement. He quickly rose and ran into the room. His wife still looked like she was in pain. He stood and looked. "We're not finished here; wait outside, Brady!" The child was wrapped in a blanket next to his wife but she still acted as if she was in so much pain. He wanted to pick the child up but he knew Claire's temper, so he went out of the bedroom door to wait, again. For what seemed like an eternity, he leaned against the wall and tried to listen but with his wife crying along with the baby, he could hardly make out what was going on.

"Maureen, no, no, Maureen! Oh my God, no!" Brady ran into the room, only to witness his wife slumped over the side of the bed. She was covered in blood-soaked sheets. "I can't stop it, the blood keeps on coming. God forgive me, I don't know what else to do."

Brady picked his wife up and held her in his arms, rocking her back and forth. "Maureen, come on now, give me a wee sign; please, God, bring her back to me." But as loud as he was begging, his baby girl's cries were louder. Claire was trying her best to attend to both of them until Brady stopped and put Maureen's lifeless body down on the bed. His hands slowly moved Maureen's auburn hair away from her face and covered her with the quilt her ma had made for her. He sat in the old rocker next to the bed until the sun went down, over the hills behind his cottage. Claire had taken the child out of the room and put her in the cradle; she knew to let Brady alone with his wife. She tended to the child in the cradle and sent word to the parish priest.

Claire went into the dark room and saw Brady still sitting in the old rocker. "Brady, Father Fagin is here; he is waiting outside."

Claire lit the gas lantern and asked Father Fagin to come in. He put his hand on Brady's shoulder, "She's with the angels now, Brady. She's at peace." Brady got up from his chair went to say something to the old priest but held his tongue. He walked out of the room as Father Fagin was putting the oils on her forehead in the sign of a cross.

After leaving Maureen's side, Brady went over to his daughter and slowly removed the soft woolen blanket. He stared down at her small, fragile body. Her skin was pale pink as if to let the world know she was a girl, and while she had a small amount of hair, it was clear she was her mother's child. He wrapped the blanket and picked her up gently. The movement woke the sleeping child up and she opened her small eyes as if to look into his eyes. Her eyes were blue but as he looked deep, he saw flickers of green.

Brady had known Maureen from as far back as he could remember. He remembered the first time he saw her. She was a little bit of a thing but always seemed to have more strength than most girls he had known. Her family's farm was down the way from his parents' land. Brady's family had been in the lumber business in Ireland for generations. There were times when all was good and other times when the struggle was such, that one would give up—but, the O'Quinns were not the type to give up. With Brady being the eldest, the business was left to him. His younger brother had died from influenza, along with his sister. Their deaths seemed to lose his parents' zest for living and it was his father's decision to give Brady the business. The business seemed to flourish with Brady taking over the mill. After the potato famine and the war, Ireland seemed to prosper. With the prosperity, the lumber business grew. Brady hired more men and poured himself into the mill but in the evenings, he sat alone. One day while walking through the forest, he came to the open meadow and rested on a rock for a bit. He sat there quietly, taking in the grand Irish landscape until a horse with a rider came barreling by him, just missing him. As he went to scroll the rider, he noticed the girl riding the mare. Her long, red hair was flowing in the wind as her legs were wrapped tightly around the horse. He knew who she was and wasn't surprised it was her. It had been a while since he had seen her around. When he went over to County Clare, he looked for her as he passed her farm but lately, he never saw her. The next day, he went down to the pub for a stout and ran into her brother, Michael. "Do ya know your sis nearly ran me down? Tell her to mind herself."

Michael laughed, "She's a fearsome thing, don't cha know, Brady!" He told Brady she had gone to Dublin to help her aunt and was just back. "She's down at the butcher getting some mutton for supper." Brady finished his stout and walked in the direction of Rooney's butcher shop. They almost knocked each other out as they hit heads going in and out the door. It was a joke that kept on coming up after they married, some months later. Their spooning was nerve-racking for both of them; all they wanted was to be together. They would go along with the usual courtship rituals but then, they would sneak off and meet in the meadow. After they were married, Brady would rush home to see his new bride and on many occasions, would make a visit for lunch, also. He couldn't get enough of her and her of him.

When she told him about her pregnancy, he could not be happier. "You know, we have male children more often in my family. I can prove it by my six brothers. I will give you a brood of boys!"

As Brady sat holding this small child, he wondered how he could go on. His wife's body was being washed by the parish women and blessed by Father Fagin. He would bury her in the meadow that they both shared. There were people moving around him; women were cooking in his wife's kitchen and others, going in and out of their bedroom. Women were attending to the child and getting the small thatched house ready for the wake. Brady paid no heed as he sat, staring into the coal fire. The days went by as if he were in a daze. He wanted them all to leave and after some time, they did. There was no trace of his wife; her clothes were removed as well as her toiletries. The quilt her mother made for her was gone, with the reasoning being the traces of blood on it. Her only essence was the little girl he held in his arms.

The small child was being cared for by the woman down the way. She would come in the day and stay until the late evening. When she arrived, it would be with her goat tied to the wagon. "The child will be fine on goats' milk for now. The redhead that she is will not get the bumps from the goat's milk." Brady had no idea about the bumps she was talking about and had doubts about the old women remedy, but he did notice how well the child thrived. Before he knew it, she was gurgling as she looked at him. Her eyes turned greener as her hair turned to a darker red.

Weeks went by before he gave her a name. The parish priest was at his door every other day, about getting her baptized. "Your child will be in purgatory forever if you don't baptize her." He knew he had to name her but none of the names seemed to fit her until he came upon a small box in Maureen's wooden chest. The chest was one of the things she brought from her parents' home. He had never really looked in it until now, for he always felt that was hers and hers alone. It was the box that she opened on their first night together. He remembered her opening the small chest and taking out this wooden box—the very same one he held in his hand.

As he opened the creaky old box, he saw the silver coins she tried to give him on their wedding night. "This is my dowry, Brady." He told her to keep it in the box until it will be needed. At first, she seemed hurt but accepted his decision. The coins were still there, along with a small book wrapped in ribbons. As he carefully opened the book, he noticed her handwriting along with her drawings. She had drawings on some of the pages of her garden that she planted along the side of the house—of the tree that they put their names on—by the small meadow. She had written about the love she had for him and how happy she was with the child moving inside her. Brady sat by his hearth with his face in his hands and wept. It wasn't until early the next morning, that he continued to read, and discovered the name she had chosen for her child. There were several boys' names, one being Shamus after the brother Brady lost; then, he noticed what she wrote down for a girl. *If God gives me a female child, I would like to name her Anna Catherine and call her Anna Cate in honor of my dear grandmother, whom I loved so much.*

"Well," Brady put the small book down and picked up his little girl, "Your ma has named you Anna Cate so you shall be named so." The child was baptized such and the priest slept well that night.

Brady's days went by quickly after that. He hired another woman from town to take care of Anna Cate during the day while he saw to her in the evenings. When the woman got ill, she sent her daughter, Fiona, to care for the child. The girl favored her mother in general. She was dark of hair and brown of eyes and what Brady would call "sturdy looking." The complete opposite of Maureen but she took good care of Anna Cate and seemed to generally care for her. At one point, Anna Cate was burning up with the fever and it was Fiona who stayed by her side throughout the night. Brady was beside himself, he could not lose her too. Fiona washed the child's body down, to cool her fever, and kept her drinking water throughout the long night. Brady didn't know if it was gratitude or pure loneliness but he asked Fiona to marry him. He knew he did not love her but he needed someone in his life and she seemed to care for him. Before long, she was pregnant with a child and due that December. Anna Cate was now four years old and excited about having a brother or sister. When Fiona delivered, it was a complete change from Maureen. She complained of a backache and within an hour, delivered a robust baby boy. To Brady, his son looked like he was twice the size of Anna Cate when she was a wee infant. Before he knew it, Fiona was pregnant again and soon delivered another male child. But as the years went by, Fiona's care of Anna Cate had turned. There was a constant mention of Brady's attention to Anna Cate and not the two boys. "I thought you would be happy that I gave you two sons but all ya do, Brady, is give your attention to your girl child." At first, Brady ignored her and thought her to be a silly woman but then he noticed the way her treatment was to Anna Cate. The child was made to do most of the chores around the house, and when she was not doing that, she would raise her voice to the point that Brady would rise from his chair. He started taking her on his trips to visit merchants in the other counties. She was a well-mannered child and easy to travel with. She asked questions about everything and he explained with detailed answers but when they got home, she paid dearly for it, more dearly than Brady knew. Fiona knew she was going too far when Brady was around, so she waited until after he left for the mill, that her true wrath came out. Anna Cate's only salvation was at school. She was enrolled in the convent school in town. During the week, she would spend some nights at the convent with the nuns. They seemed to engulf her in kindness, mainly because her mother had been a former student there. They were her protectors along with her dad and one point, she had thought about becoming a nun.

Fiona was pregnant again but this time, the pregnancy was hard on her. Her boys were demanding and were "rough and tumble," as Brady put it. As Fiona complained, more and more, Brady asked Anna Cate to spend her nights at home more. This proved to be one of the hardest times for Anna Cate. The boys had sensed their mother's feelings toward Anna Cate and it escalated, more and more. At one point, Anna Cate asked them to stop running through the house; the boys stopped, started to laugh and pushed her against the wall. Surprised by them, Brady was standing by the front door and witnessed it all. He grabbed the boys by the back of their shirts and took them outside to the woodpile. Even with Fiona's objections, he spanked them with his belt.

Anna Cate stayed at the convent during her schooling and spent most of her time with her father after that. Brady did not feel comfortable leaving her with Fiona. As she grew, she was the image of her mother and was noticed by the workers at the mill. She became close to her cousins and would spend time with her mother's family, from time to time. It was on one of these occasions, that she met George Sheedy. He was a handsome, tall boy with dark, thick hair and blue eyes. Whenever she was around him, he was constantly teasing her and making her laugh. She was seventeen now and certainly noticing boys. Brady would take her still, on his trips to other counties and it was on this particular trip, that she met Patrick Finnerty. He was a man in his early twenties who built furniture for a living. He bought wood from Brady on occasion. Patrick—Paddy as they called him—was building bookshelves for the county building. He needed a lot of lumber and wanted to talk with Brady about it. Paddy could not take his eyes off of Anna Cate; he had trouble paying attention to Brady. He asked them to stay for dinner that evening, and Brady agreed.

Paddy's house was one of the larger houses in the county. His parents had died in an accident and left him the house and farm. The last thing Paddy wanted was to farm; he hated it as a child and hated it even more, now. He wanted to create and liked working with wood. As Brady and Anna Cate went into the home, they were surprised by the home. Paddy had built furniture throughout the house and added bookshelves and cabinets to the rooms. The parlor had beautiful, dark wood shelves, up to the tall ceilings, while the kitchen had cabinets built in each corner and around the washbasin. The icebox even had a cabinet built above it. As they sat down in the parlor, a woman came in from the kitchen. She was, Brady guessed, Paddy's spinster sister. She appeared to be much older than Paddy but had the same features as her brother. Both had golden-brown wavy hair and hazel eyes. Paddy introduced his sister, Ilene, to Brady and Anna Cate. She extended her hand and smiled welcomingly. You could tell she had been a very handsome woman at one time. During their dinner, it was apparent Paddy was taken with Anna Cate.

The next morning, Fiona asked Anna Cate about her dinner at Paddy Finnerty's home. "Oh, it was lovely, he had a beautiful home and we also met his sister. She seemed very nice."

Fiona saw it as a chance, "You know you're of marrying age and you shouldn't be a burden on your father. At least the boys earn their keep at the mill." Anna Cate looked at her with a puzzled look; she had never felt that her father thought as her being a burden on him. "Oh dear, he would never say so, to hurt your feelings but he does tell me so," said Fiona.

The rest of the day, Anna Cate went about her business. She helped Fiona clean the house from top to bottom. "My goodness, what's got into the lass, Fi?" Fiona just laughed. The following week, Paddy paid the mill a visit though he had not needed any lumber; his sights were on other things. As he drove up to the mill, he passed Brady's house and saw Anna Cate talking with a young man. The man was tall in stature with brown hair. He looked to be in his late teens or early twenties. Brady's house was a small one-story white house with a thatched roof. It was plain in detail and small for a man such as Brady. Paddy's plan was to feel out how Brady felt about him starting to see Anna Cate. He thought that if he was indifferent to the courtship, he would know at the beginning. His chance came when he was alone with Brady. They were in Brady's office as Paddy tried to bring up the subject. For some reason, he never could bring himself to directly come out and ask Brady. "Man, are you trying to say something, get on with it!"

"I'd like to court your daughter; have permission to start spooning."

Brady was taken aback and could not speak for a while. His thoughts went to Maureen; for some reason, he never wanted for her leave. He knew it would come someday, but not now. "I will have to speak to my daughter," Brady said.

"Brady, you know I am a prosperous man. I know the age difference but I promise I will take good care of her, you have my word."

Brady had hoped she would marry someone close to the mill and he would see her often. Paddy lived clear over in the next county and it would be a day's travel to visit.

He would leave it up to Anna Cate; she was old enough to make her own decision. For days, he contemplated speaking with her but it never seemed the right time, until Fiona said something about Paddy. Brady had confided in her about Paddy's request and Fiona knew how to get the conversation started. "Brady, don't you have something to speak to Anna Cate about?" As he sat in his old rocker and stared at the coal-burning hearth, the lost feeling he had once felt, came over him again. It had been so long ago, that he felt that pain in his heart; the same pain he had some times, before sitting in his same old rocking chair. He glared at his wife with dagger eyes; the same wife he had married because of that deep loneliness he had felt, the same wife he had tried to love but could not. She had been a thorn in his side that got deeper as the years went by and now, she revealed what she was trying to accomplish.

"My dear Anna Cate, Paddy Finnerty has asked permission to start courting you. I know this is something that I am to decide but I would like to know your heart about this." She was surprised by the request. He had only met her once, and she could not see how his feelings could be so inspired. She looked at her father who was staring into the fire and then looked up at Fiona. Fiona's lips were tight—as if she was smirking—as she nodded her head. Was she really that much of a burden on her father?

And so the spooning began. The first was a carriage ride along the meadow, along with Brady's good friend, Frank O'Connor. The couple would be accompanied by Frank for the first three outings. Anna Cate was uncomfortable and Paddy felt too old to be spooning. Although he was only six years older than Anna Cate, he felt spooning itself was outdated for the year 1928. He asked Brady if they could forego the usual engagement time length and plan the wedding. He stated that his business was picking up and he needed to devote more time at home. Though this tugged at Brady's heart, with Fiona pushing to have the wedding, Brady agreed. Fiona seemed excited for Anna Cate and offered to help with every detail.

The wedding took place on a warmer than usual day of July. All of the town's people were invited; well, those who were members of the local parish and those few who came from County Clare. Since Anna Cate had no sisters,

Ilene stood in. The reception was short as Paddy wanted to return home before dark. So, Anna Cate kissed her Dad goodbye and left with Paddy Finnerty. Brady held back the tears so as to not be noticed but in his heart, he knew he had lost dear Anna Cate. She was the first one he wanted to see after a long day's work; she was the caring that he did not have from Fiona; she was a piece of his heart.

****

The ride back to County Clare seemed long and frightening to Anna Cate. No one except her girlfriend at school had given her a clue about this night. What her friends said had almost made her ask to go back home. "You're like County Clare, Cate."

She looked at him, puzzled, "Ya know, Paddy, my name is Anna Cate, not Cate."

Paddy laughed, "It's too much for me mouth to say so we'll just call you Cate. Ilene and I talked about it."

Anna Cate was true to the saying of a red-haired woman temper, she swelled up and she started protesting. "Well, ya know, Paddy Finnerty, my name is my own and always has been; I don't need you to change it for me. You'd better call me by it or I'll not answer to you." But Paddy just laughed and ignored her plea.

As they drove to the house, he got out first and helped her out of the new auto he had just purchased. He picked her up without saying a word and she grasped onto his shoulder. It was the closest she had been, even with all the courting. Paddy put her down quickly and kissed her hard. She could feel his breathing increase, so she stood back and asked him to wait. "Paddy, please give me a minute, I need to use the loo." He mumbled some words she could not hear and took her bag. That night, her anticipation of what was to come was short-lived. For something that was so anticipated, Anna Cate thought it was too short of a thing to be worried about it, for so long. Before long, Paddy was snoring away and she could finally sleep.

Upon waking the next morning, she sat up and had to remember where she was. Paddy was gone and she was in the house alone, or so she thought. As she went into the kitchen, Ilene had prepared breakfast. "I have made you eggs, sausage, and potatoes with liver pudding; sit and eat your breakfast. You just let me know if you want anything else, Cate." Anna Cate looked at her and thanked her for breakfast. She thought not to start off on the wrong path with Ilene. So, she quietly ate her breakfast. "I'll be going to tend to the chickens; ya see the water pan over there for the cleaning up." She wondered if she could go home but she had made a vow before God to love and obey. She missed her Dad and needed him to confide in. He was the only one who she could talk to. She had learned through the years that Fiona did not feel for her the same way she had when she was small. Cate started in the bedroom first. She had brought a quilt from her home that had been made by the women at the parish. There were several things that her mother had, that Paddy saved for her. One was a large wooden box. In the box were some of her mother's personal papers. There was a small book with a drawing of the garden they once had next to their house. Her mother kept a journal of sorts. Sometimes, the days followed one after the other and other times, she would not write for months at a time. Cate took her wedding dress, the same her mother had worn on her day, and placed it in the box. She was grateful to Paddy for bringing it in, the night before, along with some of her other things. Cate started moving things around, put her clothes in the closet and rearranged Paddy's trouser and shoes; tables were moved and curtains were taken down. "What are you doing?" asked Ilene. "I'm attending to my room," Cate said. "Well, this is Paddy's room and Paddy's house," shouted Ilene. But Cate just went on ignoring her.

Dinner that night presented itself in sheer silence. Paddy sat leaning over his food as if to shovel it in. He had picked up the discontent the moment he entered the parlor. He was used to his sister's moods but his bride seemed as moody as she was. It wasn't until weeks later, that he encountered what some would call a catfight like no other. Trying to surprise Cate one day by bringing her flowers, he walked into the kitchen and saw his sister Ilene and Cate on the floor, pulling each other's hair. Cate was covered in what looked like flour and Ilene looked like someone threw milk on her. They were yelling and rolling around on the floor. "My God, women, what in the almighty are ya doing?" They both got up as fast as they could and loudly began speaking about what the other had done. When the air cooled and both were cleaned up, he sat them down for a civil conversation. Cate had felt this was her kitchen and hers alone but it had been Ilene's all the past years. Paddy remembered what his mother had told him when he was a tot of a boy, "A home can only support one woman." He knew there would be trouble. Ilene was not what some would think—she was a spinster, that was a fact but she had been betrothed to someone in her early years. There was the misfortune of the Great War that took his almighty soul and she never regained her vigor again. Paddy knew that if his house were to be calm, he would have to deal with this. After all, as the saying went, "No worse thing than a bad-tempered woman," and he had two of them. He explained to Ilene the best he could. He wanted this to work and he knew if Cate was unhappy, he would be also. Ilene lived in the house down the path, a house he built for her after his parents died. It was small, in comparison but comfortable. Ilene was older than Paddy by five years. When their parents died, Ilene became the caregiver. As with the Irish legal system, Paddy became the heir to his parent's property. The main house on the property was a two-story thatched-roof home. The home had wood-floors made of reeds wood and had electricity installed weeks earlier, before Paddy and Cate's wedding. The home Ilene lived in was still without electricity. This caused a resentment that started with Ilene and only added to the jealousy she felt. Cate was used to new conveniences, as her Dad had it for several years at the lumber mill but when Paddy went to visit the mill, he felt Cate should have the same with her new home. Paddy was set in his ways as to his daily life. He had relied on Ilene to take care of the small livestock such as feeding the chickens, pigs, and tending to the garden. She was an expert to such but Cate had never tended before, so he left the duties to Ilene and let Cate have her small garden next to the house.

For a time now, things seemed to calm down and the small bickering was few and far between. Having only been married for a few months, Cate suspected that she was with child. There was no sickness but just a tiredness that consumed her. She hesitated to bring this to Paddy's attention until she was sure. She felt that Ilene was not the one to tell, and no one except Fiona to speak with. She asked Paddy if he would take her to visit with her father. At first, Paddy took it as if she were unhappy with her new home but she persisted, so he planned on a Saturday to make the trip. As always, Brady was glad to see her and as always, Fiona was absent of response when they arrived. Cate had trouble getting Fiona alone but when she finally did, Fiona confirmed what she had suspected. Cate wanted to tell Paddy first but that afternoon, Fiona blurted out Cate's condition. "Well, Brady, you were old when we were wed but now you are to be a grandfather."

At first, Brady and Paddy looked at each other while Cate looked at Fiona, surprised. "Well, I really wanted to tell Paddy myself but I guess you did it instead!" While Paddy sat without a word said, Brady smiled at his daughter. He pulled out his best brandy and offered a toast.

On the ride home, Paddy sat in silence. "I'm sorry, Paddy, I wanted to tell you myself. I asked Fiona to not speak of it, I just wanted to be sure before I told you and felt with her having been with a child, she would know if I was."

Paddy stopped along the roadside and kissed Cate. "When do we expect the wee little one?" he asked. Cate told him around the end of December, she thought.

As it was the way of living in County Clare, Cate would have her baby at home with the help of the local women. While Paddy had made some of the furnishings in their home, their bed was the same one his parents had used. The bed was small for two adults and at the time, was uncomfortable for Paddy. He vowed that his child would be born in a bed built by him. The next week, he went back to visit Brady and inquired about buying some wood for the post of the bed. He wanted to find wood that would carve easily and knew Brady was able to get his hands on other kinds of wood than that native to Ireland. Brady put him in touch with a man by the name of Paul O'Connor who collected old building materials. Paddy made his way to Mr. O'Connor's barn on the outskirts of Dublin. The man was a rough old man who was not well kept and had lines on his face, that indicated he had lived past his time. After rummaging through piles of old boards, the old man guided Paddy to the back of the building and pointed to six posts that were some ten feet high. Paddy could tell the posts had been painted at one time and were in bad shape. "I found these in Dublin; the building was being torn down. They say they came from South America and are a Mahogany in wood. I can sell them to you but they will cost you, they're solid." Paddy was not familiar with the wood but knew any wood could be carved. When he found out the price, he started to walk away. He knew he did not have that much to spend and started to leave. "Young man, do you always give up so easily?" the old man turned and laughed.

"I do not require six columns, only four; they are old and need work..." Paddy said. When he left, he had agreed to pay half the amount of what was first asked and to pick up the post when the transport was found.

The entire way home, he had his hand to paper, to design what he was going to carve. The excitement welled in him. His mind could not decide as to which design to use. The posts were tall and would have to be cut in order to fit in the room. He wanted the bed to reflect something about Cate—something unique to her—so he would study her as she moved about her day. Her favorite past time was working in the garden; she loved flowers and was proud of the entire garden produce. Though she loved the flowers in her garden, her heart was in the heather that grew in abundance in this land of Ireland. The color was breathtaking and brought pleasure to her heart. Paddy thought, somehow, he would bring this small flower into the weave of his carving of the mahogany post. As soon as he finished his supper, he was off to the work shed. He knew his time was limited, for he wanted to finish in time for the child's arrival.

Time had somehow helped the underlying rivalry between Ilene and Cate. The two had begun to work together. While Ilene had the experience of keeping a house, Cate would ask Ilene questions that she already knew the answer to, in order to make her feel useful. The two were trying their best to make life easier for Paddy, for they both loved him in their own way. All was peaceful and quiet which allowed Paddy to make use of his time, until one day when all hell broke loose. He heard screaming as he had never heard before. It was Ilene throwing things out of the front door of Paddy's house. "Where's my dowry?" She was so upset, that Paddy was afraid she'd throw something Cate's way and hurt her. Pieces of small furniture were flying out the front door, along with some of Cate's things. "She's taken my silver coins. I went into the chest and my dowry is gone! She took my coins!"

Paddy knew this day was coming, he just did not expect it so soon. "Hold your horses Ilene; I took the coins, not Cate. I needed them for something and will pay you back when you need them."

Ilene started to cry, "Oh, that's it, isn't it, you think I may never wed. You think I am too plain for any gent. I'll show you, Paddy." Ilene stormed away and went back to her cottage. Paddy thought that surely she would get over it but she stayed in for days, before emerging from her place. She no longer came to eat with them and only spoke when spoken to. On one occasion, when Paddy did try to speak with her, she turned and walked away. He threw his hands up as if to give up but she spoke as he was walking away. "Do you mind speaking to me about just what you did with them, Paddy?"

He knew that if he told her, it would just make things worse. "I told you, it was for my trade; that's all you need to know."

A calmness came back to the Finnerty home as Cate began to get heavy with the child. The tension was still there but Ilene stayed mostly to herself. Frances O'Brady, the town's midwife, came up to check on Cate's condition. "Your time will be soon," she said, being a woman of few words. To Cate, there were no words of reassurance or for that matter, no instructions. While visiting her father, she asked Fiona some questions but she had none either. In the back of Cate's mind was what had happened to her mother. She knew from the time she was small that her mother had died in childbirth while having her. She also knew that the common thought was that one would follow the mother when it came to matters of birthing a child. If your mother had a long labor, you would too. It was a worry she put out of her mind. To Cate, when times were trying for her, she chose not to dwell on them. She did this with her dealing with Fiona, and then Ilene.

One evening, she was sitting by the hearth, embroidering a blanket for the baby, when Paddy came in from the work shed. He was grinning from ear to ear. "My darling, I have a surprise for you." Cate started to giggle, for Paddy was always bringing her flowers or something new he had made for the house. He turned her chair around to face the front door. "Sit, my lady and behold!" When Paddy came back, his handyman from the town was with him. They opened the door wide and went outside. When they returned, they came in with a large piece of furniture. At first, Cate did not recognize exactly what it was.

It could hardly fit through the door and was in sections. "I've made you a bed, a bed for your birthing of the wee one, Cate."

As they brought in each piece separately, Cate wondered how it was all going to fit in the room. Their bedroom wasn't that small but the posts of the bed were so large, they touched the ceiling. There were eight sections of the bed. Paddy had made them fit like a puzzle.

It was something to behold, for Cate. From the time they were married, Cate began to love him more and more each day, for she had such a soft heart. At first, the age difference was a bit hard to get used to but she found him to be such a good-natured soul. He kept her safe and warm and Cate knew he would be a good dad for her child. From the first night she laid her head on the bed, a peace fell over her. She tried to talk to Paddy about a dream she had but knew she would never be able to explain it. She had dreamed as if she was floating on the clouds in the heavens, and then the realizations hit her as she suddenly started to fall but in an instant, she fell softly into a soft cloud that engulfed her. Cate woke up in a cold sweat, only to realize that her time was upon her. Paddy had gotten up early that morning to go down to Clare to deliver some goods and she was alone. She was sure that her time was not for a while yet, and had assured him that she would be fine. After all, Ilene was just down the way. She tried to get up from the bed and stopped as she noticed the blood beneath her. Her thoughts went to the worry she had possessed since she learned of her own birth. She picked up a blanket and put it between her legs and made her way out the door and down the path. The morning was cool and damp and with her bare feet, she was careful not to slip on the moss. Her gate was somewhat off as she made her way over the stones. "Ilene, it's Cate, please, Ilene! My time is upon me." Ilene, hearing the banging, ran to the door. At the sight of her gown, she knew Cate was having problems. "My god, girl, let's get you back in bed and I'll get Mrs. McCaulley from the village."

Ilene was able to get Cate up the meadow and over the stone fence but as she opened the door to her bedroom, she was taken aback by the massive structure. Cate stood at a standstill as the pain began again. "And what may this be, Cate?" Answering in between breaths, Cate told her of Paddy's gift to her and how he had been working on the bed since they found out about the child. It wasn't long before Ilene put the timing together with her missing dowry money. "So, this is what my coins paid for; my own brother, doing this to me. I'll be going down to get Mrs. McCaulley. Get yourself on your bed, Cate." Ilene went back to her cottage and started to pack. She packed three bags, all that had meant so much to her. She put on her hat and coat and started down the path to the bus stop.

Paddy came home late that night and was of no fear about Cate until he saw the front door open. He could hear her cries when he went through the front door. Running back to the bedroom, his fears took on a panic. Cate was sitting up in the bed, holding on to one of the posts of the bed. She was crying out in pain as she crouched down to her separated legs. "I'll be getting the woman for ya, Cate!"

But when she got her breath about her, she said, "No, Paddy, I know I have no time. You will have to birth me. My child is coming; help me, Paddy. Don't leave me!" Paddy had birthed many of his farm animals but this was different…This was his wife, the woman he loved and cherished. But this was also the woman he had next to him every night but had never seen without her clothes. She was a very modest girl when they were first married and she remained so through their time together. When he lay with her, he did so in the dark and under the coverlet. "Paddy, get something to cut the cord and some blankets. Hurry, Paddy." He ran into the kitchen and fetched what he thought she may need. Her screams became louder and her breathing became labored, "Oh Paddy, please help me, Paddy." Paddy said he would get Mrs. McCaulley but Cate asked him not to leave her. As she screamed again, she strained; he could see the head of his child between her legs…She held her breath and then started to pant and strained again. Cate's head went back down on the bed and she held her thighs with her hands. With another strain, the child's shoulders came out as if they were popping into the world. Paddy held his hands together as he caught the child before she fell to the bed. His callused hands were now holding his little girl—the same hands that had worked so hard on the bed where his wife rested to regain her strength. In those hours of pain, her thoughts were on her mother, and Cate prayed she would not sarcoma to the same end. Cate rested her head on the pillow and thanked God for giving her life to take care of the wee one. Paddy stood down on the bottom of the bed, still holding his daughter in his hands. The moment was one of the most intimate ones the couple had ever had. It created a bond that would do more to unite them, than any other.

"Paddy, give me the child and run down the way and see if you can get Mrs. McCaulley to help me." He gave her the child that was still covered in blood, handed her some blankets and a pail of warm water. As he walked by Ilene's, he noticed her front door open. Her house had been ransacked as if thieves had broken in. At first, he thought harm had come to Ilene but when he saw her bureau opened and her clothes gone from the armoire, he knew she had left.

He went down and fetched Mrs. McCaulley. As they were walking back to Paddy's house, Mrs. McCaulley made the comment that she had seen Ilene at the train station. "Paddy, do ya know, she was in such a fright that her nighties were hanging out of her satchel." Paddy made no comment to her. Mrs. McCaulley had years of experience, she was the one that was called when it came to childbearing and also taking care of the deceased. As she entered the room, the first thing she did was to cut the cord and clean up the afterbirth. She then checked Cate to make sure there was not too much bleeding. "Child, how did you do this by yourself with this being ya first?" Cate smiled and told her that Paddy had brought the child into life. This was not done as the man of the house was not permitted to see his wife, until after the child and mother were presentable to be viewed. As Mrs. McCaulley cleaned the child, Cate voiced her concern as the woman seemed to scrub the skin off the small child. "Oh, my dear, these little ones are tough, you mark my words; she'll be fine." After placing her in the cradle Paddy built, she tended to Cate. She seemed to scrub her as hard as she did the child; she put cleaned linens on the bed and washed the previous ones in boiling water. She then scrubbed them with milk soap to make them soft again. When the child was trying the breast, she left Finnerty's home.

The relationship changed between Paddy and Cate. No more was the nervousness of conversation among them. Whereas before the baby, their lovemaking was during the darkest of the night—usually when only the shadows of their bodies were visible—but now it was not unusual for Paddy to come home during lunch for Cate. Their relationship had changed from the usual serious conversation to one of constant humor. He found laughter in everything about them. They both decided to name their first child after Cate's first mother, and she was christened Maureen Finnerty when she was two weeks old. Cate knew not to take the child out before she was baptized but afterward, the locals from the village were invited to see the child.

Paddy Finnerty had one of the largest homes in the small town. His family had owned the land since recorded records. After Maureen was born, Paddy received a letter from Ilene; she was in Dublin at their Aunt Mary's home. She simply stated that she was fine and the letter would be her last contact with him. He was furious that she left Cate the way she did. Ilene had also stated that she knew now that her dowry money was "in the four-poster bed," she said. Paddy had gotten to the point after what she had done, that he really did not care if he had ever saw her again. Cate was more forgiving than he, "Paddy, you must forgive her, she was upset. You must realize how much those coins meant to her." But Paddy never brought the subject up again. After spending so much time on the bed, he threw himself into his work. He spoke to the people he had put off because of the bed and regained some of their orders while others, he lost. But he persevered and brought in more orders. His work kept him busy for most of the day and some nights too. He hired help to work the farm since Ilene was gone and she was the one who usually attended to the chickens and sheep. Since his acreage was vast, he decided to buy some cattle instead of using the land for planting. His parents had almost lost the farm during the potatoes famine but since they had invested in sheep, the farm was kept in the family.

As soon as Cate and the baby could travel, they went to visit her father. He was waiting for them as they drove up. His smile was ear to ear and as soon as Cate was out of the car, he grabbed his grandchild. "My dear Cate, you have made me the happiest grandpa in the world. I'm so proud, dear girl!" As Cate looked at her, Dad had tears in his eyes. They walked into the house as Fiona sat, staring at the hearth. Cate had not seen her for some time since her Dad was the one to visit them usually. Fiona's hair had since turned gray and she had let it grow without upkeep. The first thing Cate noticed was her hands; her fingers were bent and halfway closed into her hand. Her Dad was at the stove, cooking the supper, while she sat in the wooden rocker. Cate handed the small child to Paddy and went over to help. "Don't be doing that, ya da will do it." But she did not listen to her and started to set the table, while Fiona talked under her breath words that were unclear. When supper was ready, her stepbrother came running in. They sat at the table as if they were shoveling the food into their mouths. Brady seemed annoyed but Fiona seemed to follow the trend. It had been a while since Cate had seen her stepbrothers—they had grown so much. They were tall, with dark hair like their mother's, and big-boned like her. Her Dad was small in stature for a man.

Before leaving that day, Brady held Maureen and sang her the same song he used to sing to Cate. Paddy left them together for a while, for them to talk. "Anna Cate, I was so worried for you when I heard you were with a child."

Cate knew that he was; she could tell when he visited them. "I know, it was on my mind the whole time but for some reason, I knew I would be fine. I prayed to my ma and asked her to watch over me and I felt her with me."

Brady started to cry, "She is with me, too."

Life went on as little Maureen grew and seemed to change as the weeks went by. She was the spitting image of her mother with a head of full red curls and large green eyes but between Paddy's wavy hair and Cate's auburn hair, there wasn't too much of a chance she would end up with anything else, When Maureen was six months old, Cate found herself pregnant again, she was so pleased to be expecting another child. Though she had stepbrothers, growing up, she had always felt like an only child. Even though she got along with her other siblings, she never really felt connected to Fiona's sons. Paddy had built his business to the point of having backorders on his furniture. Along with hiring some men from the village, the farm seemed to prosper also. Paddy had employed an old fellow that had lost his farm during the potato famine. The gentleman's name was Colin McClary and since losing his farm, and his wife's death, he had spent his time with daily visits to the local pub. But Paddy saw something different in the old codger; he knew if given half a chance, he may prove his worth at farming. Colin seemed to somber up, almost immediately upon taking on the new task. Paddy made fit the old shed behind the barn for Colin. He put a wood panel on the wall and enhanced the wood floor for Colin. With a bed and a wood-burning stove, Colin had more comfort than previously, when his nights were spent sleeping in the pub or in friends' barns. On Sunday, Colin had the day off to attend church and spend the rest of his day at the pub with his old friends.

Life seemed to move along smoothly for all in Paddy's life. He thanked God for his wife and family. The prosperity of his business and the farm seemed incidental to him, as compared to just sitting by the hearth in the evening, holding his dear Maureen and watching Cate do her mending. He wondered sometimes about Ilene and there were times when he thought about a trip to Dublin but quickly put it out of his mind, as he remembered about her abandonment of Cate during her labor. Though the parish priest preached about forgiveness, Paddy still held that stubbornness as to not forget her actions. Cate grew larger with this child than she did with Maureen and with that, the old fears came back to her, the fear of her mother's childbirth death. As she was only a month away from delivery, she received a telegram that her stepmother, Fiona, had died. Paddy urged her not to travel but she thought about her dear Dad and had to go. So, Paddy packed them up and traveled in the truck. The roads along the way were not as smooth as he liked but he took his time slowly, to the point of others' constant blowing of their horns. But Paddy was only worried about his Cate. As they drove up to Cate's family home, her Dad was standing outside, as if he'd known she was about to arrive. Cate got out of the truck as soon as it came to a halt and ran over to her Dad. Even though she had seen him every few months since her marriage, she now noticed how her father had aged. His hair was now white and his skin seemed ruddy, with aged wrinkles. He hugged Cate as if not to let her go. It was Paddy that finally spoke, "Brady, I'm so sorry about Fiona."

Brady pulled out his handkerchief to wipe his nose, "Thank you, Paddy, she's been sick for quite a while." That afternoon, the house was filled with people from the town. Brady was a pillar of the community and had people from the adjoining counties that came by. By the end of the evening, Cate was longing to rest and her stomach felt harder than usual. Paddy and Cate spent the night in the room that Cate used as a child. Fiona's boys had moved out of the home long before and only two remained at the lumber yard, still working with Brady. Around two in the morning, Cate woke after a bad dream that she was somewhere in the middle of the ocean. She sat up in the bed and was about to cry out until she became to realize that her water had broke. The only pain she had was in her lower back. She hated to wake Paddy but could not let him sleep in a wet bed. When he woke up, he muttered all the way down to the laundry about traveling so late in her condition. "Paddy, I'm ok; remember, I have done this before."

Cate asked Paddy not to wake the whole house but Paddy knew to get help. He knocked on Brady's door and he opened it in a startle. Brady had been up all night with worry; when he saw Cate, he was only reminded about his dear wife. Cate was so much like his Maureen; she was small in stature and with the same features, with that red hair and green eyes. Cate was so much heavier with the child this time than with her firstborn. Brady got in his truck and drove down to the local village. Unlike some other towns in the county, this one had a doctor. He banged on Dr. O'Quinn's door as hard as he could, "Doc, you have to come, my daughter is with a child and having pains; please, you have to hurry."

Doc gave him a smile, "I'll get my bag and coat and will be right with you."

By the time Brady and Dr. O'Quinn got to the cottage, Cate was having continuous pains. "I'll take over now; you'd best wait in the parlor." Paddy had felt he should be at Cate's side like before but he followed the doctor's instructions. After what only seemed like a short time, the house had the crying of a child going through it. The two men stood up, not with the excitement but more due to the fear in them. The men knew of the history of this house and hoped it would not repeat itself. But when the doctor came out with a smile on his face, relief settled in them. Cate had a round-faced baby boy that looked to be more than a newborn. Doc O'Quinn said it was the largest baby he had delivered. They named him Shamus after Paddy's Dad. He was born with a head full of dark hair and bright blue eyes.

Shamus seemed to have a jolly personality from the beginning. He was such a happy child, even in temperament. Cate's Irish twins were inseparable from then on. They were great playmates and great company for each other.

After the last child, Paddy thought Cate should hold off on another child for a while. She was only 18 years old when they married and even though she seemed to fit motherhood, he still felt that he should give her a rest for a while. Life seemed to ease by, for Paddy and Cate. As the years went by, Cate became more beautiful. She loved her home and grew in love with Paddy more each year. His abilities amazed her as he made handcrafted furniture for some of the elite in Dublin. Orders were placed and Paddy had to hire men to help in. He took two young men from the next county and started to train them in the furniture craft. Slowly, they learned the use of tools and woodworking trade. At first, his patience was short but he knew he needed help, and the only way to get the orders out was to get help. His children were growing and life was good.

When the children were first enrolled in the local parish school, Cate found out she was pregnant again. There were times when she thought she would never have any other children. Paddy was reluctant after Shamus was born; the birth seemed to worry him about Cate having another child but as time went on, she thought that maybe she unable to have another one. When this pregnancy came, she was thrilled. This pregnancy was different than the other two. She seemed to show right away and her morning sickness lasted all day. It was a relief that the children were in school all day since she felt so bad during the day. Her sickness lasted for what seemed the entire pregnancy and then—all of a sudden—it stopped as fast as it had started. Though she was large with Shamus, she was larger with this child. Paddy was in a constant worried state as he saw his wife's belly grow larger. He insisted she sees the doctor in the next county over. The doctor was young but favored by the locals. In the morning, he took Cate over for a visit. He lived in a two-story building on the edge of town and used the back of the home for his office. Paddy had made a call from the local pub the day before, to let him know they were coming. This was different from most since doctors had always come to the home but since he was a county over, they went to him. Dr. Gordon was a young, tall, light-haired man with early balding; he was thin in stature with a kind smile. "How are you, Mrs. Finnerty; you look like you are further along than your husband said." Both Paddy and Cate looked at each other. He asked her to come in to the other room and told Paddy he would be out after he examined Cate. As Cate walked into the other room, she noticed the table. She had never seen anything like it; a straight black table without any covers or even a pillow. At first, she was hesitant but stepped on the stool and sat on the table. "I will need you to lie down and pull your blouse up. I want to listen to your baby's heartbeat." Cate had never heard of such a thing; everyone she knew had called the doctor when the pains started and that was the extent of the doctor when you were having a child—except, of course, unless there was a problem. She pulled her blouse up and he put something in his ears and a round, cold thing on her stomach. He moved it around her stomach for what seemed like a long time. As he did, his half-smiling mouth turned to a frown as his eyes grew wider. He took the metal piece out of his ears and put it to the side. He started to rub his hands together fast and said, “Sorry, my hands are usually cold. I need to examine your stomach.”

He put his hands on her stomach and pushed gently on it. He started with the top of her stomach, to the bottom, which made her feel uncomfortable. He picked up the earpiece again and listened again until he heard a knock on the door. “Is my wife ok?” asked Paddy. The smile returned to the young doctor’s face. He walked over to the door and let Paddy in. “Mr. Finnerty, I believe your wife is having twins. I could hear two distinct heartbeats and I will need to get a better determination of a due date for your babies.” All of this was new to Cate; with her other pregnancy, she never calculated any due date. She felt she knew herself well enough that she could determine when she was near birth. But after they left the doctor’s office, she had a specific date in mind. With Cate and Paddy living in the next county, Dr. Gordon arranged for Cate to stay with the widower Mary Kate McDowd. She had been the town midwife for years and had birthed many a baby. He knew she would take good care of Cate. Paddy was upset at the fact of having his wife stay so far away but he knew she’d be better off. They arranged for him to be called as soon as anything happened. He took Cate over to the widow’s home, one Sunday afternoon after Mass. He asked Father John to give her a blessing before leaving and prayed to God to take care of her. As soon as he got back to town, he walked into the pub for a stout but never made it to ordering it. A message had been left that Cate was about to deliver, so he raced back to the truck to go back. As he arrived at the widow’s house, Dr. Gordon came out to greet him. “Paddy, you have a boy and a girl. Cate is fine and the babies look good. I want her to stay here for a few days, to keep a check on them all. She did great and went faster than I expected. I’m glad you brought her when you did. You can go see her now.” Paddy was so proud of his wife. When he walked into the room, she was sitting up in bed, holding a child in each arm. Cate named the boy Brady, after her father, and the little girl Maggie, after Paddy’s mother.

The twins thrived and were fine, as long as they were together. Cate kept them together in their cradle as infants and later on, as they moved to their bed. They were inseparable and were in great humor, as long as they were together. She knew that it was not a good idea but they seemed so happy being together. With Maureen and Shamus in school during the day, she devoted her days to the house and watching out for the babies. The winter was harsh, the year following the twins’ births, and with that came a fierce sickness. It spread through the schools and came home to Cate’s twins. The sickness seemed to settle in their chests. At one point, she had all four of the children sick. As she came out one evening to Paddy sitting by the hearth, she started to cry. She sat down on the small stool next to Paddy and put her head in his lap. “The wee ones are having trouble, Paddy; their breathing is labored, you best be getting the doc." Cate was exhausted from worry and caring for the children.

Paddy went to get Dr. Gordon but when he went into his office, it was so full of people that he nearly walked out. As Dr. Gordon came out of his office, he noticed Paddy. "Paddy, what's wrong?"

Paddy told him the children were all sick but the twins were having trouble with their breathing. "Doc, can you help us?" He gave him some medicine and told him to use a mustard plaster on their chests. He wanted him to boil water and put them under a tent, using the vapors.

Paddy quickly went home, running into the cottage and stopped as he went to the child's room. Cate was holding her child, rocking her back and forth. She was wrapped in a blanket, covered completely so that Paddy could not see her. Her grip was so tight that he could hardly remove the blanket from her face. "My baby, my poor little girl. The angels have taken her." He stood there for what seemed like hours and finally left the room. He checked on the other children and saw to her twin brother, Brady, before going back to the child's room. Cate was still sitting in the same rocking chair but this time, she was silent and still. "My dear Paddy, I'm so sorry, Paddy." Paddy knew her pain and felt the loss in his heart. He knelt down and embraced his wife and child. A proud man he was but not so proud to show his loss. The tears came and so did the sobs but he knew that the child was to be blessed, and he left for the parish priest.

The next day, the child was washed and put in her cradle that Paddy made. She was anointed with oil by the parish priest and given last rites. Little Maggie was buried next to Paddy's mother in the family plot. There was only a graveside service since the sickness was still spreading through the village. Cate sat in the parlor, surrounded with her other children, as one by one, she was consoled but it brought no comfort to her. That night after the other children were safe in their beds, Cate finally put her head down in the bed Paddy had made for her. She lay there still and turned to her dear Paddy to hold on to him, for the strength she needed—the strength that only he could give her—for he knew that her pain was the same as his. Her heart had been broken and a piece of her heart had gone with the child. The local priest had given her last rites after only some months ago baptizing her. When she was taken from the house to the family plot, Cate could not bear to see her buried and turned to go home to her children.

As with the birth of her firstborn to the death of her child, Paddy and Cate held on to each other in body and soul. In the birth of Maureen, they went to a closeness that most married couples did not have. Paddy had birthed their child; in a point of human nature, they achieved closeness and with the death of their daughter, they clung on to each other like never before.

The farm seemed to prosper through the years. Cate and Paddy's children grew stronger as they helped with daily chores with the farm and for some years, life was good. Age seemed to agree with Cate. She became more beautiful, the older she got. Her girlish looks turned to a more gracious attractiveness. One Sunday, after mass, Paddy ran into a young man who had seen Ilene in Dublin. "She's getting married, ya know, surely ya know, Paddy." Paddy shook his head and tried to stop the conversation but the man persisted. "The man's a bit of a gambler and a womanizer but she's going to marry him anyway." Paddy was torn between going to get his sister and putting the conversation out of his mind. He had never seen this man before and thought he may have been mistaken, so he never thought about it again. That is until he received a telegram from Ilene.

PADDY, I HAVE MARRIED A MAN BY THE NAME OF SHANE MCFADDEN AND WILL BE COMING HOME WITHIN THE MONTH. PLEASE HAVE MY COTTAGE PREPARED FOR US. I LOOK FORWARD TO SEEING YOU SOON. – ILENE

"Well, I've not heard from her for years and now she's coming home with a husband and wants to have the cottage ready. She must be thinking she's a lady or something, don't ya know." The cottage had been used for storage for the past years. The first thought on Paddy's mind was whether they were coming for a visit or something more long term. It was a visit he was not looking forward to. He cleared out the front room, cook's room, and bedroom but left the other rooms for storage.

One evening when they all were in bed, a knock on the door came. As Paddy opened the door, he was shocked to see his sister Ilene standing next to a man, who Paddy would describe as a city slicker. Ilene was dressed as he never saw her before. The dress was of green velvet with a hat that looked like it had a bird's nest in it. The gentleman beside her was dressed in a suit of brown tweed with a brown-velvet vest and a cap to match. The man's hair was combed back with a look of slick oil to keep it that way. He had a thin mustache over his top lip with curls on each end. To Paddy, he looked like the devil was here to visit Ireland. He walked the two over to the cottage and opened the door for them. They had brought enough belongings for what looked like an extended stay. "Where's your man to tend the fire, sir?"

Paddy started to laugh, "Well, sir, if ya look in the mirror over there, you'll see him plain as day." Paddy laughed to himself as he walked back to tell Cate about their guest.

The next morning as Cate was preparing breakfast, Ilene walked in. She was dressed in a long robe made of blue satin. Cate was taken aback with Ilene's looks. Her brown hair was now a bright red and her face was painted, all ready with red rough, and lips to match.

"Shane will be rising and will be expecting his breakfast. He is used to having his eggs cooked in hot lard for two minutes only, four of them. Cook his sausage in the white pudding with potatoes on the side and a slice of that bread you make. I will be back in an hour with Shane." Cate stood there, wiping her hands in her apron. She had children to get ready for school, Paddy's breakfast to prepare and chickens to feed. Before Ilene left, she turned and said, "Oh, make sure the children are gone from the table before Shane has his breakfast; he is not keen on kids."

That was the straw that broke the camel's back, to Cate. As Ilene walked back to the cottage, Cate went after her. "Ilene," saying it louder, "Ilene." When Ilene finally turned, Cate said, somewhat nervously, "We have cleared out the furniture and cleaned up the cookstove in the cottage. I think it is ready for use. You may borrow what fixings you need and cook your husband's breakfast. I have to tend to the needs of my children," and she turned and walked away. It was not in Cate's nature to behave so rudely but her main memory of Ilene was when she walked out on her when she was about to give birth. She had told herself to be a forgiving person, and maybe if Ilene had acted differently, her nature would be more accommodating but for now, the bitterness was taking over.

Shane had protested most of the night. He claimed he did not know how to make a suitable fire so Ilene made it. The coldness of the cottage kept him constantly complaining about fear of sickness. It kept Ilene on edge all evening. The worry of coming home was one thing but Shane's spoiled nature was not helping. She knew Cate would be upset with her but was surprised by her comments. To Ilene, Cate had always been so sheepish; age had changed her. Ilene fixed breakfast as well as she could from memory. Her marriage had been spent in motels throughout Ireland. Shane had come from a wealthy family from the north and when his father died, he had sold the land and the home site as well. That's when Ilene had met him. The night when she left Cate in labor, she took the train to Dublin to stay with her aunt. Paddy knew she was where she was but never tried to contact her. She stayed with her Aunt Mary and worked at the local goods shop. One day, while working, Shane McFadden came into the small store. He was like no other man she had ever seen and Ilene could not help staring at him. Though she was not a beauty, she had learned from the stylish women of Dublin. As she left that evening, he followed her home to her aunt's house. Her aunt was now a widower and had lived in the home left to her by her husband. Aunt Mary had married Brogan O'Shea, a local Dublin lawyer. She had a very large home in downtown Dublin. As Shane watched her enter the front, his thoughts went to money. He had gambled away most of his inheritance or spent it on his lavish lifestyle and knew he would need to find a way to find more cash. The next day, he visited the shop again and asked Ilene to dinner, that night. Ilene was so excited, she sat by the clock and watched the minutes go by. She had not been out for what seemed like years. She met him at a local tavern not far from the shop. As they dined, Ilene noticed the women looking toward their table but Shane seemed just interested in her. He asked many questions and by the time it was over, she had told him her life story. He knew that she had a dowry and also that her aunt was ill and had no children of her own. Shane would visit Ilene and have long talks with Aunt Mary who confided in him about her wealth. "You know, my dear Mary, I have so much experience in these matters. I have handled all of my family's estate; you should let me see your holdings so that I may advise you." Feeling that Shane was a trusted soul, she gladly handed over her accounts. The sum of her holdings was more than he sold his family estate for, and he had figured out a way to get it. Though Mary trusted him with getting advice, she did not give him authority to assets. This stumbling was short-lived for Shane. Mary had expressed leaving something to Ilene upon her death, so Shane saw it as a perfect time to ask Ilene to marry him. It would give him a place to live, with Aunt Mary's servant to wait on him. Also, he figured the old lady would not be around much longer. He talked Ilene into getting married quickly, without too much fanfare, and asked if he could move in with Ilene's aunt until they found their own place. As time went on, his funds were depleted, so being desperate, he planned Aunt Mary's demise. She was old and in poor health so no one would suspect anything if it looked like natural causes. But first, the paperwork must be done for Ilene to inherit her estate. He thought about poisoning the old lady but knew it might catch up with him, so his thoughts went to an accident instead of something as bold as poisoning. He had to make it look right and he had to get the papers in order first. His plan was to get dear Aunt Mary to think of Ilene as her heir but he was soon to be disappointed since she had left all of her estate to St. Bernard Catholic Church. She had said it was the church where she was baptized and whose graveyard she would finally be buried in. So, he drew up a document stating that the estate was to be left to her niece, Ilene since she was the one who cared for her in her later years. Shane had it worded just right. He went to the library and looked up wills and made sure there would not be any question about how it was worded. Now, he had to get her to sign it. Aunt Mary took to having a drink of port in the evenings. She was consistent about only having one glass so he helped her along but added a powder he acquired from an old friend. He tried to make sure Ilene thought that he was interested in her but the longer the charade went on, the harder it was for him. At times, it was all he could to make sure she thought he was in love with her but having the truth be told, he was getting near to despising her. He thought about Aunt Mary and Ilene having an accident together but he knew the inheritance would be hard-pressed to get the money so he endured her for a while more.

One evening, when Ilene was out at one of her meetings, he used the powder on Aunt Mary and sat in the parlor with her until her small head fell down to her chest. As he went to try to wake her, she mumbled some incoherent phrase. He quickly picked up a pen and put it in her hand. Slapping her in the face, she woke enough so that her penmanship would look close enough to her somber signature. When Ilene came home that night, she was surprised to see Aunt Mary slouched down in her chair with a pen still in her hand. "My goodness, Shane, what's to be wrong with Aunt Mary?" When Ilene tried to get her up, she could hardly get her out of the chair. The two of them nearly carried her up the stairs and Ilene got her ready for bed. The next morning, the old aunt did not rise until nearly ten, claiming a sickening headache. It took two days for her to feel well enough to come down for supper.

Now that he had acquired her signature, having Ilene to inherit her full estate, Shane had to get moving on her accident. Every Tuesday, she rode out to the widow Higgins's house for tea. They had been friends since they were in grade school and had kept in touch for all their years. The friendship had grown closer since they had both lost their husbands. Shane's main problem was with the servants. They were always around, in and out of the house, and the stables. His plan was to get into the stables and loosen the wheel of the carriage enough, that when it went over the rocky road, it would surely break and turn over. Though Aunt Mary had a car, she insisted on using her old carriage when riding out in the country. She could leave on the old road behind the house and get out of town by the side roads. When doing so, it reminded her of her youth. She was by herself and felt young again.

The week after getting her signature, she was off to Bridgett Higgins's house. It was a sunny spring morning and the heather was in full bloom. Thomas, the stable hand, had the carriage ready for the short journey. As he was completing his chores, Shane went out to the garage to speak to him, "Ok gent I'll get her ready, you are wanted to deliver this letter for me at the post. I'll be needing this done, good man; please hurry along." Thomas had been suspecting of Shane from the moment he first met him but he knew he had to listen to him. Shane went into the stable and closed the door behind him. He quickly loosened the hinges on the wheel of the carriage but not to the point of being noticed. It would take some time and hard riding for the wheels to come completely off and Shane knew the road to the widow Higgins's home. It was steep and rocky. He went back into the house to get Mary moving and gave an excuse about Thomas, which no one except Mary heard. He hoped he was covering his bases for later.

"Oh Shane, you're so good to me, looking out for my needs the way you do." As with most women, Shane seemed so caring and they believed him to be a gentleman in the best sense of the word. As she went down the alley behind the house, he hoped that he had not loosened the hinges too slightly, for there was no clanging sound at all.

When he went back into the house, Ilene was just getting home. "Have I missed my aunt? I was going to go with her." Shane thought that it may have been even better for him if they both succumbed to the same accidental death but he knew he would have a much harder job getting hold of the property and money. Time seemed to pass slowly all afternoon and it was hard for Shane not to show nervousness so he went to the usual place—the pub down the way. He figured he would have a few and maybe find a tart also. Women were always easy to find for him.

The bell rang at the door around three that afternoon, when Cathleen, the maid, announced that there was a constable at the door. Ilene thought something may have happened to Shane. There were times when Shane McFadden had been known to be in the fight or two.

"I am sorry to inform you, Mrs. McFadden, that your aunt has been in an accident out on Dartar Road and she's been taken to the hospital. I believe her condition to be grave and they would like you to come at once."

She went out to get Thomas to drive her to the hospital and when she asked him, he replied, "I was afraid of something happening." She wasn't sure where exactly Shane was but had no time to go from one pub to another looking for him.

When she got to the hospital, they rushed her down to a room to see her aunt. Aunt Mary was covered with blood from what looked like a head wound. Her clothes were muddied and torn and she looked to be asleep. As Ilene went to touch her forehead, the doctor walked in. "I am sorry but your aunt has had a fall from her carriage. She appears to have hit her head and is unconscious. We are going to do some tests and get her cleaned up. I will not know anything until we get the results of the x-ray. If you would wait outside, they are going to get her cleaned up to take her for an x-ray." Ilene ran out to the car and told

Thomas to go find Shane. It seemed to be getting dark outside when Shane finally arrived. "Sorry, Ilene I was in the middle of a card game when Thomas found me. I am sorry about your aunt; you know, things happen." Ilene looked at him; Shane seemed to know what had happened already. "Oh, Shane, she is going to be fine; that doctor just came out and said she was awake now and I can go in to see her in a few moments."

Aunt Mary was let go from the hospital in a few days. They had warned her that she should let the doctor know if she had a headache. She had a concussion and they wanted to make sure that she did not develop any other symptoms. She was sent home by ambulance and put to bed for a few days. Shane had not succeeded in his endeavor but Ilene had given him another idea. "Ya know, the doctor said she's to be watched in case she shows some bleeding on the brain; the x-ray did not show any but he said it may still cause some difficulty."

So, Shane immediately went to the library to look up the symptoms. He found that a severe headache was one but another was prolonged sleeping, resulting sometimes in death. "The patient would fall into a deep sleep and will be unable to arouse. This, soon, could be followed by death." His plan was to give her a powder, double the strength this time and help her along with her pillow. Shane thought surely no one would suspect him now, after her accident. With the servants attending her, it would be hard to get to her. He would have to have this happen when everyone thought he was nowhere near the house. He told Ilene he had some business to attend to and would be out until later that night. He left the house in the afternoon around three and watched from a distance as everyone went about their normal routines. Thomas had left with the car to run some errands for the cook and Ilene was sitting in the parlor, doing her embroidery. The upstairs maid was in charge of checking on Aunt Mary. As Shane waited, he saw her sitting with the cook, eating her supper and since Thomas was still gone, Shane could make his way upstairs through the servant entrance without being noticed. He removed his shoes and went upstairs to the old lady's room. With the help of the powder he had given her earlier, she was sound asleep and snoring loudly. As he walked in and shut the door behind, she moved ever so slightly, so he waited a bit more before taking the pillow on the chair next to the bed and putting it over her face. He was surprised as to her strength and how much fight she had in her. Surely the double powder would have knocked her out but he then noticed that she had not drunk all of the tea he brought her earlier. Time seemed to pass slowly until finally, she had succumbed. He put the pillow back in its place and emptied the teacup and wiped it out. As Shane went to leave, he heard rumblings downstairs and he knew he had to go before someone saw him. As he left the house, he breathed a sigh of relief.

He knew he must make his presence known someplace else in case he needed an alibi. He went back to the restaurant of the Belmont Hotel, where he was earlier in the day, and then went back again to the bar in the hotel. He complained strongly to the young man attending the bar; he was to meet a business associate and had been waiting all afternoon in the hotel. When he left, Shane felt his bases were covered, nor was he surprised when he saw an ambulance at the house. "What the matter, Ilene?"

Ilene was sitting sobbing to the point she could hardly speak. "Dear Aunt Mary's gone, they say she must have died in her sleep. When they checked on her, she had died. Father Ryan is with her now." Shane thought he must do things slowly now as to not appear too anguished. Ilene would be surprised when she found out that everything was left to her and Father Ryan would be even more so since he thought he would be getting it all. Shane could not wait to see his reaction. The church had never done anything for him and he had no regret for his actions. Shane thought to himself about having to stay with Ilene for a bit more. It was hard being around her and if he did not have a tart or two to satisfy him, he would surely go crazy staying with Ilene. There were times when he felt sorry for her. She was always waiting on him, hand and foot but he had taught her a thing or two that he learned from his whores, down the way, and she was only too glad to please him.

The wake was the next evening with the funeral the following morning. The usually quiet house was turned into one with singing and dancing until the later hours of the morning. There was food on every table and drink in every glass. Those who could sing sang and those who could not sang even louder. All had big heads the next day but were still in attendance when Mary Dolan was buried that morning. When Ilene and Shane returned to the house, Father Ryan was not far behind, along with the local solicitor. Ilene asked them in and offered them some food. "No, no my dear, we are fine. There's the matter of the will that we need to get to. Now, I'm not trying to rush anything; it's just that Mary spoke to me about this matter."

Ilene said that she would get Mary's papers. "She told me where everything was when I first came, so I know about her wishes. I'll just be going now," said Ilene.

"Yes, yes my dear, she told me how she left you something also."

Ilene went upstairs, got the box out of her Aunt's closet, and brought it down. Ilene knew what was in the will; her aunt had shown it to her several months after she moved in with her. When she opened the box, the first thing she saw was an envelope that had "The Will of Mary Dolan" on the outside of the envelope. When Ilene had gone over her aunt's will before, it was in a document that was folded and on the outside, it said Last Will and Testament of Mary Dolan. "Oh, I have never seen this before," she said as she handed the envelope to Father Ryan, "I am sure this is just something she wrote later."

As he opened up the document, his eyes widened and he looked over at Ilene. "There must be a mistake—it looks like she did some changes. It looks like the date was some weeks ago. Ilene, did she tell you about this?" He handed her the paper.

I, being of sound mind and constitution, leave all of my estate, properties, and assets to my niece, Ilene McFadden. I do this in appreciation of the care she has given me in my later years.

Mary Dolan

It was simple and straight to the point. Father Ryan could tell on Ilene's face that she had not known anything about this but he was not so sure about Shane's expression. He had a smile on his face that reminded him of what the devil would look like. "Well, Ilene, I guess your aunt has changed her mind about giving her property to the church. You know, even when her dear husband was alive, his intention was that the church should get his estate but I guess she changed her mind. May I have a copy of the will so that I may show it to our Bishop?"

That was the last thing Shane wanted. Even though Mary had signed the will, she did it while under a powder and her signature was not as clear as the original will. Shane remembered when he got her signature, she had fallen asleep in between her first and her last names and he had to arouse her by slapping her in the face. "I'll take care of that, Father; I will get you a copy," said Shane.

The week after the funeral, Shane suggested they leave Dublin and go on an extended trip. "Ilene, let's go to Paris for the spring. My girl, you've been through too much. Let me show you Paris. Besides, you need some color in your life and a new dress will make my lady happy." She laughed as she walked away and said, "I'll get my bags!" There was more work to do before they left; the first thing was to get Ilene's signature, in order to put the house in his name. He would then put the property up for sale and reap the benefits after. His plan was to ask a fair price for the property so that the funds would be coming his way quickly; when he had the funds, he would finally be able to sit in one of those card games he heard so much about. He needed clothes to look the part and needed to stay in the right hotels in Paris in order to get in the game. As soon as he won, he would say goodbye to Ilene.

The plan was going well so far; he had gotten the signature, spoke to a seller for the house with the posting to go out the week after they left. He talked to the bank about a loan, with the house as collateral, and left a note for the servants to tell them that they were no longer needed, except for the housekeeper—to come by once a week to clean. All was going well until they were getting ready to board. Father Ryan came running after them as they were getting ready to get on the gangplank. "Mr. McFadden, Mr. McFadden, I need to speak with you; stop!" Shane told Ilene to get on the ship and he would follow. As she started to protest, he rose his voice and she left. Almost out of breath, he rambled, "I never got the copy and now you're leaving. I need the copy."

With that said, Shane responded, "Not to be disrespectful, Father, but I don't have to give you anything." He turned and left. As Shane got up to the top, he turned and tipped his hat.

As Ilene walked into the room of the hotel, she ran through the sitting room, to the large ornate bedroom, to the powder room with the large copper tub. The room was decorated in blue and gold with large windows looking over the city of Paris. She ran over to Shane and kissed him hard. "Now, now, dear lady, I've business to attend to. But here, I will give you some money and you can go and buy something for yourself." Shane gave Ilene several large bills. He told her to watch how the ladies dressed here and treat herself. Ilene never asked Shane where his money came from. There were times when he seemed to always have money, and times when he would ask her for as little. She thought that to be his business. Ilene walked down the streets, taking in all the sights. She did as she was told and took in how the women dressed. To her, they were too colorful with bright hair and rouge. Their dresses were too daring for Ilene but she wanted to please Shane. When she went into some dress shops and inquired about the prices, she quickly turned around and walked out. She had never spent so much on one dress and would not do so. Ilene decided to go several blocks over, to see if the prices were lower. She found a salon and went in; the women talked her into changing her hairstyle. Her hair went from a chestnut brown to a bright red. "Now, you look like you are from Paris!" When Ilene went to pay, the women noticed the abundant cash in the pocketbook. Ilene thought to herself, *Shane will be so pleased.*

They directed her to go to the shop the next street over, and see a woman named Lilly. In the window of the shop were several dresses—one in a bright green and another in a scarlet red. Not only were they revealing but they were very ornate, with beads and pearls sewed on them. But Ilene went in anyhow. A woman, with what looked like the same colored hair as Ilene, came running over to her. “Oh, madame, please come in. I had a call you were coming and I have the perfect dress for you. It is the latest fashion and will fit you perfectly.”

When she brought out the garment, Ilene shook her head. “No, I can’t wear something like that. It is too revealing for my age and I need something less ornate. Perhaps this isn’t the store for me, after all.” But as she turned to walk out, the woman met her at the door. Ilene thought she must have run quickly to try and stop her from leaving.

“Mademoiselle, please let me show you some other dresses. Please come with me.” By the time Ilene left, she had three dresses, two hats, and a fancy pair of shoes.

When she arrived back at the hotel, Shane was nowhere to be found. She decided to get dressed for dinner and wait for him. She took a long, hot bath in the large copper tub, put on one of the dresses with a hat to match, and her new shoes. It took several hours to get to the point she wanted to. As she looked into the large mirror, she smiled. *I don’t look like a farmer’s daughter anymore*, she thought. She sat on the small sofa so that Shane would see her as he walked in. Outside, it was growing darker so she put the lights on in the room and sat again. She waited and waited but there wasn’t any sign of Shane. After drinking several cocktails, she fell asleep and did not wake up until the next morning. She realized that he had not been home all night. She felt like a fool, and when she looked at herself in the mirror again, she thought she looked like one too. She pulled the dress off without caring if it ripped or not, and put on one of the dresses she brought with her. Feeling a bit normal now, except for the bright red hair, she went downstairs to inquire if perhaps there may be a message. When she realized he had not even left her a message, she left the hotel and went to look for him. She walked the streets, looked in all the bars and gambling halls and saw no sign of him; as the evening grew dark, she went back to the hotel and waited. The next three days, she did the same thing and went looking and never found a trace of Shane McFadden—not until the gentleman at the front desk told her that she had received a message from St. Paul’s Infirmary. She was to come at once; Shane had been hurt. There wasn’t any explanation about how he was hurt, or how badly.

When she walked into the hospital, she was met by a nun and was asked to follow her. The sister did not speak, not even when Ilene asked about Shane but when Ilene walked into the room, she realized that Shane had been in one of his usual fights. His eyes were blackened and his lips were split. Apparently, he had broken his arm. His eyes were so swollen that he could hardly see her. “Madam, there is a constable outside that would like to talk with you, if you will follow me.”

The gentleman in the hall was not in uniform but dressed in a tailored suit. "My name is Detective DeSauusure and I wanted to let you know—as soon as he is able, he is to be arrested. He owes a gentleman quite a lot of money due to gambling debts and has an assault charge against him."

Ilene was taken aback. She knew Shane could have a bad temper but she never would expect this. "Can you tell me exactly how much his debt is, sir?"

The detective cleared his thoughts and said it was in the thousands of francs. "Your husband was gambling quite strongly, he lost several million franks but continued to gamble even after that. They gave him credit for a while, in a form of an IOU, but then had to ask him to leave and that's when the fight ensued. I will have to take my leave, madam, please excuse me."

Ilene turned and went back to Shane's room; it was then, that she noticed the handcuffs that were connected to the bed rail. "Would you like to tell me where you got all the money from?"

He explained that he won the money from playing cards at another parlor. "Ilene, don't worry about it; look, they are going to put me in jail as soon as I am released from here. Girl, you've got to help me get out of here. We'll go home and forget this. If you don't help me, I may go the jail for quite a while."

Shane had concocted up a plan for Ilene to sneak in, late at night, with a tool he had in his suitcase. He wanted her to bring all their bags from the hotel so that they could get away that night. "I've never done anything like this before; what makes you think I will do this, Shane?"

Even with his eyes so swollen and cuts on his face, he was able to charm Ilene, "Because you love me, Ilene."

In their short marriage, he had never said he loved her but always remarked on her love for him. He was right, though; she loved him deeply and he knew that she would do it. With Ilene's upbringing, she had gone by the rules she had grown up with—the rules that were set in her by her parents and the church—now, she was helping a felon escape. In a way, she felt excited by the thrill of it all. She waited until 2 am the next morning and made her way into the hospital. She went through a side door that she noticed when she was there before. It was where the orderlies would come out to smoke. As soon as one went back in, she quickly went in before the door shut all the way. She wore a black dress with a scarf over her newly dyed hair. She would step into a closet or room when someone was coming. It had to be done as quietly as she could. Not knowing how exactly Shane was going to get out of those handcuffs scared her most of all. If he was caught, she would be charged also. When she did enter his room, he was waiting for her. "Quickly, give me the tool."

She was amazed at how little time it took him to undo his handcuffs. "There's a car waiting for us around the corner, let us hurry."

As they slipped into a room to hide, they startled an old man in the room. "Nellie, is that you? Have you come to see me, Nellie?" he cried out.

Ilene went over to his bed and patted the old man. "Hush now, Nellie is here now, hush now," she said softly.

The old man started to laugh, "My God, woman, you're not my old dog Nellie."

Shane grabbed her arm, "Let's get out of here, now." They made it to the car where an old Frenchman was waiting for them. "Take us to the train station as soon as possible." If they made it on the next train to the coast, they could make it over to England without being found out. Ilene had made the bed look like Shane was sleeping in it; she knew he would not be discovered until the next morning and they should have enough time to make it back to Ireland. They caught the next train out and were able to get to the coast where they could get a fishing boat to take them to either England or Ireland. All they wanted was to get out of France, so Shane would not have to go to jail. Ilene thought, *Surely, they would not be looking for Shane if all he did was owe someone money; it wasn't like he murdered someone or something*. Ilene knew what she was doing was wrong but she attributed what she was doing to her wifely duty and taking care of her husband. All she wanted to do was to get back to Dublin and start making some changes in what was now her house. She would envision details of what changes she would make. It kept her awake at night and filled her with excitement when she thought about it. She knew her Aunt Mary had money in the bank and now, it was hers. She may not have her dowry that Paddy owed her but now, she had all of Aunt Mary's money and even her home.

Shane and Ilene made it to the coast, to the small town of Calis and from there, they were able to get a fishing boat to take them over to England. Ilene was nervous about where they would get the money from to make it back to Dublin since she only had what was left from the money Shane had given her for clothes. They barely had enough to pay for the train, much less the boat ride over to England but Shane told her not to worry; he would make sure they'd get there. When they got off the boat, Shane asked her to go into a tavern in the town and he would meet her there. He had inquired from the fisherman about where to eat when they arrived and gave Ilene directions to the tavern. "Ilene, be a good lass and meet me down the way." As she walked up the street in the small city of Dover, she turned and looks down at the riverfront to see Shane walked back into the boat with the old fisherman. She stood for a while to see if he came out but turned and walked quickly up the street. After what seemed like a short time, Shane came into the tavern; he walked over to her and said, "Let's go, quickly now; come along." He grabbed her arm and pulled her up from her chair. She started to protest but stopped as she noticed a constable coming in the door. The last thing she wanted to do was to attract attention. They walked up the hill to the rail station and took a train destined for London. She noticed that Shane looked disheveled and had a cut over his eyebrow. As she sat on the train next to him, she noticed his hands had bruises on them. When he went to pay the engineer, he took out a wad of money. Ilene never asked where any of the money came from.

Their trip to London seemed long as they rolled through the countryside, and it was the engineer who woke her up. Shane was nowhere in sight. She went through five cars before she found him in the lounge car, playing cards at the table with three other gentlemen and a woman standing behind him, whispering something in his ear. "There's my darling girl, gentlemen, and she's dressed in the best of Paris," he said, slurring his words. He stood up and said he was taking his leave, to the other men. One man stood up in protest and said any man of character would not leave a game before it was finished. "I guess I don't have much, do I?" and he laughed as he turned and escorted Ilene back to their car. The train was getting ready to stop. He told Ilene to get her things because he did not want to run into those men, and they should make their way quickly to catch the ferry to Dublin.

They caught a cabbie to the dock to get a ticket for the ferry, just making the ship. Before it left, they raced onto the ferry and made their way to the upper deck to have some supper. For once, Ilene began to relax; she had a good meal and hardly said a word to Shane. He seemed his happy-go-lucky self and acted as if his situation in France hardly bothered him at all. They made their way home in the wee hours of the morning. Ilene was surprised since they were not greeted by any of the staff of the house. "Oh, I let everyone go—all except Millie but she was only to come by once a week at that."

Ilene was furious; the staff had been with her Aunt Mary for years and she planned on keeping them when she set up the house the way she wanted to. "You had no right to do such a thing, this is my house and I will have whomever I want here."

After saying so, she turned and started to empty her belongings from her case. She felt Shane's hand, pulling her arm back behind her; he swung her around and put his hand under her jaw, in order to put her face in front of his. "I am your husband, I am the man of this house and you will do what I tell you to do." When he removed his hands, she fell down to the floor and started to cry. Shane walked out of the room and went out of the front door. It was two days before he came home.

In the two days that he was gone, she had two visitors; one was the parish priest, Father Ryan. "May I have a word with you, Ilene?" She asked him to join her for tea and they sat in the parlor quietly at first but then Father Ryan asked, “My dear Ilene, do you think it’s a little strange that your Aunt Mary—God rest her soul—why did she change her will so suddenly?” Never before had Ilene ever thought to be disrespectful to a priest but Shane had clearly rubbed off on her. “Father, what are you saying? I hope you are not implying anything.” Father Ryan started to laugh, “No, no, nothing like that but your aunt just always seemed so proud to be doing this for the church. It was always mentioned every time I saw her.”

Before answering, Ilene cleared her throat and waited to say that her Aunt appreciated what she had done for her, “You know I took care of her and looked out for her; where was the church then?” She had hoped that was all there was to be said but Father Ryan persisted. “I believe, Father, you should take your leave now; I’ll show you to the door.” It wasn’t an hour later that Mr. McGregor from the bank was knocking on her door. She looked through the sidelight and he saw her. She could not imagine why he was at her door and opened the door to welcome him. “How do you do, Mr. McGregor?” she said as she left him standing outside.

“I have a matter to discuss with your husband and need to speak with him as soon as possible.” She explained that Shane had to go out of town on business and she would let him know when he came back to be in contact with him.

Mr. McGregor was about to tell her that he saw him in town last night coming out of the pub. “Well then, I’ll leave you for now and please let him know that I came by.”

Shane finally came home that evening. He was in such a foul mood that Ilene stayed to herself until the next morning. At breakfast that morning, she noticed several pieces of silver missing. When she brought this up to Shane, he blamed the servants. Only two weeks after being back home, the trouble began. There were nights when Shane stayed out all night and slept most of the next day. Their relationship seemed to flaunter; he hardly noticed her. One Monday morning, Mr. McGregor stopped by the house again. Ilene was not going to answer the door but he saw her as she walked by. “Good day, Mrs. McFadden. I need to see your husband and I must say the matter is urgent.” Ilene asked him in to the parlor. Shane was upstairs, sleeping. The night before, he was out all night and only had been home for a short time. He went to the icebox, took out some leftover mutton, and went upstairs to bed. His words were few, mostly muttering to himself and not even giving Ilene a look before going to bed.

“Mr. McGregor, Shane cannot see you now; he is indisposed presently.”

Mr. McGregor started to laugh, "My dear lady, I would guess he would be. I saw him last night going into O'Connor's Pub and I saw him again, coming out this morning." Ilene knew that the downstairs of O'Connor was just that, a pub, but the upstairs was used for what her aunt called "them ladies of the night." "It would be in your best interests to go upstairs and get your husband."

Ilene excused herself and went upstairs to wake Shane. He had fallen asleep in his clothes and she could see the rouge stain on his shirts. She shook him hard and he swung his arm up to hit her. Ilene moved, just in time. "What the bloody do you want, woman?" he shouted.

"Mr. McGregor is below, looking for you, and he said he would wait until you came downstairs, no matter how long it took."

She left him, thinking he would clean himself up and come down. But they sat there waiting for what seemed a while before the front door flew open. "I caught him climbing down the trellis, Mr. McGregor," said the man dressed in a black suit.

Ilene jumped up as the man grabbed Shane by the back of the shirt and put handcuffs on him. "What do you think you are doing? You have no cause."

Mr. McGregor asked her to have a seat and he would explain. He asked that Shane be taken outside to the car. He came over and sat by Ilene, "Sorry, Mrs. McFadden but your husband owes a lot of money to the bank and some other people in Dublin. When I told the constable about him owing my bank so much, other things came up also. Apparently, he's been gambling quite a lot and causing trouble at O'Connor's Pub. He will be in jail on 7th Street and will go before a judge sometime tomorrow. I'll take my leave now." He turned and left. There was no sympathy in his voice and she had no idea what to do next.

That afternoon, she contacted a local solicitor to look into what Shane had been up to, and what she found out shocked her. The next morning, Mr. O'Neal met with her before Shane was to go before the judge. He told her that Shane had taken out a loan on the house, and had received a large amount of cash the day before they left for Paris. He was supposed to start paying back the bank and had not done so. He also took out some small loans from several people and they were mainly the ones that had put complaints against him. The total sum against him was several thousand dollars, and he would remain in jail until this could be paid. Ilene knew her aunt had money in a local bank, so she went to the steel box upstairs to get the key to her aunt's deposit box. What she discovered was that the key was gone and so was her bank book. She walked over to the bank to speak with the manager and was told the deposit box was closed out by Shane, several days before, along with her aunt's accounts. "I'm sorry, Mrs. McFadden but your husband closed these accounts out."

Ilene became furious, "But the accounts were in my aunt's name and were to be left to me." The bank manager explained that Shane had the proper papers to be able to close the accounts and take the money out. The only thing she could think of was to sell the silver her aunt had acquired, along with her jewelry. She went back to the house and started to go through her aunt's things. When she started, she noticed quite a lot of things missing. Her aunt had three silver chests and two had nearly half the contents missing. Along with the silver, several pieces of jewelry were missing as well. She took the pieces she had and went to a local shop that bought such pieces from patrons. As she walked in, she spoke to the gentleman behind the counter first, before looking around the store. But when she did look around, she noticed a gold watch under the glass. She asked to look at it and knew when she opened the small clasp, that it was her uncle's watch. She felt sick suddenly and left. As she walked out of the shop, she ran to the alley on the side of the building and got sick. She felt betrayed and angry. She felt the same as she did that night when she found out her dowry was gone. Here she had a house to live in—one she thought she would die in—and now she was about to lose that one, too. A man had taken it away from her. She could not decide whether to help Shane or not; she thought about letting him rot in jail but she really did love him. He was the first man to show any interest in her. She could dismiss the nights out if only he came back to her the way he was before. She cleaned herself up the best she could, took out a small bottle of cologne and swallowed a small amount before going back into the shop. They settled on an amount, and she went to the courthouse to visit Shane.

The amount she collected was not enough to pay all that Shane owed but it was agreed that Shane would be let out if he promised to start paying back Mr. McGregor's bank. As they left the courthouse, neither Shane nor Ilene said a word to each other. As Ilene went to fix tea, she heard the front door slam. It was at that instant, that Ilene knew her days were numbered in her aunt's house.

****

Her skin curled from the first time Cate saw Shane McFadden. Whether it was his slick, black hair or the skinny mustache—to Cate, he looked like the devil. Ilene was something to behold, also, with bright red hair and her shinny Paris dresses. They both looked so out of place, walking around the small farming town. People would stop and stare. Some remembered Ilene, some spoke but many ignored her since they knew about her departure that night. Paddy was taken aback by Shane, whether it was his demeanor or just the fact of his reputation that seemed to follow him. They moved into the cottage where

Ilene had stayed before; the farm was totally Paddy's, as granted by his father. Being the only male heir, Paddy would take care of Ilene as his parents wanted him to do until the time came that she be married. When she left that night, he washed his hands of her. He knew she was staying with her Aunt Mary. Cate asked Ilene and Shane to have dinner with them the next evening. While in conversation, Paddy asked how Aunt Mary was. Ilene, almost choking on her supper, said, "I'm sorry, Paddy. I forgot to write to you but Aunt Mary had an accident and died, several months ago. I thought you would have heard by now."

Paddy sat there, staring at her. He slammed his fist on the table, "My God, woman, are you without any feeling at all? She was my aunt too." The children sat, wide-eyed at their father who hardly raised his voice.

"Don't ya be saying things to my wife, man." The children started to cry as Cate took them to their bedroom. When she got back, Ilene and Shane had left.

"Paddy, are you alright?" Paddy sat with his head in his hands. Cate started to pick up the dishes as he grabbed her hand, "He's trouble, ya know; mark my words, Cate, my dear."

The next morning, Ilene was over to take a tray to Shane for breakfast. She sat at the table, smoking her cigarette, while Cate prepared the food. "Will ya be going to church, Ilene? I'm sure Father O'Brien would like to see ya this day."

Ilene laughed, "No, no, Shane isn't religious, so we won't be going."

As Ilene started to leave, Paddy came in from the barn. "Well, I see you're back, Ilene. You be best to remember cooking. I'll not have Cate cooking for your husband." Ilene picked up the tray to walk out but Paddy stopped her, "I guess the church is happy they have the house now. I don't understand why they did not summon me, since I was in the will, to see that Aunt Mary's wishes were to be carried out." Ilene turned and walked out.

That afternoon after church, Paddy visited Father O'Brien. He asked him to make an inquiry about the house and the reason the church had not contacted him. "I'll be getting back with ya, Paddy, just give me some time." Paddy left, walked by the local Pub, and noticed Shane sitting at the bar. He hesitated but went in to have a pint. As he sat next to Shane, Paddy thought he'd get some matters straight while he had Shane by himself. He sat at the bar and started to speak but Shane was interrupted by a woman of questionable values. She came up to him and put her arm on his shoulder. "Hello, Paddy you sure do have a nice brother-in-law here." Paddy got up and left.

That evening, Father O'Brien came by the farm. "I've found out some information about Mr. McFadden, Paddy, and I don't think you'd be liken what

I'm about to tell you, lass." Father O'Brien told him about the money problems Shane was having but said that was a minor account to the other things in question about him. "It seems the house and estate were supposed to be to the church but only a few weeks before, your Aunt Mary left it to Ilene without letting anyone else know of her wishes. Shane's name was added some days after she died, at the request of Ilene." He told Paddy that the banks and some unsavory characters were after money that Shane owed them. "The man is no gentleman but a scoundrel. Your aunt died in an accident of questionable causes. They went to Paris for a short time and returned, some said, penniless. He then borrowed more money and gambled that away, too. When they could not pay for the loans, they lost the house and all your Aunt Mary had. I'm sorry to tell you this but it sounds like your sister has gone through a lot." Paddy wasn't so sure that he felt that bad for Ilene.

As he approached Ilene the next day, he told her he knew about the house and what Shane had done. "You know, they are looking into Aunt Mary's death. You need to be careful, Ilene. I don't think you know what your husband may be capable of. I also did some checking about his background, where he grew up. He went through his father's estate also, after his father died in a hunting accident that he and Shane were on. Be careful, Ilene." He had warned her and hoped that she would see what kind of man he was but they stayed on and pretty much stayed to themselves. Ilene would ask for money, now and then. Their food was provided to them from the farm and they made the cottage livable again. For a while there, Maureen, now ten years old, would go and visit her Aunt Ilene. At first, Cate saw no harm in it but then Maureen would come back with stories Shane had told her. When she started being disrespectful to Paddy, Cate knew where it was coming from. She forbid her children from visiting their aunt unless either Paddy or she was with them. It was after that, that things changed. While hanging out the wash, she noticed Shane watching her. He was sitting on the fence post, chewing on some sour weed, staring at her. She ignored him at first but one night, she saw his figure outside the bedroom window. She thought she should say something to Paddy but she hesitated. She noticed Shane from time to time, staring at her, and as she caught his glances, he would smile widely at her. Cate was in hopes they would leave the farm. Her skin crawled whenever she was around him but they seemed to be there for the stay, as Paddy put it.

After supper one night, Ilene knocked at their door, "I'd like to speak to Paddy, alone if possible."

Cate turned to walk into the next room but Paddy stopped her, "No, anything said can be said in Cate's presence."

Ilene stiffened her upper lip and sat at the table. “I’ll be in need of the dowry money now; you owe it to me and it’s past due.”

Paddy sat down at the table and folded his hands. “Ilene, the money was intended to be given to you when you married through the proper channels. In Ma and Da’s will, it states that the dowry is presented to your husband on the day of your marriage, following the church service. Since you made the decision not to get married in the church and did not go through the proper channels, I am not beholden to give it to you.”

Ilene stood up; her face grew almost as red as her hair, “How dare you! That’s my money, not yours. I need that money and you spent it on that monstrosity of a bed for her. This isn’t the end of this, Paddy!”

From then on, Ilene and Shane kept to themselves. There wasn’t a word spoken between them. When Ilene would see Cate, she simply looked the other way. One day, Paddy had to deliver some furniture to a store, two counties over. He would be gone for two days. Cate wanted to go with him but the children had school, and she dare not leave them with their aunt. She asked Paddy if Mr. McClary was staying on the farm that night. “That’s a strange question, you know he stays here during the week. Is there something wrong, Cate?”

She went over and kissed him, “No, Paddy I was just checking.” The day Paddy left, the weather was cold and rainy. He had packed up the furniture for delivery and covered it with a canvas covering. He had a local boy ride with him to help with the delivery. As he pulled out the farm road, he had an uneasiness about him but shook it off, as if he was just worrying about the weather.

Cate drove the small truck to pick up the children from school. As they all piled in the front seat, she had Maureen hold the baby until they got home. The rain was coming down softly and before heading up the meadow, it started to turn to snow. She felt relief, having made it up the hill without sliding on the wet mossy road. When she got into the house, the first thing she did was to have the children sit for some hot tea. Tea every day was a daily ritual and on this cold day, the children needed the warmth. Maureen was to serve, as the younger children had more warm milk than tea. To Cate, it was a practice of table manners that she insisted her children have. Afterward, their lesson plans were to be completed as she prepared supper. She made sure she had prepared the things they liked, warmed mutton stew over mashed potatoes and sweet carrots. She even made a cake earlier, that she topped with warm vanilla sauce. As the night grew darker, she asked Maureen to help get the children to bed since she was going to take a plate out for Mr. McClary. Cate told Maureen she would be back in for prayers, as soon as she delivered the plate.

In a way, she felt relieved that the McFaddens were next door even though they were not talking to them. Ilene had become exhausting as all she thought about was pleasing her spoiled husband. Cate kept the children at bay when it came to Ilene since there was not a kind word said about Paddy or Cate. She could see the light on in the small cottage but could not see anyone through the window. She went into the barn, carrying the lantern, and walked to the rear of the barn to knock on the door that connected the living quarters, where Mr. McClary stayed during the week. As she went to knock a second time, she felt a heavy object hit the back of her head that flung her to the floor. Blackness came upon her and for a short moment, she lifted her head to see a figure standing there. As she tried to rub the warm liquid from her face, she noticed the figure running out the door through the flames…

Maureen saw the flames coming from the barn. She ran into the cold night and heard the horse's squeals as the animals tried to find a way out. As she ran up to the barn, she pulled the half-opened door all the way out as two horses came running past her, and nearly ran over her. Shane came running out of the cottage, telling her to get back, "The barn's about to fall in," as he went up to her to grab her.

"Where's my ma, I don't see her and she's not in the house!" Shane carried her back and held her as she tried to get away. The flames were high in the sky and the smell of burned animals engulfed the air. Maureen turned to look around at the house as the children peeked out the small window.

****

Someone was shaking Paddy hard as he awoke from a sound sleep. He rose up quickly as he could not see the figure standing next to the bed. "Sorry, Paddy, but a postman came by with a message for you to go home quickly. There's been a fire at your farm. Don't be fretting now, the fire was in the barn, not your home. I'll put on the kettle for you." Paddy got up as fast as he could, put his goods in order, and went running down the hotel stairs. He told the innkeeper he'll pass on the tea. The truck was parked in the back of the building; he got in and drove as fast as he could. When he was several miles down the road, he realized he had left his helper there but thought he would send someone to get him after finding out how bad the fire was. His first thought was to get home. He drove for what seemed an eternity until he reached the top of the hill, beyond his farm. He could see in the distance a small resemblance of the barn, still smoking but then he noticed several car lights and a group of people walking around with torches. He thought at first that they must be helping Cate. As he drove the large truck down the narrow road to the house, the town folk separated to let him through. The grimacing look on their faces caused a panic in Paddy.

His good friend, Colin, walked over and opened the door of the truck. "Where are my children? Was anyone hurt, Colin?"

Colin put a hand on his shoulder. "Paddy, your children are inside, they are all well. We can't find Cate or anyone else. She was not in the house at the time of the fire and the children said she went to take a plate out to your man." Paddy turned and ran over to the burning barn with Colin behind him. Colin grabbed him and pulled him down to the ground. "No, Paddy, it's still hot." As he sat sobbing, his friends and neighbors prayed for dear Cate and Mr. Dorn.

Paddy buried Cate next to their sweet little girl. The family plot was on the highest point of the farm and was surrounded by sweet heather. "Da, did the fairies take Ma to heaven?" asked Maureen.

"Yes, child, the fairies are watching her now." There were so many people in the house that Paddy thought he would go crazy. He was tired of speaking to everyone and just wanted to be by himself. The children were taking it so hard, he could tell they felt the same. Ilene was going around, speaking to everyone, and it seemed like it was a party instead of a funeral. Paddy noticed that Shane was nowhere to be found.

The sky was growing dark and some of the people were leaving, when he noticed a man coming in, who he did not recognize. He spoke to Ilene and then walked over to him. "Paddy, first let me say I am so sorry about your wife and your man. Let me introduce myself, I am Detective Tully from Dublin. I have been called in to do an investigation on the fire. Is there someplace we can speak in private?" Paddy led him to the back of the house, where he had a small area where he did his accounts. The area was no bigger than a closet but it had a door and no one would hear them. "I believe your wife was dead before the fire."

Paddy was shocked and could hardly mutter a word in response, "I don't understand, sir."

Detective Tully cleared his throat, "It seemed that when the body was prepared for burial, they noticed that your wife had a large gash in her head. This made them suspect that she died from that gash. Before burial, we examined her and decided that the cause of death was from the blow to the head and not the fire. I will be doing more of an investigation. I need to know if you know of anyone who may have wanted to do harm to your wife."

"Everyone loved Cate," Paddy could not think of anyone who would have ill will against Cate. "Before I left, she asked me if Mr. Dorn would be staying here while I was gone but I couldn't understand because he was always here during the week. Did something happen to him also?" he said to the detective.

"No, it seems like he had too much to drink and had maybe passed out."

But Paddy knew this not to be true, "No, no, he never drank while he was here. Oh, he is at the pub on his nights off but when he worked for me, he never drank. He's been working for me for years."

Detective Tully sat for a while, refilling his pipe, "Anyone else you can think of, Paddy—oh you don't mind me calling you by your given name, do ya?" Paddy shook his head. "I do know about your sister's husband. I have someone back in Dublin looking into him. When I was asking around town, the priest told me what he had found out." Detective Tully stood up and extended his hand to Paddy. "I want to keep this to ourselves as much as possible. As far as the people I've talked with, I've asked them not to say anything. I don't want the person who did this to leave town. I will find out more tomorrow and let you know. I thank you for your time, sir."

When Paddy went back into the front room, most of the people had left and his children were asleep on the settee. Maureen was the only one still up. She was helping Ilene clean up. "Thank you, Ilene, but I can get the rest of this." She turned and asked Paddy if maybe she and Shane should move in to help with the children. "No, I can manage fine." He turned and picked up the children and put them to bed. When he returned, Ilene had left. Maureen was looking out of the window, crying. Paddy put his arms around her and held her tight. "It will be ok, Maureen, your ma's in heaven with the angels." But the only thing on Paddy's mind was that someone had killed his dear Cate.

"Da, I can't think about her dying in the fire. Not dying that way." Paddy wanted to tell her but felt he should keep things quiet for now.

That night, his mind kept him awake through the night—*who would ever hurt Cate*? He went over and over it, all night long. When he got up the next day, Ilene was in the kitchen preparing breakfast. "Ilene, you don't need to do this, I will take care of my family." She asked the children to get ready for school. "Someone has to look out for you and the children. Let me help." He hadn't the strength to deal with her right now. Two days later, the detective stopped by the farm again. Paddy had taken the children to school, and the little one, he dropped off at his good friend Colin's house. He saw the detective's car coming up the drive and wondered if there was any news as to his wife's death. Detective Tully got out of the car and stood with his hat in hand, looking over the burned barn. "Paddy, I found some very interesting information on your sister's husband, Shane McFadden. I will need to talk to her to see if she knows anything about that night. It seems that Mr. McFadden has been in some trouble before. He has a reputation in Dublin. It seems that there have been some questions about your aunt's death. Apparently, the investigation of her accident revealed that the wheel of her carriage had been tampered with. They said the accident could also have been attributed to the way the hinge was bent. Then, there is the fact that the will was changed shortly before the accident. The church has been looking into that. Is your sister at home now? I saw Shane down in the town and I would like to speak with her alone." Paddy told him she was home and pointed over at the cottage.

Detective Tully knocked on the door softly at first, waited, and then banged hard. He could hear her muttering to herself as she walked to the door. "I'm here, don't ya be banging my door down."

Ilene stepped back as she saw Detective Tully standing at the door. "Good day, Mrs. McFadden, I believe we met some days ago at Cate's funeral. May I have a word with you?"

She told him to follow her and asked him to have a seat. "May I get you some tea, Detective?"

He replied that it would not be necessary. "I would like to ask you some questions about your husband and hope maybe you can put some light about what happened that night." He noticed Ilene wringing her hands, as she rose up from the chair and walked over to the window. "I was in the bedroom that night, resting. I felt bad that day and went to bed early that evening."

The detective thought it strange that she would be so nervous if that was all there was to the story. "Where was your husband that night?"

Out of nowhere, she started to cry, softly at first, and then to the point of being unable to speak. He handed her his handkerchief and tried to get her to calm down. "I saw him go out there, I saw him, ya know. He was always looking at her. I saw him go into the barn." Detective Tully wanted to make it clear that she was talking about the night of the fire. "Yes, that night; he went to the back of the barn and he grabbed a hoe, I saw him do that, too."

Shane McFadden was arrested that evening. He was on the second floor of the local pub with a woman of ill repute, as Detective Tully put it when he was interviewed by the local paper. He was taken immediately to Dublin to face the multiple charges against him. Not only was he charged with two murders, but he was also being charged with forgery since the signature of Aunt Mary's will was being questioned. Shane had sent numerous telegrams and made calls, when allowed to, to Ilene. She had not visited him or tried to get in contact with him. He had no money and needed a lawyer. A man by the name of Rory Quinn came by to see him. He must have been all of twenty years old and just finished with his schooling. But where he was, at that point, he had no choice but to hire him. He told him that he would find a way to pay him, somehow. Rory left that day and came back the next afternoon. He walked in with a brand-new briefcase, nearly empty; he took out a few papers and dropped them on the floor and nervously picked them up. "Sorry, Mr. McFadden, I am a bit clumsy, please be patient with me, sir." Mr. Quinn sat down, folded his hands and said, "I have some disturbing news for you. It seems your wife is going to be testifying against you; apparently, she claims that she saw you that evening, going to the barn and picking up a hoe before you went in."

Shane became enraged as he stood up quickly, knocking the chair to the floor. Two guards came in quickly and held him down. "No, no, she's wrong. I never left the house that night. I fell asleep in the parlor on the chair. Please let me go, I won't cause any harm. Let me talk to my barrister."

A guard stayed in the cell while Shane spoke to Rory. "I'm afraid that's not all, they have moved your case to the Special Criminal Court where your case will be heard by three judges."

Shane knew enough of the legal system to know that his chances of getting out of this were worse, going before the Special Criminal Court. "Please tell my wife that I need to speak with her as soon as possible." But Rory said that she has been advised not to speak to her husband. Shane felt he had to get to her, somehow, and he knew that he had no one to call. He had burned his bridges with his family, friends and even his wife, apparently. He could not understand why she would lie about him. He had done a lot of things in his life that included killing someone but he would never hurt Cate. He was in awe of her; she was the prettiest thing he had ever seen. He wondered why someone would hurt her. His mind was going crazy, trying to figure it out. Rory had told him that if he was proved guilty, he could be hanged. His eyes teared up as he thought about it.

Paddy had friends from the town to help with the debris from the barn. They asked him to stay in the house while they worked but he would come out from time to time. For the most part, he worked in his shop. He knew he needed help with the children but hesitated to have Ilene there. She had proved to have bad judgment her whole life and he wanted to make sure her way of thinking was not passed to the children. At night, it was unbearable to sleep in the bed he made for Cate. He would wake and go to hold her, only to find an empty space. He remembered the birth of their first child, Maureen, and how he brought the child into life. It made them so close and Cate wanted only him to birth their children. When the twins came, he was upset at not being with her during her time. He would wake up some nights, wet with tears, and other nights, calling out her name. It went on for weeks until he moved a small bed to the back of the house and started sleeping there.

Paddy's business had slowed down. Where he used to have back orders he now had just enough work to get by. The farm was gone since most of the animals had perished in the fire, and his willingness to get back to where he was had left him. He gave into Ilene when it came to helping with the children.

The trial was coming up, and he knew it would bring back all those feelings he was trying to get over. He was asked to attend and be questioned along with Ilene. Ilene seemed as if she wasn't the least contrary to having her husband in jail. She went about her business almost gaily every day. She would cook breakfast and sing while serving. She mostly stayed at Paddy's all day and prepared supper, before returning to her cottage. On one occasion, Paddy came in and found her sleeping on the bed he made for Cate. He went over, pulled her up, and asked her to get up. "This should be my bed, Paddy; after all, it was my dowry that paid for it."

Paddy shook his head, "My God, woman; let it go, will ya."

The day was a rainy cold day in Dublin. Paddy had checked into the hotel, closest to the courthouse. He had arranged a room for Ilene also. His funds were getting low and he had no idea how he would make it over the next few months. The trial started with Shane's Barrister opening with a defense for Shane. His defense was shabby, at best, since he had no other defense except for the fact that he had fallen asleep and never left the cottage that night. Paddy testified that he left the day before to deliver some furniture. He also stated that he thought Cate seemed worried about something, that she asked if Mr. Dorn would be there all night. When Ilene took the stand, she stated what she had told the detective. She went into detail about Shane's activities, his womanizing, and their trip to Paris. She sealed his fate in a matter of 97 minutes. Of the three judges, one from the High Court, one from the Circuit Court, and a third from the District Court were all unanimous that Shane was guilty. The sentence was announced by the High Court judge as Shane stood to hear his fate, "Shane McFadden, you are to be hanged by the neck until death." Shane's knees went soft and he fell back in his chair. He turned and looked at Ilene with a look of helplessness as she stood up from her chair. Her face was blank at first but then she smiled at him and turned to leave. Most of the people in the courthouse never noticed anything, except for Paddy. His gut feeling was that something was amiss with this all along, and now, he knew what it was.

The ride back from Dublin was a long and quiet one for Paddy. Ilene seemed almost kiddy. As they rode along, she hummed and talked about everything but the trial. "Paddy, now that this trial is behind us, I think it's a good time for me to be moving back in. I can get me bags this evening and have breakfast on the table come morning." Paddy did not say a word; his eyes were straight on the road and never left.

When Paddy returned home, he went to pick up the children from Mrs. Bromley's house. She was a widow that never had any children of her own but loved taking care of Paddy's children. He asked if she would consider helping him full time, from now on. "But, I'm not understanding ya, Paddy; your dear sister, Ilene, seems like she would be the one to do that. Oh, I'm not saying I wouldn't love to help."

Paddy told Mrs. Bromley that Ilene would be leaving and would not be returning. He went back to the house, fed the children, and put them to bed. He brought in the covering he used when he delivered furniture and started to dismantle the bed. Piece by piece, he carefully took each piece apart. When he made the bed, he made it like a puzzle so that each piece would fit together without putting a nail in any of it. As he took down the posts, he cleaned and polished them, and wrapped them up carefully to protect them from any damage. When he was almost finished, he turned to see Maureen. She was standing there, crying, watching him. "I'm sorry, Maureen, I'm not able to shut an eye while in this bed; my heart tugs at me, girl."

She walked over to him and started to help him. Together, each piece was wrapped and marked. "What are ya going to do, Da?" He told her that he was taking the bed to Dublin to leave it with a man he knew. The bed would be sold.

The next day, he took the older children to school and the little one to Mrs. Bromley. He had gone by to see Mr. Conley when he was in Dublin for the trial. Mr. Conley knew Paddy's work and knew his fine craftsmanship. While in Dublin, he went by the jail to pay a visit to Shane. If he told anyone of his visit, they would think it strange but for some reason, he thought Shane may be telling the truth. He had his suspicions and even though there was anger in his heart, he had to see Shane. Paddy had never been in a jail before and thought it to be very much like a zoo; instead of animals in cages, there were men. He was led to a room where a single chair was in front of a room with bars. He heard the bar door opening and closing, and then Shane came in the room across him. A guard remained behind him and was able to listen to everything. He said, "My God, what are ya doing here, Paddy?"

Paddy had no idea where to start, "I've got a question for you, Shane; if you did not kill my Cate, who do ya think did?"

Shane started talking without hesitation, "I did not touch your sweet Cate, Paddy. I have gone over and over this, it is all that is on my mind, and I've had a lot of time to think but I think Ilene killed her. I think she did it because she hated you so and was so jealous of Cate. She hated you because you spent her silver coins, and she hated Cate because you used them to make her that bed. It was brought up to me, almost daily. She ruminated over it so that it consumed her. It was like something that was eating her inside. I'm sure it was a way to get back at me. I lost her aunt's house. I borrowed money on it and lost it all. This was all vengeance, and now I'm going to hang for it." Shane started to cry like a baby, "Paddy, I didn't kill Cate." Shane wiped his eyes, "Sorry, old man, but I don't want to die."

Without a word, Paddy got up and left. He went over to Barrister O'Quinn's office and asked to see him. He was trying to schedule an appointment when Mr. O'Quinn came out of his office. "Hello, Paddy, are you well, sir?"

Paddy asked to speak with him privately and he followed him to his office. His office was in disarray with papers scattered about. Mr. O'Quinn quickly moved the papers off the chair and asked Paddy to have a seat. "I've been to see Shane McFadden just now, and I believe him. I don't think he killed Cate and Mr. Dorn." He told him of the conversation and asked him what was to be done about it.

"As you know, Paddy, Shane McFadden is an unsavory character at best. What makes you think he is telling the truth?"

Paddy thought it to be strange to be turning against one's sister but the reason was there. "My sister's actions speak of almost a relief at Cate being gone and Shane's soon to be hung. She possessed envy and vengeance toward Cate, Shane, and I. By killing Cate and blaming Shane, she got what she wanted—revenge."

He spent nearly the whole day in Dublin and got home late that night. Mrs. Bromley had brought the children home and when Paddy walked in, Ilene was in the parlor. "Where's the bed, Paddy? What have you done with it?"

Paddy went in to pour himself a whiskey and came back to deal with Ilene. "I'm selling the bed, Ilene. It was made for Cate and now that she's gone, I can't rest my head on it."

She threw down the cup she was holding, "If you sell that bed, I want what's owed to me, Paddy. You give me back my silver coins!"

"I think you need to visit your husband before they hang him, don't you?"

Ilene looked shocked that Paddy would suggest it. "I have no intention of seeing him after what he did to Cate and your man."

Paddy thought that was a fine answer coming from a woman who left Cate while she was having a child. "Well, suit yourself then."

Ilene left to go back to her cottage. By the next afternoon, she had changed her mind, "I'll be going to see Shane. Will you be able to carry me there?" Paddy arranged to take her the next day since time was short, and there were only a few days left before Shane would be hung. The trip was in silence, Paddy had not a word to say. Ilene wondered why Paddy would even care about Shane.

Ilene walked in through to the front office. "I'm here to see my husband, Shane McFadden." She turned to say something to Paddy but Paddy had not followed her.

The warden got up from his chair and said he would take her to her husband. She was escorted to a room with a table and two chairs. The room was a small room without any windows and two exits. She sat down in one of the chairs, waiting for what seemed to be too long. The door finally opened and Shane came in, dressed in a black and white overall with chains around his ankles and wrists. Without saying a word, he sat down, nearly falling from the chains. The guard that brought him in left out of one door and the warden excused himself out the other door. "Well, well, so you've come to see me."

She smiled at him the same smile she had on her lips when he saw her in the courtroom. "If it wasn't for me brother, I'd not be here. He shamed me into it. It may not look good for me not to come."

Shane put his hands on the table, making a loud scraping noise as he leaned forward to her, "Why, Ilene, why did ya lie about me? I didn't kill Cate and ya know it."

Ilene laughed, "Let me put it this way, darling Shane. You took my house, my money, and my Aunt Mary, and then you took for yourself several women that I knew about and I'm sure some I did not. So, you're going to pay. They are going to hang you by the neck until it breaks and then, from what I've been told, you're going to shit in your britches."

Shane tried to move his hand but then he remembered to try to be calm. "Tell me, Ilene, tell me before I die; tell me why you did it—why Cate?"

She stood up and turned as if to leave but turned, suddenly, "I'll tell you why, Shane, I could get back at everyone that way. I could get back at Paddy for spending my dowry, I could get back at you for taking everything away from me, and poor darling Cate, little miss perfect Cate; she isn't so perfect now."

Shane figured she had started and he wanted to hear what else she had to say. "What about Paddy's man, why him?"

Ilene sat back down, "Oh, he was just in the way. It was perfect timing and I've waited so long, and with Paddy gone, there was no better time. I planned it perfectly; you know the devil's in the details."

The door opened and the warden came in. "I'll take my leave now, goodbye Shane."

She turned to walk out and the warden grabbed her arms from behind. "You best be not taking your leave, Mrs. McFadden; you're under arrest for murder. We heard it all."

Paddy sat in the room next to where Shane and Ilene were. He heard how Ilene planned to kill Cate and that she mainly wanted to get back at him. Paddy wondered how she could have such vengeance against him or Cate. He shivered when he thought about her around his children. He left the jail and walked over to his truck. A pain came into his stomach and he vomited, standing next to his truck. "May she rot in hell!" he murmured to himself. His own sister—he wondered how she could do something like this to him. Granted, her only gripe would be him spending her silver coins, the dowry she had but after she turned 30, he figured she would never be married. His mind kept on going over things as he drove home and by the time he reached his house, he felt relief that she would be gone.

Several days later, he received a call that someone wanted the bed and was going to be purchasing it the next day, so Paddy planned to make the trip back to Dublin the next day. The children were out of school that day for a holy day of obligation, so he asked Maureen to accompany him. She had never been to Dublin and since she was getting older now, he wanted to buy her some new clothes. Maureen was definitely her mother's child; she had hair just like Cate's—a silky auburn. Her eyes were green like the hills of Ireland. Since Cate's death, she was Paddy's right hand; it was Maureen who looked out for the children with the help of Mrs. Bromley.

Paddy and Maureen left early that morning before the sun rose. It was a trip that took nearly one hour, over some of the roughest roads in Ireland. He stopped at a small village on the way for breakfast. Paddy wanted to make a day of it, for just the two of them. As they approached Dublin, Maureen was amazed at the building the crowds of people. People were rushing to work and the cars and carriages were holding up, getting to where you wanted to go. Paddy drove down a small alley and parked his truck. They walked around to the front of the building and found they were too early, so Paddy decided to take a walk and show Maureen some of Dublin. They went through parks and looked in store windows. Paddy stopped at a sweet shop and bought Maureen some taffy and some other sweets, to take home for the other children. As they walked back to the furniture store, they walked by a clothing shop. "Let's go in here, Maureen." He was going to use some of the money from the bed for new clothes for Maureen.

When they entered the shop, they were greeted by a short, plump woman. She walked from the back of the store, and as she turned to the side to pass the table of clothing, Maureen giggled under her breath. Her smile was bright and cheery as she spoke to them, "Please have a chair, young lady, and I will fetch some things for you to look at."

A young girl came out with a tea set and offered them some tea, "Would you like lemon or milk, madame?"

Maureen laughed, so she could hardly answer, "I would like milk please and two sugars." The woman came out from the back of the shop and had several dresses for Maureen to look at. Maureen went back with the woman and tried on all the dresses and walked out to let Paddy see her. The woman told her to walk out, let her dad look at the dress, and then turn to show her dad the back of the dresses. She was able to get two dresses and chose the ones Paddy liked the most. They left the shop and headed over to the furniture store.

As they walked over to the furniture store, Paddy heard someone calling his name. When he turned to look, he saw it was the warden from the jail. "Hello Paddy, how are ya, lass?"

They shook hands and he asked if he might have a word with him. "Maureen, go on over to the store and see Mr. Kelly, I'll be right there."

The warden told him that Ilene would be in jail for the rest of her life but Shane would be getting out soon. Paddy looked surprised. "Well, Paddy, we could not prove a thing. Ilene tried to tell us he killed her Aunt Mary but there was no proof and we could not be believing what she said. He did swindle some men out of their money but that's all we could prove, so he'll be getting out soon. Just wanted to let you know, Paddy." Paddy felt that he should feel relieved but it brought back the memories of Cate dying. He wondered if he would ever get over it all.

Maureen walked into the large store. She looked around at the store and walked through the different rooms. Each was like a room in one's house. They were all in common; the furniture was in sequence, starting with a parlor or living room as some called it; next, there was a dining room with a large table, fit for a banquet; across from that, was an area for the cook room with newly styled stoves, not like the one at the farmhouse. She walked back into her favorite room—the bedroom. Some were in bright colors and some looked like a queen's room. When she was almost at the back, she heard a woman's voice; as she walked around the corner, she noticed a rather tall lady, nicely dressed, with a large hat on. Her back was toward her and she suddenly stopped speaking. Maureen went over, passed the woman and man standing there, and walked up to her mother's bed. It was covered in a green-satin coverlet, that she had never seen before. She slowly removed it and started to cry. At first, her sobs were faint but then she felt her heart was about to burst in her chest. The feeling hit her like it never did before. Her cries were for the mother she lost. No more would she see her mother lying in that bed, no more would she be greeted by her smile. Her loss remained somewhere deep inside, and only now surfaced. As she stood, leaning over the bed, the woman came over to her and put her hands on her shoulder. "Now, now, dear child. The gentleman told me about your loss and I promise you, time will make it easier. Your mother will always remain close to you; she's in your heart, she's a part of you, and you will still be a part of her, also." She walked Maureen over to a chair and told her to sit. Soon after, she was handing her a glass of water and drying her tears. Paddy had been in the front of the store, talking with the owner about the sale of the bed; when he heard a small cry, he realized it was Maureen. He went rushing back but stood aside while the lady spoke to Maureen.

"We'd best be on our way, Maureen." He helped her up from the chair and started to leave.

"Dear sir, if I may introduce myself." He turned and walked over to her. "I am Lady Weston. My husband's estate is outside of Canterbury and I will be taking the bed to England. Mister Kelly here will be shipping it for me and has explained to me about the assembly of the bed. I have never seen such craftsmanship before." When Paddy heard the name Lady Weston, he reminded Maureen to courtesy and speak to Lady Weston. "I was wondering if it may be possible for you to come to Weston and assembly the bed. I, of course, would take care of any passage and would also like this child to see that the bed will be well taken care of." Paddy was leery at first but he accepted her offer. He had never been to England and thought it may be a treat for Maureen.

He left the information with Mr. Kelly and told him to contact him when the arrangements were made. Maureen's emotions became calmer, and they made their way back to the truck behind the store. They rode in silence until Maureen spoke, "Sorry, Da, I tried not to get so upset but I miss her so much."

Paddy put his arms around her, "Lass, sometimes it just hits ya, all a sudden. It's ok now, don't ya be fretting. Look forward to our trip now."

Two weeks went by before Mr. Kelly contacted him. They were to leave the following week on a ferry bound for Liverpool, where they would take the train into London and then on to Canterbury. There, they would have a car take them to Weston. Maureen had her two dresses bought weeks before and Paddy made sure to bring his tweed suit. On the ferry, most people stayed inside, unobservant of the raging sea but Paddy and Maureen stayed outside to take in the sight. They got off the ferry and took a car to the train station, where they boarded a train to London. The closest train station to the home had one small building and only one track but they were surprised as they arrived at Victoria Station. People were bustling everywhere. Men were dressed in their finery and women were dressed very much like Lady Weston. Paddy had never seen such. They both watched as people passed by. Neither spoke, just stared, until Maureen let out a giggle. Then, they both looked at each other and started to laugh out loud. The gentleman next to them cleared his throat and they stopped. The rail ride to Canterbury was long, due to the constant stopping. But as the train stopped in the small towns, Paddy and Maureen took it all in.

A car was waiting for them as they got off the train. A young man, dressed in a black suit, was holding up a sign with their name on it. He took the small bag they had put in the back of the car. Paddy went to sit in the front of the car but the young man insisted they go to the back of the car. "No sir, please sit yourself in the rear and your daughter, too. If ya don't mind." They were being chauffeured to Weston; both sat upright and waved to the people walking on the streets. As they made the turn into the estate, they looked for the house. "No sir, the house be up the way, sir. We've a ways to go." The long drive was lined with large trees in a lined row, perfectly equal in separation. They went through another gate and over to the left, they saw Weston. It was a very large manor house—the largest house Paddy had ever seen. Even in Dublin, the houses were not as large. The driver drove back to the rear and stopped the car. A woman in a maid's dress came out to meet them. "The Lady said you'd be coming this day, I'll show you to your room. Please follow me." Paddy went to get their bag but was told the lad would bring it to his room. They went into the door and walked down the hall to a staircase. They were put into two rooms, side by side. Maureen's room had a single bed with a small table next to it. The room was simple but clean. When she went next door to see her Dad's room, it was almost identical. They were told the washroom was down the hall. "You'd best be staying in your room until you are called. Don't ya be roaming around the house, now? I'll bring you some tea and some supper." They stayed in the room, ate their supper together, and went to sleep. Early the next morning, Paddy was summoned for breakfast and to begin working on the assembly of the bed. The maid that they met the evening before tapped in Maureen's room, brought in a tray, and told her Lady Weston wanted to see her at ten o'clock in the library. "I will fetch you moments before, so be getting yourself ready for my lady. Mind your manners and remember to speak to her only when spoken to. In case ya don't know, you courtesy when seeing my lady." Maureen wondered if this was the same woman she met at the furniture store. She seemed so nice and caring but the way the maid spoke, Lady Weston seemed so regal and not at all as she remembered. She brought both of her dresses and saved her favorite one for this occasion. Her Dad let her buy some ribbons for her hair and she wore it up, to look older than she was. She ate her breakfast as fast as she could and dressed quickly. She sat on the bed patiently, until the maid came in. "Off with you now, follow me, and I will tell you when you can go into the library. If you see anyone walking by, do not speak until you are spoken to." The maid was muttering something under her breath as she walked Maureen through the long hallway to the stairs. They walked downstairs to another hallway and then up another set of nicer stairs, lined with colorful carpets. The rooms at the top of the stairs opened up to a large room. It was one of the largest rooms Maureen had ever seen. The ceiling was white, with smaller squares of carved wood. Each square was different. Maureen walked in and stopped to look at the ceiling. The maid grabbed her and said, "Come on with you, girl." The hearth went almost up to the ceiling and was carved stone. She knew not to stop and hoped she would see it again. They walked up to a pair of closed wooden doors as the maid told her to stay there. She went in and shut the door to Maureen. She knew to stand still but looked over to see a young man, standing there and looking at her. He smiled at her and almost forgetting herself, she went to speak to him, until the doors opened and she was pulled in.

She stood there, in what seemed to be another large room. This one was all in wood, except for the ceiling that had painted maps. She gazed up, studying them until she heard the soft voice of Lady Weston, "I'm so glad you've come with your father. You look very pretty today. Please come with me; I'd like to show you something."

Lady Weston took her hand and she walked them upstairs. The stairway was enormous, with each stair-rail being done in a carving of an animal. There were squirrels, foxes, deer, and the likes of animals she had never seen before. They walked upstairs to a room and she opened the door. Paddy was standing there, next to the bed. "My dear, this is where I put the bed. I wanted you to see the room I have selected for it. I promise you, we will take good care of it." The room was massive and the bed looked like it was made for it. Maureen held back her tears this time, and as they rode back to take their train, she remembered what Lady Weston had said to her about her mother always being with her. She was always in her heart.

Chapter 2

Emily strolled down the street, window shopping, while her cousin Clara was meeting with her advisor. Emily was to meet her at three o'clock for tea. Some of the shops looked so inviting at first but she was disappointed when she went in. She stopped to cross the street and noticed a large furniture store across the street. Each window was set up to a theme, with one being a library featuring bookshelves, desk, and accent pieces. But her eyes grazed on one, the large four-poster bed. The bed was beautifully designed with cravings on each post with the design extended to the headboard. With all the beds that Weston had throughout the estate, none compared. As she crossed the street, an automobile honked at her. When she entered the shop, she turned as a gentleman asked if he could assist her. "Yes, I would like to look over the bed you have in the window."

The man cleared his throat, "Yes, yes, we have just received that piece yesterday. Can you follow me?" They walked down a hall to a locked door. He opened the door which opened to the room that the bed was displayed in. People walked up and down the street outside.

"I am very interested in purchasing the bed, please give me the price. I will also need it shipped to my home," she said.

"Yes, of course; there is one complication with your request. The bed was made by a furniture maker but he would have to be the one to set it up in your home. It's like a puzzle."

After leaving the establishment, settling on the purchase and shipping, she stopped and gazed at the shop's window. As she saw her reflection in the window she pondered how her life had changed so quickly…

Emily Baines was promised to Robert Bedford Weston from the time she was twelve years old. He was a distant cousin and was to inherit the Weston estate along with the title. Emily was tall in stature and even at twelve, was destined to be a beauty. She had long, wavy, blonde hair and deep-blue eyes along with an eye-catching smile. Her father often remarked that she did not inherit an English smile and then would laugh about it. Emily attended the right schools and was presented at court when she was eighteen. Though fourth cousins, she did not care for Robert as a child; she thought him pompous and selfish. Things changed when he started to court her. While out in public or even at social events, the demeanor was different than being alone with him. Their engagement was announced to the family on Christmas Eve and in the papers on New Year's Day.

After many parties, the wedding took place at the family Chapel on Weston, June 1st, followed by a reception in the east garden of the Weston Estate. Emily was now Lady Emily Baines Weston. Robert and Emily occupied the house set on the north pasture of the Weston Estate. The house was a smaller replica of the main manor house at Weston. Emily had, at her call, a lady's maid, two kitchen cooks, and a butler that also served Robert's needs. There was ample space, and eight bedrooms for entertaining any overnight guests. Emily and Robert were expected to attend all the family functions at Weston, and Robert was consulted about any family business. The estate had been passed down when the title was bestowed on Robert's great-grandfather, along with the massive estate. Emily knew that at one point, she would become the headmistress of Weston and she was prepared to do so. She was a work in progress, as her father put it. Even when not agreeing with Robert's mother, she kept her opinions to herself. She knew never to get too attached to any of the servants and to keep family concerns only to the family and not spoken about, to anyone else. Because of this, the only one she could confide in was her husband and, sometimes, her mother.

Emily expected her first child the following May, after being married for less than a year. Robert was thrilled and she was nervous. There were times when she pondered how she got to this point. Her life had been planned for her; she had no control over making her own destiny. She knew nothing about children, only being around them occasionally. She was an only child and her father was the main person in her life. Her mother had always been sickly and in the last five years, had taken to her bed. There was even doubt as to her attending her own daughter's wedding. After numerous physician consults, a diagnosis was never made as to the cause of her illness. Emily knew her mother would be no aid to her when her child was born. She felt better when Robert hired a nurse to move, to stay, and attend to the child and his wife. Emily was in her confinement for two months before her son was born. He was a large, chubby baby boy that seemed to have an easy personality. They named him Charles Bennington Weston and one day, he was to inherit the Weston estate. The child was so even-tempered that when the physician confirmed she was expecting another child, she thought surely it could not be as difficult as some made it out to be. Little Charlie—as she called him when she was alone with him—was a joy to be around. He was always gurgling and when he started to put words together, he would laugh at himself. The only time Emily heard him cry was when he fell while learning to walk.

When her time came, she thought it to be as before but the pains lasted through the night into the next day. The doctor suggested that they transport her to the closest hospital but as they were getting ready to transport her, the pains suddenly became sharper, and she delivered. They named him George and he proved to be the complete opposite of his brother Charles. He was constantly crying and had to be rocked in order to get to sleep. When sleep finally came, it only lasted for a short time. Emily went through three nurses before one finally stayed. Her name was Florence and she was able to handle George. There were times when Emily would find any excuse to get away from the constant crying. At night, George kept the whole house awake. This increased the tension between Emily and Robert. Robert would spend nights at the main house and Emily started to feel more alone than usual. She knew there would be times when Robert would be gone, on family business, but she never expected him to not want to be around his family. "I can't work when I've not had a good night's sleep and no matter where I go in this house, I can't get away from the constant crying." Emily took him to a specialist in London to make sure he was in good health. His weight was good and he seemed to be on track for his age but to Emily, he seemed like a most unhappy child.

One afternoon, Emily was sitting in the garden, watching the boys play when a car drove up. She called Florence out to watch the boys as she went to attend to the arrival. It was a young man who brought a post, addressed to her husband. As she went to put it on her husband's desk, the telephone rang. "Lady Emily, there's a call for you; they say it's an emergency." She quickly went into the library and picked up the phone. There was static on the connection but she could make out what they were saying. Lord Weston and Lady Weston were on holiday in Italy, and while the gentleman on the phone could barely speak English but she could make out that there had been an accident. He was saying the automobile had gone off the road; Lord Weston was killed and Lady Weston was hurt badly. Emily lost the connection but did manage to get the name of the hospital where Lady Weston was. Robert was on his way back from London and was to arrive that afternoon. Emily went to tell Florence that she was going to meet Robert at the station. She called the household staff and explained the situation, and had her maid pack her clothes in case she was going with Robert to Italy.

Emily was standing on the platform as Robert got off the train. He looked surprised to see her there. "Robert, your parents have been in an accident in Italy and…and I'm sorry but they said your father has died." With that, she forgot herself and burst into tears. Robert grabbed her arm and escorted her to the car. All he asked was if there was any other news. She replied that that was all she was told and they rode home in silence. She thought it odd that he did not seem to have any emotion. He quickly got out of the car without waiting for her, went into his library, and shut the door. Emily started to go upstairs to check on the children and she heard George crying loudly. "Please, George, not now," she muttered.

"Can't you keep that child quiet?" Robert yelled. Robert ran up the stairs past her, called for his valet and slammed the door of his room. Emily went to attend to George and heard the front door shut. He had left before she had a chance to speak to him.

There wasn't a call or any information relayed to her. It was only when she went to church, that she found out from the priest that Lady Weston was being brought home, and was expected to arrive the next day. She was so embarrassed at being left out, that she was in tears when she arrived home. Robert had turned out to be exactly what she thought him to be. As she looked to the future, she felt it would be a very lonely one. Emily knew that she should be at the main house when they arrived but decided not to. She could hear her father saying that her stubbornness would do her no good and she would be the only one to suffer because of it.

She did not see Robert until three days later. She came in from being out for a walk and happened to look in the library, where he was sitting at his desk. "Good of you to tell me you're back," she said as he continued to ignore her.

She turned to leave and he finally spoke to her, "The funeral is tomorrow at noon. Mother has broken her back and is in terrible pain. I need you to attend to the guests that will be arriving tomorrow. You will need to get the staff to be prepared with meals and attending to our guests' needs. You will also need to come to the main house as soon as you can." He got up to leave, turned around, and said, "Please leave George here with Florence but bring Charles." It was this that changed Emily. She grew more protective of young George. She did as she was told, packed her things, and instructing the household staff of Weston. She ordered the cooks to prepare for some 46 guests that would be arriving. The rooms were made ready, food was ordered, and a menu was set. After going over the details, she went up to visit Lady Weston. When she tried before, she was told she was sleeping and asked not to be disturbed but when she entered the room, she was shocked. Lady Weston's face was still bruised and she had a large gash on her left cheek. Her arm was broken and she was unable to move her legs. Emily stood there, hardly able to speak. "Is that you, Emily? Come over here, my child." Emily went over next to the bed and put her hand on her shoulder. "I'm glad you're here. I don't think I will be here long. My pain is unbearable and I want the Lord to take me." Emily started to cry. She remembered coming to Weston as a child and Lady Weston being so kind to her. "You know, I chose you, Emily. I wanted you to be the mistress of Weston. With that comes not only the title but a lot of responsibility. Please be patient with Robert. Underneath that brash persona, there's a scared little boy." Emily left, feeling a little puzzled; she could not see Robert being scared of anything.

The day of the funeral was a chilly, rainy fall day. Emily stood next to Robert as relatives and family friends watched, as Lord Weston was lowered into the family plot. Robert stood there without showing any emotion. Emily was in attendance along with many of her cousins. As the funeral went on, Emily looked around at those in attendance. She realized then, that of all her family, she was the one chosen to marry Robert; she was the one to be given the title. But with all those around her, she never felt so alone.

After they all had gone, Emily took Charles and went back to get George. She had been away from him for three days and wanted her baby back. She instructed her housemaid to pack some of George's needs to take with her back to Weston, not knowing whether they would remain there for any length time. She thought she may be back at Brighton. Emily would not separate her children, nor would she let Robert. She took little George to see Lady Weston. She was doing poorly and she thought that seeing the children may perk her up. Little George seemed to take to Lady Weston and her to him. Charles acted like he was bored visiting, so Emily set him off with his nanny and stayed a while with Lady Weston. "My dear, I will need your help and hope I may count on you." Emily assured her she would be there for her. She felt more comfortable there now than she had ever before.

After seeing Lady Weston, she went upstairs to put the children. There were no rooms set up for the children, so she asked the housemaid to show her all the rooms in the house. She picked three rooms on the east side. The two rooms on the outside were to be the children's rooms with the room in the middle to be the nanny's room. They were the brightest rooms in the house and got the afternoon sun. As she was going down the main stairs, she met Robert on the way up. "I did not know if you would be here."

Robert had not said a word to Emily about any future plans since the accident. He thought her to be imprudent for assuming any changes. The first year after their marriage, she was almost absent from any of his daily plans. There were times when they hardly spoke a word during their time together. Her daily activities were mostly where the children were concerned and not Robert. He became so used to the routine, he rarely thought of her. His nights with her grew less as time went out. She never approached him about it and seemed perfectly fine with the arrangement. "Emily, may we discuss your intentions as to your plans?"

Emily turned to speak to Robert, "I've been asked by Lady Weston to stay and help her with her needs. I made arrangements for the children to take two rooms on the west wing of the house, along with a room for their nanny to stay. I will also be arranging for my lady's maid to be at my disposal." She turned and walked away. She felt more strength than she ever felt before. She knew, even though hesitantly so, that Lady Weston would approve of her plans. As she walked away from Robert, she listened for a reply to her statement but heard none. She thought he would rebut George staying but he made no reference to the fact.

For some reason, George's crying episodes were fewer than before. His persona calmed, the longer he was at Weston. Robert left for London, soon after the funeral, and did not return for several weeks. Tending to the death of Lord Weston took longer than Emily thought it should. When he returned one late afternoon, he announced to Emily that Weston would be having a ball that included a three-day celebration. Robert was to be titled and Emily would now be addressed as Lady Weston. Robert's visit to London included a visit with the King and his advisors, who decided that because of the death of Robert's father, he should attain the title, and his wife become Lady of the Manor house of Weston. This was not discussed with Emily or his mother, Lady Weston, before going to London. At first, Robert thought Emily would be thrilled by her bestowed title but she simply excused herself and left the room. She hesitated to go into Lady Weston's room and thought best that she wait until the morning to visit her. That evening, she had supper in her room next to the window, as she looked out at the grounds of her new home.

Robert took this as a childish action, feeling she did not have the knowledge of what was just given to her. Emily knew all too well what the title entailed—she knew her life would be different now—no matter where she went, her presence would be noted. She wasn't quite sure if she was happy about having so much responsibility. From the time she reached what her mother called "the age of reason," she had been promised to her cousin Robert. Her mother and grandmother spent their time preparing her for this, and when they thought that she was learning so well, she was really resenting every minute of their preparations.

"I will be visiting Her Ladyship this afternoon for tea. Please tell her of my intentions." She decided to see her alone and leave the children to their play. Emily planned an outing for the children outside of Weston, she could watch the children play in the garden. When she had all in place, she had her lady's maid announce her. “How are you today, your Ladyship?” She smiled back at Emily as she picked up her cup of tea.

At first, Lady Weston was quiet as the conversation lagged but she stopped in mid-conversation and looked out at the children. “My dear, I assume that you believe me to be contrary to Robert’s decision. Please understand this is expected; this shows that he has the attitude to do what is expected of him. I know you will do what is expected of you and you will honor the position you will hold.” Emily had not expected her to be so complacent. “Emily, you know your grandmother and mine were sisters. I know you were taught well.” Lady Weston was still unable to walk—her wounds were healing slowly but she was still unable to stand on her own. A nurse was still taking care of her full-time and to Emily, she needed to remain.

That evening, she asked her lady’s maid to have her favorite dress ready for dinner. She decided not to eat with the children but rather to dress for dinner in the evening. She felt she should at least try to have a better relationship with Robert. She asked the kitchen to prepare his favorite meal and told his man to have him dress for dinner. When she came downstairs, he was standing, looking out the window with his back to her. She walked over and stood by him, “I’m glad we can have this time together, Robert.” He drank his drink and walked to the table. The room was large enough for a banquet-sized table that held over 50 people. At the end of the room, the doors opened to another room that held a table for 30 people. The house was large enough to entertain quite a few people, and rooms to accommodate as many, to stay for occasions like the ball coming up. Emily had never planned such a large event. When Emily tried to converse with Robert, his answers were mumbled or were one-word answers. She hardly touched her plate. When he finished his meal, he excused himself and left. She went back to the room she had stayed in since moving to Weston.

The next day, she met again with Lady Weston. At first, when she arrived, she tried her best to keep calm about the situation but as she spoke, the tears welled up inside of her. She got to the point that she could hardly speak. “Now, now, my dear, calm yourself. I will help you with this.”

Emily explained that she had no idea about the expense of such a grand event or really where to start. “I’ve not updated my wardrobe since my trousseau. I have not such a grand ball-dress as I will need for such an occasion.”

Lady Weston instructed her about getting the house ready for such an occasion. She told her to start by bringing in more help for the cooks by going to town and having the extra help come out a week before the guests were to arrive. “Mrs. Mayfield will give instructions for the food preparation. Meet with Miss Castle on housekeeping, she will have all the room prepared for the guests and Mr. Mason will assign the footmen as to their duties. You will need the house decorations to be updated, and that can be done by Grayson's in Canterbury, and you will need to go to London to have some dresses made for you as soon as possible. I will give you my lady's name and have an appointment made for you. I have an account there, so you should not have any problems." Emily drank in the information and as she was getting up to leave, Lady Weston asked her to sit for a while. "Emily, please sit. I'd like to talk with you about Robert." She slowly sat back down. She wanted Lady Weston's advice but she wasn't so sure about talking to her about Robert. "My dear, I know Robert's hard to deal with. He's always been so aloof. He's been that way since he was a small child. He was our first-born and I'm sorry to say we spoiled him so. He never seemed to let anyone get close to him. Please listen to me, you must persist in trying. He has always seemed to be alone, never letting anyone get close to him. He must be a very lonely man, Emily."

To Emily, Robert just seemed a very arrogant man, not lonely, but the remark stayed with her. Every chance she had alone with him, she tried as Lady Weston asked her to do. There were times when she felt defeated and other times when there was a glimmer of hope. Her days were busy with the upcoming events. Her trip to London was a success; she ended up ordering ten dresses which consisted of two ball gowns, two day dresses, and six dresses suitable for dressing for dinner. Along with the dresses, she purchased three pairs of shoes and four hats at Harrods. When she and her lady's maid returned, it took two autos to carry her purchases. While in London, she made another appointment to have a tweed day jacket and skirt for the annual hunt.

As Emily came into the receiving room, she met Robert as he was going to his office. "What do we have here, Emily?"

She asked her lady's maid to see that the boxes were put in her dressing room. "Yes, Robert, I needed to get some things. Lady Weston gave me the name of her dressmaker and made several appointments for me. Please excuse me, Robert; I need to dress for dinner." She walked away quickly and expected Robert to say something but there was only silence. When she did come down for dinner, Robert had left for London. Emily sat at the large Mahogany table; staring at the seat at the other end, she wondered if her life would always be like this. Even with two small children, a house full of servants, and seeing to Lady Weston's needs, she felt so lonely inside. Staying busy was her only relief but the nights were sometimes unbearable for her. She still stayed in a separate room than Robert; since she moved to the main house, Robert had not asked her to his bedroom. There was no one to talk to; her father was her confidant but this subject would not be acceptable to him. With the position she would be attaining soon, speaking to anyone about such a personal matter would appear as a weakness; she thought about confiding in the estate's minister but he would go right to Robert about the matter. Emily had hoped that Robert's newly acquired title would finally help his disposition.

On the days before the ball, the house was buzzing with people arriving; some were her relatives, along with Robert's, while others were dignitaries from all over England. Emily's father came but her mother had taken to bed and sent her regrets. Emily was not surprised; at least she could spend time with him alone. As soon as she found the time, she asked her father to walk with her to the south garden. It was a place where she could sit and talk. The south garden was a sculptured garden of evergreens, some designed with the shapes of the animals located on the estate. There were small settees where Emily could sit with her father and talk. At first, the conversation went to the children; he inquired about George and wondered if he crying had stopped. Emily assured him that George's crying had definitely slowed down, and since the children were on the other side of the house, everyone was able to sleep soundly. He commented on the fine job she was doing with her life at Weston, and as she was thanking him, she began to tear up. "My dear, please tell me he is good to you!" he said in a gruff.

"Oh, father, he doesn't hurt me or anything like that. It's just that he doesn't have anything to do with me or the children."

He smiled at his daughter, "Emily, you have to realize how busy he is; give the man time, I am sure he will come around. You are to be supportive right now, cater to his needs, and do it so that he notices." The short talk gave Emily a new outlook and she went back to the house with a renewed outlook.

The next four days were some of the most exciting days of Emily's life. There was the afternoon hunt on the southern corner. The land was full of wildlife, with the morning consisting of duck hunting, followed by a supper at the hunting lodge, followed by an afternoon of rest for the women and cards for the gentleman, which led into an afternoon deer hunt. The women made their way back to the house to dress for dinner, while the men followed later that evening. Dinner was served at 8 pm that evening to give the men time to return home. The next day was a day of rest in the early hours so that one would be ready for the large dinner served over several hours. The eight-course meal was served by nine footmen; it included part of the local game from the hunt, to fresh seafood imported in for the occasion. Wines were including with each course and before the evening's festivities, the men adjourned to the library while the women played bridge in the card room. With the rooms being close to one another, Emily could hear what sounded like a muttered argument coming from the other room. It persisted to the point of someone leaving the room and slamming the door. "What in the world is happening, ladies?" said one of the guests but in a short time, Sir Bryon Nobles had Emily's lady maid come in and ask to speak to her. "Sir Bryon asked that Lady Bryon see him in their room." Emily went over whispered in her ear and she took her leave.

The evening went on without any mention of the incident. Lady Weston made an appearance, long enough to congratulate her son on attaining his new title, and made a short speech about Robert's father. Emily and Robert danced the first dance as the others followed. Emily had greeted all those in attendance and it seemed that the night was over. It had all gone by so quickly to her. As she turned to see her lady's maid standing behind, she was greeted by "Good morning, your ladyship!" She smiled to herself; she was now a woman with a title, a title that she would have to her grave.

Guests started leaving early that morning and Emily was busy making sure their needs were met. As soon as Robert said goodbye to the last guest, he was off to London. Emily caught him as he was about to leave. "I'm sorry, something's come up and I have to leave as soon as possible." Emily turned and wished him a good trip. He stopped her with a touch of his hand on her arm, "Emily, thank you; everything was lovely." She smiled and asked him before leaving the room about Sir Randall leaving. "It's the reason I have to leave so soon. Apparently, there's trouble with Germany again. They've a new chancellor, one that could be a threat to us if we don't watch him. His name is Adolph Hitler."

Emily would hear the name Adolph Hitler every day for years to come. He was an impending fear for all of Britain. She feared for her husband and children. Emily's days were filled with the duty that her title demanded and overseeing her children's care. Her and Robert's life seemed to change for the better. When he was at home, he seemed to not want to discuss the looming situation of war. Emily listened intently to the radio and anticipated the coming of war. She remembered the last war and how it affected her life as a child. Her father was past the age of service, and her mother would put it out of mind as she did everything else. Emily's main experience was listening to the conversations that followed. She was fearful as to how her life would change but was naïve as to how much.

Shortly after the announcement of the new chancellor of Germany, events seemed to change rapidly. Robert was busy with business in London and attending meetings. Some of these meetings were held at Weston but as large as the manor house was, there were nights when Emily could hear those arguing clearly, across to the other side of the manor. She knew better than to ask Robert, as his mood was foul following these encounters. He had a look of constant worry about him and these were times when his mind was clearly far from where he was, whether it was the nervousness of the times or just the remembering of the prior war. Robert's mother—who was now addressed as Mary, Dowager Countess of Weston—suddenly became ill. She had held on since the auto accident as best she could but worries were taking the best of her. She felt it necessary to use tea time as a time to secure what should be done before the world changed. She instructed Emily on preparations by keeping a surplus on hand of the bare essentials. "Emily, you must start to keep the pantry full, and you must find a secondary place to store dry goods. You will need to keep the household fed and warm for however long this insurgence will last. Think of your children." This time, which used to be so relaxing for both Emily and the countess, now was unsettling for both women.

On September 3rd of 1939, Britain declared war on Germany. Emily heard the announcement on the radio that was set up in the atrium. She quickly went to find Robert in the library, sitting with his head in his hands. At first, she thought he may be crying but when he looked up at her standing there, he said, "We may just find out what hell is like before we die."

As the Lord of Weston, he was not required to serve but felt it his duty to do so. He assured Emily that his service would be confined to London which would be a command position solely, away from combat. The following day, he had the servants, footmen, and even the livery meet in his library. He asked that the men meet separately with him. "Gents, as you have heard, we are at war with Germany; I know that some of you may want to join the fight and I wish you would make your plans known to me. I will be serving and will be taking my leave soon to London. I have asked Rev. Moore to say a prayer for all of us gathered, and for England…"

The next morning, Robert, along with his footman, left for London. Before leaving, he instructed Smitty, the blacksmith, to watch out for the estate. Smitty had been his playmate through his younger years. Robert's father had not encouraged such a friendship but Smitty had good skills to teach Robert. Lord Weston worried about his son being too much to himself as a child, whereas Smitty was what Lord Weston called "a boy's boy." He was always fishing, hunting, or anything to do with the outdoors. Smitty also knew horses from the time he was old enough to ride one. He taught Robert so many things Lord Weston did not have the time or the wish to do. When the time came for Robert to go to London, he knew Smitty would see to things. London was only 70 miles away from Weston but with the war moving so quickly, Robert knew he would not be home for a while. Weston was relatively safe for now; the only disadvantage was its closeness to Dover, where headquarters were.

Emily was worried about her children, and of late, concerned about Lady Weston. Mama, as she liked to be called by family, was growing weaker as the weeks went on. The doctor had been to see her more often than not, and Emily could tell by his demeanor that the outlook seemed contrary. Emily would spend afternoons encouraging her to take leave of her bed and get some fresh air. At times, her plate was nearly untouched and about the only substance she would take was her tea and crumpets. The doctor said it was better than not having anything at all. On one occasion, Emily insisted that she take a nice, long bath, hoping to lift her spirits. Her lady's maid prepared the bath and assisted her in getting undressed. She was asking Emily if her lady's maid could help lift Mama but Emily insisted on helping her with the task. To both their shock, she was as thin as a rail when lifted. She had kept her ill body to herself with letting anyone know. The following days were some of the hardest days Emily had ever endured. Mama had labored breath and did not respond to anyone's voice. The doctor said it was only a matter of time.

In the evening, as the rain fell hard against the leaded glass, Emily woke up in a fright. She thought she heard someone calling her. She took the light from her bedside and checked on both the children. They were both sound asleep and even the hard rain had not woke them. She went down to check on the nurse sitting with Mama, and as she entered the room, she noticed her head down, snoring loudly. As her eyes went to mama, Emily was surprised to see her eyes open. She appeared to be awake. Emily held her hand and tried to speak to her but Mama looked straight up at the ceiling, smiled ever so slightly, and closed her eyes. To Emily, it was as if she saw someone she knew and as soon as her eyes closed, she breathed her last breath. Emily had never been around death before and had never seen anyone die but for some reason, she felt a peace come over her. She stayed next to the grand lady until daybreak when the nurse finally woke. "Oh, my lady, I am so sorry! I didn't mean to fall asleep, please forgive me." But Emily told her to call for the doctor and dismissed her. She was glad she was there that rainy night.

Robert was to come to Weston the following day and Emily had the house prepared for those who would be arriving. Whereas an event of death would usually be an occasion of several days, in wartime, the funeral was to be a short affair. The gathering of such dignitaries would be shortening due to the recent bombings in London. Robert left for London the day after the funeral. He met with young Charles and George before leaving and tried his best to explain about Mama. He felt it better to come from the Minister, as to explaining death to them. His affection toward Emily improved over the past months, and on the night before he left, he held her close to him as if he was frightened as to what was to come. Robert was somewhat attentive to his mother; when her health started to fail, he would spend afternoons with her. Their conversations were always just between the two of them but Emily never felt left out and she never asked him what they discussed. She was happy theirs was such a close relationship; to her, it reflected Robert's character. He was a proud man, at times too much so but beyond that starchiness, he did have a kind heart. As he prepared to leave, he asked his footman to carry his goods downstairs and get the auto ready. Emily knocked softly on his dressing room door, "May I walk you down, Robert?"

Robert picked up his briefcase and walked over to her. "Emily, I don't know when I'll be home again. It may be some time. Take care of yourself and the children. You may have to make some decisions about Weston, particularly if you can't get in touch with me. Smitty will know what to do; after all, he was raised on Weston also." Emily straightened herself and walked down the stairs with Robert. The children's nanny was waiting at the bottom of the stairs with the boys. They were both dressed in their fine tweeds and behaving perfectly as their father shook their hands. "You boys take care of your mother and Weston." The main staff was standing outside in line of accordance to rank. Emily waved as Robert's auto went down the tree-lined road.

"My Ladyship, may I speak with you?" Smitty asked as Emily was walking over to the stables.

"Of course, Smitty what is it?" Smitty said that one of the farmers on the east pasture wanted to increase his pasture by 100 acres. He said he could do the clearing and this would enable him to double his herd of sheep for the war effort. Emily asked Smitty for his thoughts and he told her he agreed but felt that the solicitor should write an agreement that the acreage go back to original after the war. Emily said she would contact Mr. Wells to have the papers drawn up. As she walked away, she thought how clever Smitty was.

For a while, days at Weston remained about the same. There was news from London about the bombings. Robert would send messages to Emily mostly through a messenger. Emily's cousin, Bess, sent a telegram to Emily asking if her children could stay at Weston. They lived outside of London and she feared for her children's lives. She would follow her as soon as she had everything secure. Emily could not turn her down and had rooms prepared for them. Bess had two girls ages 10 and 13. Emily saw them the summer before the war broke out and remembered them as being well mannered. There were reports of larger cities such as Birmingham and Coventry being bombed. The children were unable to play in the open fields of Weston for fear of snipers. As the days went on, reports came in of local families losing loved ones. Every week, friends, neighbors, and some who had lived on Weston for generations were being killed. London had casualties by the thousands.

Robert was serving in the command center in London. Emily knew that it was located underground, somewhere in London but that did not mean he was safe from harm. The Blitz was every day, never at the same time—it lasted over 70 days. Robert's visits were never announced beforehand. He was not home for any holidays and would come home in the dead of night; on one occasion, he could not see the house as his driver drove down the road until the headlights of the auto were upon the front entrance. He knew on this night, the absence of a bright moon had helped but he prayed the house and all the occupants would make it through this nightmare. Even though it was after 10 pm, he still expected someone in the main hall to meet him. As he entered the house, there was only one light in the great room; even the fireplace was not burning. He stood standing, remembering how things were just last year. He heard talking from the library and walked over to open the door. Emily was sitting next to the fire with her mending. She saw the door open and held her breath. "Emily, it's Robert." She let out a sigh as she went to him. He had forgotten how beautiful she was and held her close. He felt almost like weeping but held his composure. The pressure of the constant bombing, plus the mounting loss of life was getting to him. Robert had written so many letters to families about losing a loved one, that he had to come home for some peace but what he found worried him.

The war had taken its toll on Weston. The outward appearance had changed drastically. Getting out during the day took courage. The countryside had planes flying over daily. If one stood to identify them for any length of time, you may have a German shoot before you could get under cover. So when the children were outside at all, they were under the cover of trees and were always supervised by an adult. Emily knew how much they were being deprived of the usual play where they could run and explore but their lives were more important. It helped with having the other children there. On one occasion, George was playing just under a large oak tree when they heard a plane overhead; he froze in his tracks as a spray of bullets went in a row next to him. Robert was surprised to see how pale the boys looked. They were getting tall and looked thin to him.

He walked with Emily over to the stables the next morning and realized nearly half of the horses were gone. Some of the horses had been sold to the army as workhorses. There were only six horses left and Robert hoped they would not be needed. He invested, as did his father, in thoroughbreds. Most he had raised himself with the help of Smitty. He wished he could ride his favorite Maxfly but he knew that would be too dangerous now. The horses were let out daily to the meadow next to the stables but there were only a few times Smitty rode them, and usually, it was under the cover of night. Robert was amazed at how well Emily had the house organized. She had the children busy with schoolwork during the day and their nights were filled with games or storytelling. Their favorite activities were when she started a story. She would give them the place the story had taken place, added some characters, and had the children add to the story. Each child would take the characters through different events. Emily wanted them to use their imagination and remembered doing this storytelling with her grandmother. Robert sat and watched how the stories changed from child to child. He smiled as the boys' stories had adventures and Margaret and Victoria's had romance.

That evening, after the children went to bed, Emily came back to Robert. She sat down on a small ottoman and put her head in Robert's lap. Robert thought this to be odd behavior for Emily who seemed so private in their relationship. Before the war, he would have scolded her as to her actions but now he welcomed her attention. He smoothed her hair as they sat in silence, "Robert, how are you, Robert? I worry so about you." He smiled as she lifted her face to him. "I do love you, Robert." It was the first time the word was spoken.

Robert had never expressed his love for her; after all, theirs was an arranged marriage. She felt embarrassed, having said it first but Robert pulled her up to him and kissed her long and hard. Their night together was without holding back. He felt released from the strict constitutions he had always processed. He was finally relaxed for a short time until he heard planes flying low above the house. He ran to the window and pulled the dark cloth back to see that were American planes. "Thank God!"

Robert left early the next morning. He felt relief with seeing the American planes. As his car went through the countryside on their way to Canterbury, the ground below seemed to shake. He saw as the auto went over the next hill, that the city had been bombed. He prayed the Cathedral would be spared. Robert and his driver waited under a large tree until all was quiet. They made their way into the outskirts of the city as people were running out. Stopping the car when they could go no further, they ran toward the bombing site. There were those who could walk and those lying in the streets bleeding, small children were walking around looking for someone to help them while others were speechless from what was happening around them. Robert had seen so much despair from the London bombings but he had never seen it firsthand. He was always in headquarters or tucked away in his room. He had complained about seeing the same four walls for so long, that now he wished he were back. He helped as many as he could before the realization came to him, that maybe Weston may have been bombed.

Weston was a good way from Canterbury by car but still not so far by air. He told his driver to get him back to Weston. He knew the lines would be down in Canterbury so he drove for some miles outside the city and tried to place a call. “Apparently, the lines are down all over. Let’s just drive as quickly as we can bank to Weston.” They rode as fast as the car would let them, passing fire trucks and other emergency vehicles, until they were down the long road to Weston. Robert gasped as he saw the smoke from a distance and knew it was Weston. His thoughts went to Emily and his children. “Please, God, don’t let anything happen to my family.”

As the car got closer, he saw that it was the stable that was hit and not the house. Emily was standing outside as the flames engulfed the large building. She was standing alone with the servants behind her. As Robert ran over to her, she broke down as he held her tight. “Robert, I’m so sorry but we can’t find Smitty.” He looked around at the house and saw the children looking out the second-story window. He asked the children’s nanny to go in and get the children away from the window. The stench from the burning building was sickening.

People from the small farms on Weston came over from nearby farms when word spread about the fire. “I saw the bomb but it didn’t come from the sky like the others, Lord Weston. It came across the field and hit the barn. Never saw a thing like it, no never, my lord.” Robert knew what he was talking about. The German invented a self-propelled bomb called a V-Bomb. The explosion was so severe that the entire stable was on fire and all of the occupants perished in the fire. Robert hoped that Smitty was tending to something away from Weston. Robert took Emily to her room and asked her lady’s maid to stay with her. The lines were down and he could not get in touch with headquarters but felt he should attend to matters at Weston before going back, so he sent a courier to notify them.

The household was battered by constant fear and Robert felt ineffective as head of his manor. As the hours wore on, Smitty was still nowhere to be found until the news came that they found his body in the rubble. For days, the house seemed to be silent as the realization of just what happened came to light. It was bad enough being so confined as they had been but losing someone so dear brought it all home. “When will this bloody thing be over with?” Robert yelled as he slammed his fist on his desk, thinking he was by himself. He turned and saw George standing next to a bookcase. He stared at his father with Robert noticing an expressionless look on his face. “Are you well, young George?” George stood motionless as Robert walked over to him. It tugged at Robert’s heart as he looked at the boy. He picked the young lad up and held him tight as he wept.

The funeral was the following week for Smitty. On the land which once held the stables, was now the burial ground for Smitty and the thoroughbreds he once took care of. A monument was to be erected as soon as possible. The town of Canterbury was nearly destroyed but the Cathedral survived the bombing. It seemed like each family had a member lost in the bombings. As Robert went back to headquarters, he passed through towns—some that were left with just rubble. There were misplaced people roaming all over the countryside and at times, even his fellow Englishmen proved to be as unsavory as the Germans.

- After reporting in, Robert went directly to his office. His assistant gave him a message from his commanding office as soon as possible. He thought that surely this must be about his absence while attending to his family, and was prepared to defend himself as he reported but when he entered the briefing room, he was surprised to see several officers around the table. As he walked over to them, they parted to reveal the Deputy to the Prime Minister. "It's good to see you, Lord Weston. I hope you are well and ready to help with an endeavor we have for you." Robert was taken aback as to the importance of the matter. He was trained in military matters but had never been in anything so related to combat. "I believe you spent some time in Germany as a boy and you have some knowledge of the countryside. Can you confirm with me here by looking at this map? The area marked—is that the area you are familiar with?" Robert had spent time as an adolescent in Germany. It was a summer he would never forget. His father was invited to an estate outside of Berlin to spend the summer and was able to take the family. They stayed at the estate of Baron Von Helm with his family, who had a son the same age as Robert and a daughter, two years elder. Robert's summer consisted of learning to drink German beer and nightly visits to their daughter, Prinzin Gertrude. Robert recognized the area on the map and knew exactly what they were talking about. There was an ammunition factory located near the area of Baron Von Helm's estate. The factory was located in a small town, adjacent to his estate. "We believe this is one of the biggest ammunition factories in Germany. Like so many other such installations, it was built next to a school or a hospital in order for its protection from being bombed. There is a school next to the building. Of course, the children are there during the day only. On the other side, there is a small building that is marked as a hospital but intelligence tells us that this is merely an extension of the factory. As usual, a very unorthodox thing to do, wouldn't you say, chap? What we are asking you for, Lord Weston, is to accompany the reconnaissance flight into Germany to identify the area. I know this is a lot to ask since you will be flying in during daylight and it is heavily guarded but you seem to be our best chance for this."

- There were ways in which Robert wanted to be more involved in the war, to really get out there with his comrades but he wasn't sure this was it. "Sir, I would be happy to serve."
- As soon as he said it, his hands started to shake. "Good man, good man!"
- Emily received a letter from Robert several days after he left. In most of his letters, he would ramble on as to the conditions in London, or tell about the people he ran into but this was shorter than most. She noticed his penmanship to be as if it was written in a hurry.
- My Darling Emily,
- The journey back to London was long and disheartening. My grand old England is being destroyed as this war goes on. The longer it lasts, the longer it will be to get this country back to what it once was. We must all do our part. I know this is rarely said but I want you to know that I love you and our children very much, and hope to be home shortly.
- All My Love,
- Robert

Emily was distressed by his words. Not only were they so different from his previous letters but she felt something was wrong. She tried to contact him with the contact number she had but when she was able to get through, he was not there and at other times, the lines were down. She thought about going to London herself but knew she would be in danger, and someone needed to be with the children. She finally got in touch with her cousin who worked near Robert's headquarters. She was working for the army and could find out about Robert since all other means seemed useless. It was days before she got back to her and then. The static was so bad that Emily could hardly hear her. "Lady Emily, I can't find out too much; all I know is that Robert is helping with something that is hush-hush but his assistant said he was fine and not to worry. He said he sent a letter some weeks ago from Robert, he put it in the post himself."

Emily knew that it was the letter she had received and thought it was odd she received it so fast since the post usually took weeks. The worry seemed to stay with her as the weeks went by. After the bombing of the stables, the children were confined to the middle of the house in case of another attack. They all knew they could be attacked again in the same manner as before but the only alternative was to stay in the cellar during the day. The children were pale and thin already, so Emily would have them go away from the house and try to get some sun on them through the trees or even to go to the gardens where they could not be so easily noticed overhead.

On this Sunday morning, the Minister was coming to Weston to hold services. Before the service was to start, her ladyship's maid brought her a note that he wanted to see her in the library before the service. Emily took it as being something to do with the service and paid no mind or worry about it. When she entered the library, she noticed two uniformed officers in attendance—one, she knew to be Robert's cousin. She gasped as she saw them. "No, no, your ladyship! Please let us explain." They helped her sit as they told of Robert's plight. "Robert was on a mission—one he volunteered for. If you will remember—when he was a boy, Lady Emily, he spent some time in Germany. Sir Robert helped us with a mission since he knew the area in question. He went on a mission to pinpoint the area in question and returned to London that day but when the time came for the bombing, he wanted to offer his help. He was concerned because our target had a school beside the target and he wanted to make sure that the target was cleared of children in the area. Robert's plane was in trouble and he parachuted in time before the plane went down."

Emily felt her world caving in around her; she heard her grandmother saying to her "remember your position, dear." Her position meant to always remember her position, no matter the circumstances. "Do you think he made it to safety?"

The minister put his hand on hers, "We think he has been captured by the Germans. We hope to get word confirming this soon."

Emily had never felt so alone. There were people attending to her needs. She had a house full of servants, an estate large enough to support several families, yet she had no confidants among them. She missed Smitty and their daily talks. The children were still so young and even her cousin's children, being older than her own, were no help to her loneliness. The Americans had stepped into the war some time ago and England's attacks were fewer than before. Her heart ached for Robert as he was constantly on her mind. She felt so different than she did when she first married him. He was such an arrogant man, never letting his caring side show but the war had changed him. Emily wanted to contribute in some way to the war effort but she knew she was doing so by caring for her own children and her cousin's two young girls.

On one early morning, she set out to visit the families that lived on the estate. Many had lived on Weston for generations and cared about Weston as much as the Weston family. She set out to visit them one by one. She chose one day to try and visit as many as she could. Emily saddled one of the horses from a neighboring farm that was brought over after the loss of the stables. He was over in a field within walking distance and she used Robert's mother saddle, that she stored down in the basement. She thought it best to ride to the neighbors by horseback; that way, if she did hear an overhead plane, she could take cover under the trees. The threat was always there but since the Blitz had ended, German planes were few. The war was turning around with the help of the Allies. Before the war, any visits would be announced but Emily felt she would put more people in jeopardy by doing so. The more families she visited, the grander her ideas became. Weston comprised several hundred areas and much of it was lying unused. Emily saw a chance to contribute by using the land even more than before; pasture could be expanded. There was vast timber to be used and with the help of those she spoke with, it was possible. The one thing she wanted to do was not to have Weston lose its beauty. Fields were opened to those who had cattle, sheep, and other livestock. Emily's main problem was getting the livestock to market, so she asked Robert's cousin, Sir Randall, for help. "My lady, I don't mean to be rude but I don't think Robert would agree with this."

Emily knew he would react this way, "Sir Randall, I just want to do something more for the war effort. England has to ration food and this is one way I can help. We have vast resources here."

Sir Randall cleared his throat, "I realize that but you don't know about the situation you are entering in and frankly, neither do I. I don't think I can help you." Sir Randall was hoping this would end Lady Weston's protests but she vowed to find someone to help her.

On the following day, she asked her driver to drive her into Canterbury. It was one of the few times Emily had left Weston since the bombing of the city and the Weston Stables. Her nerves were on end as the car entered the city. She gasped as she looked at the rubble from the homes and offices that were bombed. Buildings had sandbags protecting them. There were signs with arrows to the nearest bomb shelters along with other signs about looting. She noticed how fast people ran from place to place, and there were very few children playing outside. As the auto went by the City's Cathedral, she asked the driver to stop. "I'll just be a moment," she said as she started to go into the church. As she walked down, passing the beautifully carved pews, she stopped to take in the beautiful stained-glass windows. Emily knelt down; she prayed for Robert's safe return, for her children's safety, and for her old England. As she thought about her life now and how life was, she started to weep. Her tears started slowly as they ran down her cheeks until her sobs were heard throughout the large cathedral. This was until she felt a hand pressing on her shoulder. As she stopped and turned to look behind, she realized she was the only person in the church. Emily's crying had drowned out the siren. She ran out onto the street and saw the fear on her driver's face. "Come, my lady, down here," as they both ran into the shelter. The shelter was located under one of the office buildings on the other side of the street. As they ran, Emily could hear the bombing in the distance. She looked up to see a single plane on fire, heading down, toward another building. As she and her driver ran into the shelter, they followed the others down a narrow staircase and gathered close to one another. The building around them shook as the plane crashed. The lights went off and on as powder filled the room as they all started to cough, then another siren went off to signal the all-clear. Being unprepared, Emily followed those with flashlights to the upper level. As everyone got into the street, sirens rang loudly as fire trucks went to the fire, burning from the crashed plane. There were those attending to the wounded and people running everywhere. Bewilderment was the look most had. Emily felt as if she was an outsider; she wasn't any help to those suffering and did not have any skill to help those around her. Her thoughts as to Weston helping the cause were made stronger that afternoon and she vowed she would pursue what she started out to do. Weston would forgo the lavish countryside that stood idle and become a working estate to help the war cause.

With the disruption around the city of Canterbury that day, Emily returned to Weston. Early the next morning, she took her chances and saddled one of the few horses left at Weston. Even with the warnings, she left to go to the Fultons' small farm. Mr. Fulton was very adept at raising cattle and other livestock. His family had lived on the farm for several generations. They were surprised by the visit from Lady Weston. It was highly unusual for such a visit—a visit where she had not been announced beforehand. Emily felt the lack of protocol was acceptable during these times. She stated her purpose right off, and Mr. Fulton agreed. Emily had granted him more pasture to help with the increasing amount of cattle for the war effort; now, she wanted to add more. She even pondered about building a slaughterhouse on the property but knew Robert would never approve. It was agreed that more cattle be added to the estate and land was to be cleared as soon as feasible.

She felt comfortable knowing she was at least helping the war effort and that maybe, somehow, there would be an end to this one day and Robert would come home. Her fears would wake her at night and she'd go down to Robert's study, hoping she would feel some comfort in the room he loved so much. As the war went on, the children were able to get out more. Emily's cousin was able to send clothing from London for her two girls and Emily's boys. But rations and supplies were getting harder to come by. Meat was plentiful since their cattle and sheep were right there but foods such as coffee and even flour were harder to come by. "I'll not be baking the cakes I used to bake, Lady Weston," said the head cook.

"Don't be worrying about that, we'll get by," answered Emily.

Emily had reports from Robert's brother weekly of any news about Robert, "He was captured and is in a POW Camp on the German border. From all the indications, he is well. It helps that he speaks fluent German." Emily knew Robert spent time there as a boy with his father's friend, Baron Von Helm.

One evening while all were huddled in the study, Stubbs, the butler, said, "There is a gentleman asking to see Lady Weston. He says he served with Sir Robert and has news of him. He is waiting in the great hall. Shall I have him shown to the Library, my lady?" Perplexed by such a visit but anxious too, she told Stubbs to show him to the library and she would be there momentarily. Her heart was racing as she straightened herself in the mirror and proceeded to the library.

As she walked in, she noticed a gentleman standing, looking at the fire. Stubbs cleared his throat as the soldier turned to look at Lady Weston. "Your Ladyship, please excuse my sudden arrival. Please let me introduce myself—I am Captain Henry Waddington."

Emily noticed Stubbs looking at the gentleman with a slight frown on his face. "Please, Captain Waddington may we sit by the fire." He waited for her to sit and took the chair directly across from her.

As he walked over to the chair, she noticed him limping on his right leg. "Sorry, Lady Weston, I was injured at the Battle of the Rhine and I have trouble getting around right now." Emily sympathized with the young soldier and voiced her concern to him. "I have a letter of introduction that Sir Robert gave me before he was captured. I have been told he is in good health." Relief was felt immediately when Emily heard of this and she asked Stubbs to have a maid bring the gentleman some tea. "Oh, that's very kind of you, your Ladyship. I am rather parched from my journey." After drinking his tea, he presented her with a small envelope. She noticed the envelope to be stained and wrinkled and thought it to be from Captain Waddington's travels. She was anguished to see what Robert had written. Emily held the letter to her heart, took a breath and opened the contents of the envelope.

My darling Emily,

I am writing this letter of introduction for my pal, Captain Henry Waddington. He has served with me and has been my right-hand man. Please show him every kindness and make him welcome at Weston. He is recovering from an injury and needs to rest. I have offered for him to stay at Brightan while recuperating.

Your loving husband,

Robert

Emily thought it strange, at first, for Robert to refer to the Captain as a pal and the spelling of Brighton was misspelled. "Stubbs, please have a footman accompany Captain Waddington to Brighton along with any supplies he will need." Stubbs left the room as Captain Waddington declared he did not have a need for a footman, and would see about any supplies that he needed. The cottage was larger than most on Weston and was kept up in case of need of guests coming to stay. She bid him goodbye and asked him to come to tea the following day.

As she turned to leave, Stubbs asked if he might have a word with her. "Of course, please feel free to speak your mind, Stubbs."

He clasped his hands to his stomach and grumbled as he spoke, "I am sorry, your Ladyship but for some reason, the gentleman seems misplaced. I am glad he will not be staying under the roof of Weston. I sometimes have these feelings, your Ladyship. Please be careful."

Emily thought it odd for Stubbs to speak, without anything so much more than a feeling. "Stubbs, I will be careful, we all will. Please tell my lady's maid that I will be going to bed."

Captain Waddington was a tall, distinguished-looking man with blonde hair and deep-set blue eyes. Emily was trying to place his accent and planned to ask him where his family was settled. She could usually tell which part of England one was raised, as soon as they spoke. There was a great difference between northern England and southern England. She assumed that he would be getting in touch with his brigade as soon as he was settled. Besides the faint limp, he seemed to have no other impediment that was visible.

The next afternoon, he arrived for tea when expected. He again was dressed in his uniform that seemed to have been through quite an ordeal, to Emily. He looked a bit disheveled, to Emily but she asked him to sit next to the large window in the morning room. Emily had the dark covering taken down from the large window that looked over the west garden. On this clear day, the room was warmed by the sun, and even though the garden was kept up as before the war, the view still had a calming effect. "Please have a seat, Captain Waddington and let me pour you some tea." She returned his smile and poured him some tea as she felt his eyes never leave her. "Would you prefer cream or lemon, Captain?" He answered neither, which came as a surprise to Emily as a request from an Englishman. "Captain, where is your family from?" asked Emily.

"Why would you ask such a question, my lady?"

Taken aback, she answered, "Oh! I do apologize, Captain, I was just curious about your accent."

Emily tried to change the subject but the Captain held tight-lipped and did not speak. "No, your Ladyship, I am the one to apologize. I lost my parents years ago and have been in service to my country ever since. I have not settled at any place particular since then. I am rather displaced. It is why your kind husband offered me a place here for my confinement until I am well. I thank you for your kindness, Lady Weston." Emily felt awful and embarrassed by her questions. The subject would never be brought up again, she vowed.

Captain Waddington left soon after that and she did not see him for several days. When Sir Randall came by for a visit, Emily mentioned Captain Waddington to him and showed him the letter of introduction he had in his possession. "I don't think I have ever heard Sir Robert say—much less use in a letter—the word pal before. He must have certainly picked up some common language while in service. Tell me, Emily; did this young Captain have any word about Robert?"

Emily sat up in her chair and said with excitement, "Yes, he said he had heard Robert was well. He said he was in a POW Camp located in Germany near the border of Switzerland."

Robert's brother puffed on his pipe with a concerned look on his face, "I find that hard to believe, that information is classified. I would like to meet Captain Waddington. Your Ladyship, would it be possible to arrange a meeting with Captain Waddington here at Weston?"

Emily thought it would be nice to have a small dinner party with Captain Waddington being the main guest. "I can arrange something soon. I will notify you when I have an exact date."

Emily rose up from her seat, thinking Randall was leaving after his visit but he stayed seated. "Emily, we need to speak about the recent endeavor with Weston being used as a farm." She turned and sat across from Robert's brother, prepared to have a serious conversation about her plan. "You know Robert would be greatly upset with what you are doing with Weston. Your endeavor would be suitable more for a gentleman than the Lady of Weston."

Emily smiled as she explained her convictions. "Randall, I have been able to help the war effort in this venture. Weston will get back to what it once was when Robert returns and the war is over. I have done very little to Weston while producing a great deal of food for the Army." The more he scolded her, the angrier she got. He knew, by her demeanor, that it was best to leave the subject alone, for now. Her discontent was evident. He rose from his seat, kissed her hand and said he would see her soon. When he left Weston, he had seen another side of Lady Emily; one he suspected Robert had never seen.

Robert had been in the German camp for over six months now. She prayed that God would keep him in good health until this terrible war was over with.

Germany had taken over France and was pushing into Russia but recently, the tide was turning in England's favor. Whenever Emily would ask Captain Waddington about the dinner party at Weston, he seemed to always be busy. For some reason, he was going to Dover quite often. Emily knew Dover to be one of the main strategic posts for England's defense so she dismissed any concern of him not coming as often to Weston. She hardly knew he was on the estate at all.

Emily's cousin, Bess, came for a stay early that next week. Her daughters had been at Weston for nearly two years now and Emily had become so attached to Margaret and little Victoria that she hated to see them go. They were so much company to her but London was safer now than at the beginning of the war. Their schooling had moved along well, thanks to Emily having Professor Drake coming by during the week. He was a well-known professor that had taught at Oxford for most of his teaching years. Now reaching the age of 60, he retired to the town of Canterbury to live with his sister during his later years but after the war started, his sister's home was one of the first to be bombed. Professor Drake had just finished his breakfast with his sister when he walked out the door, walked over to the local library, only to turn and see the bomb fall from the sky with a direct hit on his sister's house. In a second's time, he lost his sister and a place to call home. Now, the small townhouse was reduced to rubble along with his most treasured possessions. His book collection was one of the best private ownership in all of England and now, all he owned were the clothes on his back. He was grateful to Lady Weston when she hired him to tutor the children. Emily thought him to be the answer to her prayers for the children. Even though they were homebound, especially at the beginning of the war, his teachings took them all over the world. He opened up so many things to them including her favorite sessions during the dark nights. Professor Drake taught them to think on their own. He would start with a beginning to a story, give several sentences that included a character or two, a location, and a short scenario to begin with; then, he asked each child to add to the story, one at a time. He was amazed at their imaginations and so was Emily. What started out as a chore, in the beginning, turned into something exciting later. Cousin Bess had planned to take the children back to London that summer and could see each time she visited her girls how much they had learned. Emily planned on keeping Professor Drake as long as possible but knew the boys would go to boarding school as soon as the war was over and Robert was home. She dismissed—in her mind—any thought of England losing the war and Hitler taking over England.

Several weeks after Sir Randall's visit, she received a note from him saying he would like to meet Captain Waddington. He suggested that instead of planning for a specific date for a dinner party, perhaps she could arrange for a brief meeting without him being aware of Sir Randall being in attendance. Emily thought it strange, coming from him. He suggested Emily ask Captain Waddington to come by, in reference to some kind of need for help or advice.

She had Stubbs post a note to him to arrange a time and asked for a reply of confirmation. *Surely, he will not refuse*, she thought. Captain Waddington had been there for several weeks and Emily thought his recovery should be nearly at an end. She received a reply by post a day before the meeting. She knew it would be easier had she picked up the telephone but was afraid her voice would give her away.

Sir Randall arrived the evening before, prepared to stay at Weston that night. He avoided any discussion at length about Captain Waddington and kept his topic on other happenings. Their conversation was mostly about Robert and the times they were all together as children. Emily had fond memories of Weston as a child. When there was a celebration at Weston, her family was invited. With Robert and Emily being four cousins, her family was always included, whether it was the yearly hunt, a relative's wedding, or the annual fox hunt—she was included in it all. She loved Robert's mother and was especially close to her throughout the years. "You know, Randall, I was not too fond of Robert when we were children," she laughed.

He coughed on her words and started to laugh so loudly, that he seemed to choke; the butler came into the library to ask if he needed anything. Sir Randall got his breath and said, "Me neither," and they both laughed.

It was at this point that her laughter turned to tears, "Oh God, forgive me, and I'd give anything to have him here."

Sir Randall patted her hand, "There, there, Lady Emily, we'll have him home soon."

The next morning, Emily had the servants prepare a midday meal to be served in the drawing-room that faced the back of Weston. The same garden of boxwoods and roses was kept up fairly well during these past years and was still pleasant to look at. To Emily, it had a calming effect on her, and she thought that conversation was easily exchanged because of it. Captain Waddington arrived earlier than expected. Sir Randall was still not in attendance and Emily had to get the message to him, somehow, without the Captain being suspicious. "Your Ladyship, I am here as expected. Please tell me, what may I do to help you?"

Nervously, she said, "Oh, Captain Waddington, please pardon me. My servants did not listen to me about the preparation for today's meal. Please have a seat and I shall return post-haste." She went out of the room, hoping Randall would come in shortly.

After waiting for a while, she did not see him so she went back into the drawing-room, and noticed Captain Waddington making a notation in a small book. He quickly put the book in his lapel as Emily walked back into the room. "I have to make notations, my memory has suffered of late."

Emily tried her best to keep up small talk, waiting for Sir Randall but as he walked into the room, Captain Waddington remain seated. Sir Randall walked over to Captain Waddington and stood directly in front of him where he was seated. "Captain Waddington, it is customary that you rise and salute me as soon as I enter the room. Have you forgotten your military training so soon?" Captain Waddington slowly rose from his chair and saluted the colonel. As Sir Randall turned to sit in the seat closest to the Captain, Captain Waddington took his seat once again, before allowing the Colonel to be seated first. Sir Randal bit his lip and reprehended him a second time; he attributed the matter to the soldier's war wounds. Emily kept busy, instructing the servants on several unimportant instructions, allowing the gentlemen to talk for a while until Stubbs announced dinner was served. They entered the small dining room on the east side of Weston. The room was smaller than the family dining room where guests were usually entertained but Emily felt a small environment would be more comfortable. The entire conversation was mostly Sir Randall questioning Captain Waddington about his background. Emily observed that he was trying not to be so obvious but to her, he could not be less so.

The small talk went on until the end of the meal and the gentlemen went into Robert's library for a cigar. As soon as Emily saw the gentlemen go into the library, she barely made her way up the steps before they emerged from the room. Captain Waddington came out of the room in what seemed like a hurry, proclaiming he had all but forgotten an appointment he had. "Please accept my apology, your Ladyship; I am late for an appointment in town," he explained, as he went quickly to the main hall and out the door.

"Rather odd, Lady Emily but there is something about this Captain Waddington that seems so familiar to me. I do not know what it is but in time, I can usually figure it out." He kissed her and bid her farewell.

The entire visit was strange, at best. Emily knew of the Captain's war wounds to be related to his limping from a leg wound but he had never expressed any kind of memory loss, except for his sudden forgetfulness today. Emily dismissed the event and kept busy with the details of the estate. The size of the house and the staff that ran it was enough to keep her occupied, but the added duty of keeping the estate running with the newfound war effort rarely gave her time to take care of everything. The children were busy with school during the day and the evenings were Emily's time with them. The never-ending task kept her mind off from the worry of Robert. Word would come to her through Robert's brother of information through military channels about Robert. It had now been over a year since his capture. She knew he was in a POW camp in Germany and was still alive but that was the limit of her information. At times, she would ride early in the morning to the small chapel on the estate to pray for Robert. There was something about the old chapel that gave her peace and for some reason, she felt a closeness to him. The chapel was over two hundred years old and was the original church built on Weston when the land was given to the Weston family. Since then, there were two other churches built—one destroyed by fire, and the present church located on the other side of the estate.

Early one morning while coming back from the chapel, she noticed Captain Waddington standing in the middle of the road, talking with a gentleman on a motorcycle. They looked to be arguing, as Emily held back her horse; she slowly dismounted and walked over, under some low trees. The conversation seemed to grow in anger until Captain Waddington pushed the younger man down to the ground. He continued to yell at the man loudly, as Emily tried to listen to what he was saying. She tied her horse to the tree and edged closer to listen until she could hear what Captain Waddington was saying! At first, she could hardly believe what she was hearing. The motorcycle roared away loudly and she quickly mounted her horse and rode down the trail, away from where Captain Waddington was. Her heart pounded fiercely as she rode home—hoping he did not see her—and she thought she should get in touch with Sir Randall as soon as possible. As she came into the main entrance, she quickly ran to the library to use the telephone. She was quickly informed that he was out of town and would not return until the following Sunday. Emily was frantic, not knowing where to turn. She quickly went to Mr. Drake, the children's teacher. "Mr. Drake, I am so sorry to interrupt but I must have a word with you as soon as possible." He looked startled at first, but in his usual manner instructed Charles to proceed and excused himself. Emily asked him to follow her down to the library. As she walked ahead of him, she turned every few steps to check if he was there. Her nervousness kept him to the point of almost stumbling in her footsteps. "Please, please have a seat," she said, as she tapped her hand on the chair.

Mr. Drake sat attentively as Emily wrung her hands without saying a word. "Lady Weston, may I be of some assistance to you?"

She pulled up a small chair over to him and with almost a whisper, asked, "If I tell you a word, could you find out what language it is?"

Mr. Drake was taken somewhat aback and replied, "I am acquainted with several languages and may be able to tell you now, pray tell."

"The word is drummer arch," Emily said looking around the room and repeating the word to Mr. Drake.

"Lady Weston, the word is of the German language and well, it means—the best way of saying it, stupid or numb skull. It's a slang word, at best. May I ask where you heard it?" Emily went to answer him but thought it best to keep the information to herself and wait until Robert's brother came back.

Emily's nerves grew worse that evening, thinking Captain Waddington may have seen her leave. Her thoughts would not let her rest as she tried to discover some reason for him to use the German language. She went over—in her mind—the events of that day; the young man he was screaming at, so shabbily dressed and riding a motorcycle. It was early in the morning before she finally fell asleep. Her dreams woke her up in a fright when she thought about him living on Weston. She rang for her lady's maid and then rang again quickly before she came running into her room. "My lady, is everything alright?"

Emily rose out of bed, quickly put on her day gown and asked Rose to go down and check on the children. "Wait; Rose, ask Mr. Drake to keep the children in the study and to please not let them out of his sight." Her lady's maid stood, blinking her eyes rapidly. "Go now and do what I asked you." Rarely was Emily ever short with her staff but she was in complete dismay over the situation and the uncertainly of it all.

She hoped there may be some explanation for Captain Waddington speaking the German language to another as he did. He was clearly upset and ill of temper. As Emily looked out from beyond the black curtains, she was amazed at the beauty of the gardens of Weston. Even though they were not up to their usual mannered look, the east garden was one to behold. As she did when she was upset as a child, she turned to her Bible for solace. She held the book she had as a child, that was given to her by the Vicar of her father's estate and as usual, she let it open by pulling the covering apart. As usual, she found a passage that soothed her nerves. Her grandmamma had shown her this when she was but six years old and Emily had held to the tradition still. She dressed for the day and decided to visit the Fultons' farm to check on the progress being made to sell the upcoming harvest. The farm was on the opposite side of Weston from where Captain Waddington was staying.

As she went downstairs, she visited the children and asked Mr. Drake if she could have a word with him. "Mr. Drake, please see that the children remain with you in class until I return from the Fultons' farm. If, for some reason, I am delayed, please leave them with Rose…She has instructions not to let them out of her sight."

He looked at her, perplexed by her statement, “Is there something wrong, my Lady?” he asked.

“No, no, I am just concerned about a situation and I know I am being overshadowing but that is my nature.”

After instructing that her horse be ready, Emily proceeded to the small barn that Smitty loved so much. She thought to herself how much her life had changed over the last few years. As she walked over to the barn, she suddenly mounted her horse and rode out, taking in the beautiful blue sky and richness of the green meadow. Emily rode hard as if to run from someone, turning around to see if she was being followed. As she came to the narrow road to the Fultons, she slowed her stride and trotted to the old farmhouse.

The Fultons were given land to use as pasture. Emily gave them more than double their pasture after the war started. She knew Robert would be upset by this but it was her effort to help the soldiers fighting in the war. The grain they raised was used to feed the cattle that were being raised on the northern pastures, and the vegetables were sold to help the war effort, also. Emily thought Weston would get back to normal when Robert returned, and surely he would understand her purpose in doing this. As she approached the large farmhouse, little Sarah came running out to greet her, only to be followed by Mary Fulton. She was drying her hands in her apron. “Oh, my lady, so sorry, I must look a fright!”

Emily smiled, “No matter, Mary, I am unannounced and I am the one most sorry. I should have sent you a note of my intentions.” She showed Emily in and excused herself. Emily could hear her giving instructions to her eldest daughter. She looked around and smiled as she looked at Mary’s parlor. Though her furnishing was sparse, the room was well maintained. The shelves were flanked by old china and old books while embroidered curtains covered the windows. Hooked rugs were scattered around the room and Mary’s personal touch was everywhere. There were times when Emily envied having a home with her own personal touch; even her home as a child had furnishing, not of her mother’s choice or even her Grandmama’s choosing, some over centuries old, just like Weston. A young girl came into the room, carrying a tray that was shaking along with the child’s hands. She walked over and nearly dropped it on the small table in front of Emily. Emily smiled at her as if to calm her as she curtsied and left quickly.

Mary came in shortly with a clean white apron and her hair combed and put up in a bun. “I can send one of the children out to fetch Walter from the fields? He is working close to the house today and it shall not take long,” asked Mary.

"There no need for that. Please ask him to let me know how the harvest is coming along. I would just like a visit with you now." Mary looked startled at first before realizing the tea was getting cold. She poured Emily a cup with her hands shaking as badly as her daughter. "I enjoy coming here, Mary. Your girls are lovely and the house is so accommodating." Both women seemed too relaxed as they talked about the perils of life during wartime.

Before Emily realized, the afternoon was growing dark with clouds brewing outside. "I think I should be taking my leave before a storm comes."

They both rose as Mary went to look out the window. "I believe it will be here shortly, why you don't let Mr. Fulton carry you home in the truck? At least you will be covered. We can take your horse tomorrow." Emily insisted she would be fine and left promptly. As she rode away, the sky behind her was dark; she could hear the thunder rumbling as she rode fast, down the road to the open meadow. She thought surely she could beat the rain but as she rode, the thunder grew louder. Emily's heart pounded so hard that the sound seemed louder than the thunder. The rain started to hit her hard and she found it hard to see, so she headed over to the covering of the trees but before reaching the edge of the forest, her horse rode up as the thunder clapped. The last thing Emily remembered was the ground getting closer as she fell.

The evening was fast approaching as the servants waited for their mistress's return. The more they spoke, the worse their suspicions were. The rain had stopped and the sky was growing dark. "My lady was very concerned about something before she left; like you, she did not speak of where her journey was to be."

The stableman came running in from the side door and into the cook room, stuttering to get a word out; the other servants started yelling at him. "The…The horse…it's here!" The horse was riderless, the saddle was hanging sideways, and the animal was clearly in distress. Without Lady Emily there to guide the household, Stubbs took over the order of Weston. He asked Master Charles to sit in on his instructions. He sent for Sir Randall and sent out notifications to all the local farmers on Weston, in case they had seen Lady Weston. It wasn't before too long that Mr. Fulton said he had seen her earlier that day. "Lady Weston was visiting the farm earlier today and spent a good while with my wife and my daughter. When she left, there was the rumbling of thunder in the distance. I tried to warn her from leaving but she insisted on getting back to Weston." Mr. Fulton was beside himself. "Sir, if anything has happened to her ladyship, I will personally hold you responsible…"

The dim light hanging from the ceiling was moving back and forth. She thought it to be hypnotic as she tried to focus her eyes. The last thing she remembered was the flash of lightning and the ground getting closer to her.

Emily tried to move but the pain was unbearable. She heard the clicking sound and tried to turn her head toward the sound. Even with the faint light, she could see a faint image sitting at a small table, as he slowly moved his hand to the rhythm of the sounds; some being repetitious, and some being singular. She recognized the sound—the same sound as when she would accompany her father when he sent a telly—although it wasn't exactly the same but close enough. Emily could smell a familiar mustiness, she could not quite place it; she turned her head toward the old brick wall and then turned quickly as she sensed him standing near her, looking down at her. "My dear Lady Emily, how regal you look now! Your tattered dress stained with mud and grass, the proper hair fallen into dismay and look, your bosom in full display. What a proper English lady you are." He laughed as he turned away to light a cigarette. Emily pulled what was left of her blouse over her breast. She noticed her blouse had been cut and not torn as the edges were straight. She quickly looked around to take in her surroundings. "You know I can't let you tell them what I am doing, you stupid woman. I saw you over the hill when I was having a talk with one of your fellow countrymen. Your people are weak, just like your dear Robert." He started to laugh, not in a manner as before but more like a continuous catcalling. Emily became angrier than ever before. Her skin crawled as he went on. "I mean weak, like your pompous Robert. I hated him like no other. My father would bow down to his father and him. He would praise them and put me down in front of them. I've been planning his demise for some time but he helped it along, by getting himself shot down. It really fell into my lap, so to speak. Well, now I get to have his wife. The laugh is on him."

Emily managed to sit up as he approached her, "Please tell me if he is still alive."

He stopped and smiled down at her. He reached down his hand, grabbed her chin sharply, and pulled her face up to his. "Yes, my lady, I am keeping him alive so that I can be the one to kill him—kill him with my bare hands, my Lady. That is after I tell him about what I did to you."

He started to unbutton his shirt, pulled it off and threw it on the dirty floor, undid his pants and dropped them to the floor. Captain Waddington was naked, standing over her, laughing. He grabbed himself, "I'm going to tell your dear Robert how much you like this before I kill him." He leaned over her and put his hand under her blouse and then started to undo her buttons on her riding pants. Emily's anger swelled up in her as he lifted his face and spat on her, "You bitch, you dumb bitch!" She looked up at him and with all her might, she jabbed the screwdriver she had been holding into his neck. His eyes widened as blood dripped down on her. His hands went for her neck as he squeezed with all the strength he had left. Her breath went out of her as his image fell apart.

Someone was shaking her hard—she feared when she'd open her eyes he would still be there. "Emily, it's Randall," he said while patting her face. She caught her breath in a sudden panic and rose up straight. With rapid breathing, she looked around to see Sir Randall and another soldier with him. They handed her a wet towel and covered her with a warm blanket. Emily stared at the dead body of a man she thought was Captain Waddington, with the screwdriver still in his neck. "Emily, this is Hans Von Helm, the son of Baron Von Helm whom we used to visit in Germany when we were children. The last time I saw him, he was around seven. I should have seen the familiarity."

Emily covered her face with her hands, "My God, I have killed someone." Randal came over to her, pulled the blanket around her, and put his arms around her. The soldier sitting at the table was going through all the paperwork. "Can you please take me back to Weston?"

The other soldier came over to Emily and pulled a chair closer to her. At first, she backed away. "No, my lady, I will not harm you, I just need to ask you some questions. I know this is not a proper time but I need to know more about this man."

Emily told him about the letter he presented to her. She knew her husband's hand-writing and felt the letter to be legitimate. She referred to the fact that he would be reluctant to meet with others. He claimed his reluctance to a war wound that still affected him. "He clearly played on my sympathy. I saw him speaking with a gentleman the other day while riding. I did not believe that he saw me at the time. He told me that he knew I saw the encounter. At that time, he was yelling at the young man in German."

The two men conversed quietly and then came back over to speak with Emily. "Lady Emily, I know this has been a terrible time for you but I have to ask you to not mention this to anyone. We need to keep the contact that the so-called Captain Waddington had with Germany. We now know the exact location of where Sir Robert is being held."

Emily remembered that the so-called Captain Waddington had said he wanted to kill Robert with his bare hands. "That's even more reason to keep this quiet," said Sir Randall. They told her that she would be taken back to Weston and the story would be that she had fallen off her horse and was found by a local farmer. They had the assistance of Mr. Fulton, the farmer Lady Emily had visited the day before. Both men thought the farmer to be trustworthy. His truck arrived shortly thereafter, and the men helped her out of the small shed. She was shaken as she walked out but at the same time, she felt a certain accomplishment; she knew that this had certainly helped the war effort.

When Emily arrived at Weston, the servants were standing out front to meet her. As the man of the house since Sir Robert was not there, Charles stood first to greet her. "Charles, thank you for being here. I don't see Master George, where is your brother?" He told her George said he was feeling ill and had taken to his bed. Emily's concern for herself left her quickly; before even taking care of herself, she went to George's room. She went over to speak to him and noticed his arm over his face. He appeared to be sleeping. She touched his forehead and he moaned and rolled over on his stomach. She left the room and instructed that he be checked hourly.

Her lady's maid was waiting for her with a hot bath and tray prepared. "You're always so thoughtful, Rose. I do not know what I would do without you," Emily said. She asked to be alone. She was taught from an early age not to show her inner feelings to anyone. Crying was a sign of weakness and crying in front of anyone meant giving in to those feelings, which meant weakness. She had held on to her calm manner as long as she could but she was at the end. She plunged down into the water, her head totally immersed.

She felt like she did when she was a child, spending time at the shore when before her mother had taken to her bed. The waves would sweep over her and when she emerged from the cold water, she would feel clean like her mother told her, "Let the water wash over you and wash all the bad things in life away." As Emily's head rose up, she hoped her mother's statement was true. The horror of that night would be washed from her. As her sleep seemed to come easily, her hand went to the soft pillow beside her, "Oh, Robert, come back to me."

It seemed like she had just closed her eyes when Rose was patting her arm, "Wake up, my lady, it's young George—he's feverish and we've sent for the doctor."

Emily put on her day gown and ran down the hall to the east wing of the house where the boys were. When she went in, Sir Randall was already there. "The doctor should be here shortly, Emily. His breathing is labored and the fever is high." The boys had never really been that sick in their early years—just the normal colds and short stomach ailments. One of the reasons was they were kept mostly at Weston, due to the war.

Emily's nursing skills were lacking due to inexperience as she wrung her hands, not knowing what else to do. She went over to George to touch his forehead. She took her fingers and pushed his hair back. "Don't do that, mother." Emily stood up and backed away. Her gesture was unusual at best and she was rejected by George. She attributed the statement to the fever.

George was always so close to her whereas Charles was just aloof, so pompous. George was so like Emily in the way of being so sensitive. She gathered her mother knew this; hence, that is why she tried to have Emily hide those emotions. Emily did not have to do the same to George; Robert took care of this from the time George was a toddler having crying spells. Robert would keep George either at the other end of the house or stay in London most of the time. When George was old enough, Robert would belittle him if he acted too emotional in any situation. Before Robert was missing, Emily tried to make up for what Robert lacked. Emily began to over-compensate until Robert made her aware of this, but with Robert gone so long, his warnings were easy to forget.

Emily sat by George's bedside until the doctor arrived. "Has the boy been exposed to any sickness recently?" George's nanny replied that he had not been with anyone other than his teacher and the house servants but he had been out in the storm, and came in, soaking wet. She indicated that he was given a hot bath and put to bed the night before.

"Why was in out in such a storm?"

"I do not know, my Lady; we asked him and he got ill-tempered and ran up to his room." The doctor gave him a shot and ordered bed rest. He asked if he might stay until the child recovered.

Emily's life seemed to take a turn after her encounter with the so-called Captain Waddington. George recovered from his illness but never seemed the same sweet boy he was before. Emily attributed this to his maturing. He seemed to be mad at the world. With safety returning to England, Emily decided to send George to Rathbone, a highly regarded boys' academy. He seemed to relish the fact that he would be leaving Weston. Charles had chosen to remain at Weston until his father returned. Emily felt that he should attend the same school as George but even George protested the idea. On the day George left, he said goodbye to everyone—even the servants—except his mother and brother.

For Emily, the next few weeks after George left were the most lonely she had ever been. As a child, there were endless days when she hardly saw her parents. When she was young, her parents would travel for weeks at a time and one day, her mother decided that she was ill. To Emily, she was fine, the doctor had not visited and she appeared as she always did. Ever since that day, she no longer dined with them and very rarely did she ever go out. The one thing Emily remembered was her parents' constant yelling. At times, she would visit her mother daily to read to her but as time went on, she was told to wait for her mother to summon her. This became less and less over time. As she walked around Weston, she felt like that little girl she once was, that lonely child she once was. She thought that maybe a walk in the gardens would ease her empty feeling. As she walked out of the evergreen maze into the open meadow, she noticed a car driving up the long road to Weston. She had not expected any visitors today and thought it strange that the car stopped in front of the main entrance. She walked slowly toward the house and saw from a distance, two gentlemen emerging from the auto. She could recognize the shorter man as her brother-in-law, Sir Randall, but could not identify the other gentleman. He was of a bad posture and graying hair and walked with a cane. As she went closer, her heart started to pound as she started to run toward the man; he walked as fast as he could toward Emily. Tears streamed from her eyes as Robert labored to get closer to her. As Emily was able to get a closer look, she noticed how frail Robert looked. He was so thin and had aged so much in the time he was in the POW camp. Sir Randall had said he was surprised he made it so long. She hesitated to show the emotion she felt at first but ran up to him and put her arms around him. He felt so frail to her—she could feel his bones. Emily closed her eyes and thanked God he had returned to Weston. He cleared his throat as she hung on close to him, "My dear Emily, you will break my bones if you hold on tighter." *Robert had always been so standoffish; apparently, he was still the same*, she reflected to herself.

As they walked into the main entrance of Weston, Robert held on to his brother for balance. He sat down in the first available chair in the main room. Robert looked at the staircase in the main hall as if it were a large mountain to climb. He knew that he had to make it up those steps but he also knew he could not do it without help. Sir Randall, seeing the fear, spoke up, "Lady Emily, may Robert and I have some time together in order to discuss some things? I promise I will give him back to you. I believe Robert may need an attendant." Emily said she would see to it and left the room.

"Thank you, I do not want Emily to see how weak I really am. You said you had something to discuss with me about Emily; would you like to do that now?" Sir Randall felt that the time was not right and assured him that he would be back when Robert had some rest.

Busy with getting Weston close to the shape it was in, Emily spent the days before Robert's arrival getting the house and the garden as close to what it was before the war. The Germans were pushed out of France, and England was winning the war. The horror stories told of Hitler were beyond belief and poor Robert had seen them all. Emily knew very little about his situation over there—she only cared that the was finally home. "My lady, Sir Robert wants his meal served in his room and has asked that you join him." Emily knew that Robert was weak but she hoped that after a few days of rest, he would be on the road to recovery. She dressed in a simple dress and tried to fix her hair the best she could. Her days of going to London for a new wardrobe and visiting the hairdresser seemed like so long ago. After two children and the fear of another bomb hitting Weston, she felt that she aged beyond her years.

Robert was sitting in his chair, next to the window looking out to the east garden. He could see the monument that was built honoring Smitty and all the horses lost in the bombing. He turned as Emily entered the room, "All we have lost, Emily—thank God we are all alive to see the end of this." She smiled as she walked toward him. Emily felt like a child unfamiliar to her surroundings. The last time she saw Robert was over three years ago. She had managed the estate, the children, and even made a profit by using the land around Weston to help with the war effort. She knew Robert would not approve, but she felt it kept her sane during these past three years.

Sally, one of the kitchen servers, knocked at the door softly and entered the room. She arranged a small table using the food brought up from the kitchen. She served each plate and poured each a glass of wine. "May I get you anything else, my lady?" Sally quickly covered her mouth in embarrassment, "Sorry, Sir Robert."

Robert smiled, "I guess you have to get used to me being here, don't worry, Sally."

Robert and Emily sat in silence as they started their meal, each not knowing what to say. "Charles came in to see me. Emily, you have done a fine job with him. He has grown into a nice, young man." Emily thanked him but pondered why he had not asked about George. The same feelings she had so many years ago came back—the protective feeling she always had with George. Robert could see her lips push together as her eyes looked downward. "Do you know about the letter George wrote me before I left?" Emily looked puzzled. He pulled out a leather billfold and started to unfold a torn and dirty piece of paper. "This is what is left of the letter George gave me. I saved it all these years; it was the one thing I held on to. The ink has faded and the paper is stained and torn, but I can tell you every word he wrote. When will he be home from school?"

Emily's heart softened as she saw the pride in Robert's eyes. "He has a long weekend coming up, I will send for him then."

Emily had a room next to Robert's that she moved her things into. She knew when he returned home, he would take some time to get his strength back. She felt he would ask her to join him when his health returned. George came home the following weekend. Robert came down to meet young George when he arrived. His color was much better and he was able to use the stairs. As George greeted his father, tears welled up in his eyes as he shook his father's hand. George was tall and lanky with his mother's looks. He had a head full of wavy, sandy hair like Emily's with deep-blue eyes. George always seemed to have a smile on his face. The relationship Emily and George once had noticeably changed in the past year. Emily attributed the change to adolescence. Robert and George spent their days talking about everything and anything. They would get into deep discussions and dine in the library together. Emily felt left out in the beginning but realized she was being selfish. She had the children for so long by herself and Robert had missed so much. The war finally ended and England seemed to rally at their freedom once more. Emily was surprised that Robert let the estate go on producing, as they did during wartime. Her overseeing was taken over by Robert and boredom set in. Whereas socializing was scarce during wartime it was back in full force now. There seemed to be endless parties and so many weddings. The English culture needed to make up for what they missed in the past years. Soldiers were now back in the workforce and the rebuilding began. Robert seemed to take advantage of it all. Emily had made a handsome amount during wartime and Robert saw it as an opportunity to invest in the rebuilding of London. His trips to London went from once a month to almost weekly. Robert insisted that Charles and George attend school near London. Emily felt that since Robert came home, she had lost not only her job attending to the Weston estate but also her two sons. When she requested that she accompany Robert to London, he would have an excuse for her not to go. Her wardrobe needed an update along with her appearance, so one day, she decided to take the next train after Robert left. She knew Robert was having dinner with the boys that night. The place she visited was Harrods. The store was an up-to-date clothier and a salon to go with today's styles. She stood at the door of the salon, dressed in her herringbone suit, her hair pulled up as she had worn it for the last ten years, along with her tattered black shoes. "My Lady Weston, it is so good to see you again! We have missed you!" She was taken back to a private room and told to please change into the robe provided for her in the small adjoining room. Emily removed her outer clothing, put the robe on, and let her hair down. Looking at herself in the mirror, she realized how the past years had aged her. Her skin was drab and she looked worn out.

The day was filled with the pampering she needed. When she left the store later that afternoon, she had a new boob cut and every piece of cloth she had on was new. Harrods was sending her purchases to Weston, as they used to do. She felt revived and had new energy as she walked down Brompton Road. Emily even noticed some men looking her way. She had some time before surprising Robert and the boys, so she decided to stop in a familiar shop for a cup of tea. She was famished and felt a cup of tea may relax her. She decided to sit in the back since she was by herself. She smiled to herself at the thought of surprising her family. As she gazed over at the front window of the shop, she saw what she thought was Robert walking by and thought she might be discovered. She looked down and pulled the brim of her new hat down with her hand, and stayed in that position for a moment or two until she raised her eyes over to see Robert and a woman sitting in a booth together. They looked to be deep in conversation while not being intimate. They were not holding hands; there was not any contract in that way. Emily noticed that the woman was tall in stature and not showing very much familiarity while still being attractive looking. "May I get you another pot of tea, madame?" Emily just wanted the young lady to leave her alone. She could not leave because the only way out was right in front of them, so she decided to wait until they left. "Yes, I would like another pot of tea," she said. They seemed to stay an eternity, so much so that her neck started to ache from keeping her head down. When they finally left, Emily hesitated about which way to go. If she went to meet Robert and the boys, she would have to keep silent about seeing Robert earlier. She wondered why he brought her there, to the tea room where they both frequented in their courtship. She turned quickly and headed toward Victoria Station.

Her temper flaring at first, she walked even faster than those walking down the street. She went from side to side, between groups of people, walking so quickly she ran into Robert's banker, Mr. Gifford. Emily dropped the goods she was carrying and bent down to gather her bags. "Lady Emily, are you all right? You were in such a hurry."

Feeling as though she was close to tears, she regained her constitution enough to speak to Mr. Gifford. She let out a silly laugh, "Please pardon me, Mr. Gifford, I was simply trying to make the next train."

He helped her and said, "Well, I guess you better be off then, may I help you to the station?" She said she was fine and left quickly. Mr. Gifford looked puzzled as she walked further away from him.

Emily had missed the train and had to wait for over two hours for the next one. The evening was near as she looked at the large station clock. She felt tears falling down her cheek as she thought about Robert. Theirs had not always been a perfect relationship. They were promised to each other in infancy. The times were such, that it was nearly unheard of but they both seemed to accept it. Emily thought Robert to be a pompous, cold individual. Even as a child, he seemed to think himself better than everyone—even those whose titles granted them more than his. He was never kind to Emily even as a child—he simply ignored her until she became of age to be presented. It was then, that he noticed her beauty. When she came down the staircase that evening, his feelings changed. The idea of them being married became bearable to him. But to Emily, even at the beginning of their marriage, he was never affectionate to her. The only affection he had for her was strictly in the bedroom.

Since he was back from the war, she had slept in the adjoining room. Robert had not requested her nightly companionship. He would simply join her in her bed and leave during the night. When she saw him in the tearoom, she thought that the reasoning was right in front of her. While riding home on the train that night, her mind would not stop. Mumbling to herself, she said, "So that is why he stays in London some nights." The ride from the station in Canterbury seemed endless. When she entered the manor, she asked Stubbs to help her with her bags. "My other orders will be arriving on Monday, please have these brought up to my room."

Emily turned and started up the staircase until Stubbs spoke to her, "My lady, Sir Robert called and said he would be staying in London and will return on the morning train." She stopped, unable to move, regained herself, and without turning to answer, went up to her room.

After falling asleep several hours later, she was awakened by her lady's maid, "Sir Robert has arrived from London and wishes to have breakfast with you. We have set up out on the veranda, tis a beautiful day, my lady."

She rose from her bed and asked that she tell Sir Robert she felt ill and was going to remain in bed for the rest of the day. "Please bring my meals to me and let everyone know that I do not want to be disturbed." Guilt slowly evolved in her as thought about her mother hiding from the world. She had taken to her bed when Emily was a child and had not left since. Emily knew she would have to face Robert sometime—she felt that it would be easier as time passed. After several hours of tossing and turning, she rose to pour herself a hot bath. The warmth of the water would surely mellow her spirit and pass the time. In her was the small hope that Robert would be concerned enough to come to her room and check on her health, but she knew him too well and knew he would not. Emily knew Robert loved her—in his own way—and the children, but she also knew his first concern was himself. It was the reason why she was so surprised to see him with such a plain, copious woman. Emily knew he had an eye for beautiful women so she was puzzled when she saw him with her. Her mind imagined every conceivable reason. At the end of the day, she had him having affair after affair. When her supper tray was brought to her. the lady's maid noticed that she had been crying for some time. Even with Emily trying to hide her distress, her appearance was of concern.

Emily's tray remained untouched as she stood, staring into the darkness outside her window. She vaguely heard the door open and assumed it was the maid coming to pick up the tray. "Emily, are you ill?" he asked. She knew his voice and answered him with a simple no. Hoping he would leave, she stood there for what seemed like an eternity, waiting to hear the door close behind him. With a sigh of relief, she turned to see Robert standing there. "Emily, my dear, what on earth is the matter? Are you ill?" He put his hand on her shoulder and she started to weep. "There, there, it can't be that bad. Did something happen in London?"

Startled by his question, she dried her eyes and looked up at him. "Whatever do you mean? How did you know I was in London?"

He laughed ever so slightly, as his finger moved her hair away from her eyes. "Well, besides seeing Stubbs, who helped you with your bags, you have a new hairdo and there's been a very large delivery from Harrods." He could see by her expression that Emily did not share his amusement.

She pulled away from him and erected her posture, "I saw you in London at the tearoom we used to go to. I planned to surprise you and the boys that night for dinner, but instead, you were meeting your mistress."

Robert's eyes grew wider and then he started to laugh, "Lord no, Emily, you can't be serious. You think that I am having an affair?" He walked over to fire and sat down on the small sofa. "Come sit with me, Emily," he said as he patted the cushion. At first, her stubborn nature almost got the best of her but she gave in to her emotions and sat by him. "Emily, I am not having an affair with Ann Tallon or with anyone else. Her husband was with me in the POW camp. We became good friends and looked out for each other. In the situation we were, you had to count each in a way that is hard to explain to anyone who has not been through it. Ann wanted to meet with me to talk about her husband. Captain Tallon was with me during the last days. Unfortunately, he died only days before the liberation."

Emily felt terrible for what she considered to be what her mother called "female silliness." "Robert, I feel so stupid but I thought, well I mean, I thought…"

Robert looked at her with a sympathetic look, "Say what you mean, Emily."

To Emily, there wasn't any way to say what she meant except to bluntly say it, "I mean since we have not been very intimate of late, I assumed the worst." She could tell by the look on Robert's face that she had touched a nerve.

"I think I need to explain some things to you, Emily. First, I apologize that I did not tell you this when I came back. I really did not want to talk about it, but I feel the need to do so now." He pressed his lips together, cleared his throat, and started to tell her some of the details about his internment.

Robert started to explain. “Their mission was to go into Germany and identify a bomb plant. The plant had been built just outside of Von Baron Helm’s estate. I knew the area from going there with my father. It was a reconnaissance mission, during night-time hours. We were a lone plane and thought that to be less dangerous than usual, but we were discovered—thankfully after we had sent back the coordinates of the plant. I had never had much training in airfare and it was the first time I had used a parachute. I was the only survivor; the pilot, copilot, gunner, and navigator were killed before they hit the ground.” Emily put her hand over her mouth, surprised. “I broke my leg when I landed and did not realize I ruptured my back; they, of course, did not care. After I was taken in, they put me in a basement. For what seemed like a year, I was kept alone in a dark, cold basement. The only light I had was a small window with bars. I would spend my time counting the days and making sure they were marked on the wall. Food was sent in through a small door at the top of the stairs. There were times when I looked forward to them coming to beat me. God forgive me, but there were times I felt like I was in hell.” Robert put his head in his hands, rubbed his face and looked at Emily.

“Robert, you don’t have to go on,” Emily said.

“Yes, I do, because this has to do with you, Emily. You see, the reason they were keeping me there, was because of the so-called Captain Waddington. One day, a young German soldier came to see me. When he walked in, the first thing I noticed was that he was SS and the second thing was he looked familiar. There was something about his eyes and that blonde, almost white hair. He could tell that I recognized something about him and asked me if I remembered him. He said he was the youngest son of Von Helm. He told me that he remembered me visiting, with my father. I did remember a young boy of seven or eight but hardly paid him any mind. Young Baron attended school in England before the war and claimed he spoke English as well as any Englishman. He also told me of his plans to get into England and stay at Weston.”

Emily stopped him, “And the letter?”

Robert nodded his head, “Yes, the letter. The letter was after much resistance. I won’t go into the detail of that, but I tried to word it so you would question it, but I knew that you would be glad to hear that I was alive. He told me before he left, that he would be the one to kill me, and that I should be glad that I would have a few more months to be alive until he completed his mission. I had no idea what exactly his mission was, but I knew it could cost many lives. After that, I was moved to the camp. There wasn’t a day that went by, that I did not think about him being at Weston. I talked to Stubbs and others—they had no inkling that he was not a British soldier. As you know, he would radio reports to Germany about troop movements. He spent quite a lot of time down in Dover, where he frequently got soldiers drunk and even killed a few. You did our country a service by killing him."

Emily knew Sir Randall told him about the demise of Captain Waddington by his wife's hands, even though he had never brought it up. As far as she knew, the matter was kept secret and was never to be discussed. "Oh, Robert, what you must think of me!"

He held her hand, "Emily, I don't think you know what you did. He had information about a major battle that had been secretly planned for some time. The information was next to the radio he used for transmittal. We found out it did not go through because of the storm that night. If you had not killed him, England could have lost thousands. What I think of you, my Lady? I think you are one of the bravest women I have ever known." He leaned over and kissed her hard. She responded and he stopped. "There's something else I need to tell you," he said as he rubbed his hands together. "My health is not the best. Either from when I ruptured my back or the beatings that followed afterward—well, it seems I have a crack in my vertebra that they can't operate on. I have been told that it is near my spine and a sudden movement or hard fall could paralyze me. That's why I stay in London some nights. I am nervous about traveling so much or moving too much at all."

So this was the reason he hardly touched her. It explained why he would not use his driver to go to London. The roads were still bad from the war, but the trains were where they once were before the war. "Robert, please, I understand," and she kissed him softly.

As Emily began to rise, he grabbed her arm and looked up at her, "I do love you, Emily, and always have. It's just that I never was good at showing it."

Life at Weston went somewhat back to what it once was before the war, except for the boys being off at school. Young Charles came home from London quite frequently, spending time with his father. He reminded Emily so much of Robert when he was a young man. He was exceptional with his schooling but like Charles, quiet and reserved in personality. Robert had been investing in real estate in London. He continued to farm portions of Weston and used all the proceeds to invest in the rebuilding of London. While others were destitute from the war, Robert seemed to prosper. He had a good eye for profit. Emily thought his experience in the German POW camp taught him to take chances and not be so reserved as he once had been. Emily's trips to London became more frequent, also. There were times when she would attend parties with Robert and stay in the city for a day or two. The change in her was noticeable, especially to Robert. No more of the shy young woman she once was, Emily had turned into quite the socialite. Because of her title and background, the new upper class in London gravitated to her. They found her interesting and well versed. All in her life seemed to be coming together, except for her relationship with young George. While usually being the more attentive of her two children, George seemed to find every excuse not to be around her. He rarely came home, and when she did go to London to see him, he would find something else to do. As she thought back, she realized she had not been alone with him since he went off to boarding school. George spent most of his time when he was on holiday at a fellow schoolmate's home—more than he spent at Weston. He was getting ready to go to university the next year and she knew she would see him even less. Emily wondered; for a child so close to his mother, he now seemed so distant.

Two weeks before the Christmas season, Lord Robert received correspondence from George's preparatory school. It stated that George was being disrespectful to his instructors and peers, and it was requested that a meeting be scheduled before the next semester. Robert was enraged by such a letter and vowed to scold young George severely. When he arrived the following day, Robert was there to meet him as he exited the car. He grabbed him by the back of his jacket and walked him into his study, slamming the door behind them. When George emerged, his eyes were red, and his pride was even more hurt. Emily did not see him until that evening. The plan was being made, early on, for a special family dinner in celebration of the upcoming holiday season. The dinner was for the family only, which included Sir Randall and his wife, Lady Randall, with their two children. Robert's Aunt Bess was included also, along with her constant companion, Count Marques. The family would laugh to themselves as Aunt Bess introduce the old count. They felt the title was more likely won in a card game than acquired. As Emily looked around, she noticed that Charles was present, but George had not made an appearance. She asked that the dinner be delayed to give him time. When Emily had given up any hope of him arriving, she sent Stubbs to check on him, but as he went to leave the room, he arrived. With a sigh of relief, she went to meet him as he walked in, but he walked over to Aunt Bess and kissed her on the cheek and turned and walked into the dining room. Emily felt bewildered and embarrassed standing there. It was not only noticed by Aunt Bess but Lord Robert. Robert went over to her, held her arm and said, "My dear, let me escort you into dinner." She looked at Robert with a hurt look on her face as he tried not to show his anger at his young son. When Emily would speak to him at dinner, he simply ignored her and changed the subject. His ill-manner was evident to all and he even had Charles upset with him.

Emily decided that now was not the time to deal with George and simply turned her attention to the others at the table. When the gentlemen exited to the library, George asked to be excused. He went upstairs without saying a word, and Charles followed behind him. The ladies went into the main room to have tea close to the fire. Before too long, there was a loud rumble in the east wing. Robert came running out of the library and ran up the stairs to the boys' room. The whole house could hear him yelling, along with those in the kitchen. "I'm sure all is well, now. You may go to your rooms," Emily said. Her voice was brash and her embarrassment showed. Aunt Bess and her Count made haste to leave, as Sir Randall started to go and help. Robert came running down the stairs, holding the boys by the back of their jackets—Charles on one side and George on the other.

Emily watched as he walked into his study. The guests excused themselves as Emily stood in the great hall by herself. Not knowing whether to go into the study or to her room, she stood there, bewildered. Raised voices came from the room, and she identified George yelling at his father. As she finally made the decision to go upstairs, she heard the door to the study open. "Emily, can you please come in?" She turned and walked toward the study, wondering what was wrong. As she walked in, she noticed Charles holding a rag over his eyes and George turned toward the fireplace, staring down into the fire. She sat next to Charles and put her hand on his shoulder. He looked at her with a face of disgust and moved down to the end of the sofa. "George, you have made accusations to me and Charles about your mother and I want you to tell her why." George mumbled something to himself. "Son, come over here and speak to your mother!" Robert said.

"I saw you! I saw you with that Captain Waddington, he was kissing you!" Emily tried to speak but was suddenly speechless. Tears came pouring down her cheeks as that terrible evening came back to her.

"Sit down, George; you don't know what you saw," Robert instructed.

"I'm not lying father, I know what I saw," George replied.

"Yes, George, you know what you saw, but you don't know the situation. Please sit down," said Robert. George came over and sat across from Emily.

"I think I'd better explain to you about Captain Waddington." Robert went into detail about the friendship between the two families, and about the time he spent in Germany as a child. He went on to tell them about being captured and who they thought to be Captain Waddington. He told them about the letter he was forced to write, and how he came to stay at Weston. "He was trying to get on your mother's sympathetic side and find out information about British troops. Your mother saw him speaking in German to a local from Canterbury, and she became suspicious. The night you saw her, she had fallen off her horse in a storm. Your Captain Waddington found her and brought her to the old mill building. It was this building, from where he was sending information to Germany on a radio. Your mother was unconscious for a time."

Robert stopped talking as Emily explained, "I woke up as he was leaning down, and he thought I was dead."

Emily started to go on, but Robert stopped her, "He was discovered, and your mother was saved from further harm. Sir Randall came at the right time and rescued her. He had sent a message that night to Germany about a major invasion. Apparently, he got some information from a soldier in Dover about the invasion and was about to transmit it again—since the first time the information was not received because of the storm. They found the soldier dead at the bottom of a cliff in Dover. Because of your mother, many lives were saved. She notified your Uncle Randall about her suspicions."

Emily knew he had stopped her from telling the boys the truth about what really happened to Captain Waddington. "George, why were you out there?" Emily asked.

"I went to find you. Your horse came running back to the stable and I was worried. I am so sorry, mother."

There was one question Emily was afraid to ask but she had to know the answer. Before she could ask, Robert said, "He came running back here in all that rain."

Emily remembered how sick he was with the fever and she now knew why he treated her the way he did. "I think we all deserve some brandy! Yes, even you boys!"

Robert seemed to have an eye for investment. He was able to purchase commercial properties in what were some of the up and coming areas of London. The war changed London so much. Robert invested in areas around the port of London. He knew that one day, London's port would be back to what it once was, or even better. It was one of the following purchases that sent him to Stockholm. Robert had made several trips previously but was still nervous when flying. He left that morning in a graying sky with a chilling wind. As he walked to the plane, his hat flew across the concrete. To him, it seemed like an omen because the same happened previously when he left that morning for Germany. If it had not been for someone telling him to hurry, he would have turned and walked back to the terminal. As he went to take his seat, the Captain said they wanted to hurry and take off due to the incoming weather. The flight seemed uneventful until they were to land. Robert could see the snow coming down out of his window and he knew there would be ice below. As the plane came in for the landing, all seemed well, until he heard the sound of the brakes locking below him. As the plane began turning in circles,

Robert was thrust to the back of his seat with such force, that he blacked out. Darkness engulfed him as his body twisted.

"Lord Weston, Lord Weston," someone was saying to him as they slapped his face. Robert saw a figure standing over him. He could not make out the face of the shadow standing over him. He wanted to speak but could not get the words out. Robert blinked his eyes in order to see better but fell back into the same darkness as before. Emily was called after the plane crash. The doctor that called her said that the plane had not really crashed but went into a tailspin that injured some of the passengers. "Lady Weston, your husband has been going in and out of consciousness since he has been here. Can you please tell if he has any other medical problems?" he asked. Emily explained his back condition and told the doctor just what she knew. Robert was reluctant to discuss his condition and when the subject came up, he had dismissed her questions. Emily said she would get the next plane out. She made arrangements to leave for London as soon as possible. If she could get a flight out, she planned on staying in London with her cousin. The weather was cold and rainy and there was a chance of snow. Emily packed enough clothes in case she had to stay for a while. She felt so bad for Robert; the fear that he had been living with became a reality.

Emily was lucky to get the next flight out to Copenhagen and was entering the hospital early the next morning. She inquired at the front desk and was taken down a long corridor to a room at the very end. The hospital was bright, sterile, and nondescript. As she entered the room, she saw Robert awake and alert. He was flat on his back without as much as a pillow under his head. When he turned and look at her, his eyes were empty and his face strained as he said, "Take me home, Emily."

Emily had not spoken to the doctor since he called with the news; she feared to hear about his condition. "I'll be right back, Robert; I will see about getting home."

Emily inquired about speaking to the doctor and was told to wait. She sat outside Robert's room on a small steel bench, looking down the hall for the doctor. As she leaned forward, she felt someone standing over her. She looked up at a middle-aged man in his starch white coat. He had small, round glasses and a short, crew-cut hairstyle with eyes as dull as his hair color. For some reason, he reminded her of Captain Waddington. "Can you come with me, Mrs. Weston?" Emily was about to correct him to call her Lady Weston but for some reason knew better. He seemed quite sure of who he was and could probably care less about who she was, or for that matter Robert. "I am sorry to tell you this but your husband is paralyzed from the chest down. He lost the ability to walk, urinate or even have a bowel movement. He has no feeling whatsoever and will need constant care. I recommend that you find an institution to take care of him." His statement was brief and to the point.

Emily was stunned by the doctor's lack of feeling. "I want to arrange for my husband to be returned to England as soon as possible. Can you make the arrangements?" She rose from her chair and left the office. As she walked toward the room to speak to Robert, weakness came over her and she caught herself against the wall. Tears fell down her cheeks as she realized what was in front of her. Her poor Robert had been through so much, from having been confined to a basement for over a year, to a POW camp for almost two years. His back had marks of beatings he endured, and his hands were scarred from being placed on hot embers. The pain had never stopped him since his return, and now the pain was gone but so was the feeling. Emily knew she could not go into Robert's room like this. She found a ladies' room, and as she stared into the mirror, she prayed for God to help her.

Robert was transported on a medical airplane two days later. Emily made calls to their family doctor in Canterbury to inquire about getting a nurse for Robert when he returned home. Since there was not an airport close enough to Weston, Robert would be transported by ambulance to Weston from Kent. Emily went to the hospital early that morning, dressed in a comfortable suit, with the intention of helping Robert dress for the trip but when she arrived, they informed her that she would not be needed. Robert asked that she not come into his room until he was ready to leave.

Emily was there with the full intention of helping her husband. Years before the war, she would have shrunk at doing such a thing as nursing her husband, but because of the trauma of the bombings of Canterbury, she knew so much more. Emily waited patiently for Robert; she could hear Robert grumbling at the doctor. Finally, the door opened and a stretcher came out with Robert on it. He was dressed in a tweed suit with a tie on. He only nodded at her when he saw her. They rolled him down the hall and out to an ambulance waiting. The attendants put him in the ambulance and it drove away, leaving her standing there. Emily knew what airport he was going to, so she gathered her bags and took a taxi. She felt as if she was slapped in the face. The taxi was able to follow the ambulance after speeding through the small streets of Copenhagen. He followed it, up until the ambulance entered an area that was closed off from the rest of the airport. Emily could see—from the cab—Robert being lifted into the small plane. She asked the driver to wait, and then she got out of the cab and tried to get through the gates. One of the men saw her and he came running toward her. "May I help you?" Emily explained that she was married to Lord Weston emphasizing "Lord" and requested that she accompany him to England. He ran back to the plane and inquired about Lady

Weston. Upon his return, he told her that only the doctor was allowed with Sir Robert and she would have to make her own arrangements. Her disappointment gave in to anger, the same anger she felt toward Robert in their early years. He had mellowed so much since coming back after the war, and now he seemed angry and even scared. She asked the taxi driver to take her to the main terminal so that she could get a plane back to London.

The earliest flight was not until the next morning, which meant that she would not be there when Robert arrived at Weston. After purchasing the ticket, she placed a call to Weston and asked that Robert's rooms be ready for his arrival. She had to find someplace to stay; having never been in Copenhagen before, she inquired at the information desk. The first thing she did was to find someone who spoke English, and the second was to introduce herself as Lady Weston. "I would like the name of one of your finer hotels in your downtown area," she asked. Emily was impressed by the helpfulness of the young woman. She made a reservation for her and even called a taxi to take her there; she also recommended a restaurant near the hotel. Emily thought she would enjoy herself while she could.

The hotel was one of the grandest places Emily had ever stayed. The attire she brought with her was not appropriate for dining in the hotel restaurant, much less the one where she was doing to dine. Emily asked the concierge to direct her to a shop within walking distance; she was grateful that she had enough money with her. Not knowing the length of time she would be in Copenhagen, she stopped by the bank and withdrew a large sum before leaving. The shop was a small but elegant store with only ladies' attire. Instead of the wool suits she had been wearing, there were dresses in beautiful lightweight wools with matching coats. Before leaving, Emily purchased two dresses with matching coats, hats, and gloves and a dress to wear to dinner that night. The saleslady told her that there was a shoe store just across the street, that had the latest styles in shoes. She directed her to ask for Julia who spoke fluent English.

After Emily went to the hotel's salon, she dressed in her new clothes and left for the restaurant where she had 7 pm reservations. She followed the hostess to a small table next to a window; she then pulled out the table to sit with her back to the window. The tables in the restaurant were lined next to each other with white tablecloths. The room was decorated in a satin royal-blue paper with gold trim. At first, Emily felt strange dining alone, but she then noticed another woman by herself. There were several men by themselves also. As she looked out, she caught the attention of a gentleman sitting on the other side of the room. He was a middle-aged man with dark, almost black hair, with exceptional looks. To Emily, he almost looked too handsome. She had never seen such a man. He was dressed in a dark-blue suit with a starch white shirt. Emily could see he was tall in stature since he seemed to be too large for the table he was sitting at. "Lady Emily, may I take your order?" Emily thought he must have paid attention.

Before the evening was over with, she had a bottle of wine, a five-course meal, of which she had to guess what kind of meat she was eating, and a brandy to top it off. Emily contemplated how she would make it back to her room without falling while walking in her new heels. She laughed at herself as she thought about the old black shoes she wore every day. As she started to rise from the table, she felt a little dizzy but the waiter was pulling the table out so she had no choice. "Thank you, sir!" she said as her eyes focused on the staircase going downstairs.

She walked swiftly over to the railing of the staircase, put her hand on it and was about the take the first step when a hand fell on hers. "Little lady, there's an elevator down the hall over there," said the gentleman in his American accent.

Emily turned and saw the doors of the elevator, "Excuse me, sir, but thank you for your help."

She walked down toward the elevator and was almost there when her heel caught in the carpet and she nearly fell over. Putting her hand on the closest wall to her, she pulled her leg up, trying to detach her shoe. "Please let me help you!" He bent down, put one hand on her ankle, and pulled the carpet off with the other. Emily felt something she had never felt before as his hand touched her ankle. It was a new and different feeling. He stayed down, looking up at her until she moved her foot and pulled the bottom of her dress close to her. He rose slowly, "I beg your pardon, but I didn't want you to hurt yourself." Emily blushed as she looked into the stranger's eyes; they were the bluest eyes she had ever seen. For what seemed like an eternity, they stood looking into each other's eyes, until she realized someone was standing next to her.

The waiter cleared his throat, "Lady Weston, you left your gloves on the table." He handed her the gloves and she thanked him.

"My goodness, I had no idea I was helping a princess." Emily laughed, "No, sir, I am not a princess, but thank you for your help."

Emily walked away as erect as she could manage, heading toward the front door of the restaurant. The hotel was just a block away, but to Emily, it seemed like a mile. On occasion, she would have a light-headed feeling from too much wine but drinking was not something she did on a regular basis. During the war, it was harder to come by and after the war, she only engaged in a glass or two at dinner. She must have had at least a bottle or more of wine. The waiter kept on pouring more. Emily saw the lights of the hotel and proceeded down the sidewalk, toward the entrance. She had to pass through the lobby to the desk—past so many people. As she walked up to the clerk, she hiccupped loudly; blushing from her outburst, she giggled. "Madame, may I help you?" Emily asked for her key and turned to find the elevator. Hoping there would be a message, anger came back to her. Walking quickly over to catch the elevator, a hand came across the door as it was getting ready to close. Emily looked over to see the same gentleman she spoke with at the restaurant. "Hello again, my Lady; it looks like we meet again." Emily felt annoyed that he was now at the same hotel as her. "I think maybe you need a cup of coffee; please let me treat you to a coffee and chocolate Danish. The hotel has a small bakery on the other side of the lobby, so it's very close." She almost felt insulted that he made the reference "very close," as if he were suggesting that she could not go far, but the Danish sounded wonderful, so she accepted. Carefully, she walked beside the tall, dark-haired man. As she walked through the lobby, she noticed women looking at him.

The small shop was decorated with white cabinets and counters, red and white strip chairs, and red curtains. To Emily, it looked like the perfect bakeshop. As soon as she entered, she could smell the chocolate. He pulled a chair out by a table next to the window. The river outside was lit with rows of gas lanterns reflecting the flowing water. Emily felt so odd, sitting in the faraway place next to the stranger, not even knowing his name. She was so far from Weston.

"Now that I know your name, I guess I will tell you mine," he said as he smiled. "My name is Michael Callahan from America. I have a small shipping company and travel quite a bit between America and Europe. I am not married now and have only been married once in my life. My wife died in childbirth, and we lost the baby. Swore I'd never marry again after that. I'm rich but honest and think you are about the prettiest woman I have ever seen."

Emily started to laugh, "Sir, I believe you had too much to drink also!"

They stayed in the restaurant until closing, talking about each other's lives. His was one of work and adventure. His trips consisted of business and pleasure, with frequent trips to Africa for a safari or two. To Emily, he seemed the outdoor type. He spoke of skiing in Switzerland and visiting the Pyramids. To Emily, he was fascinating at best—so unlike Robert, so unlike the men who came to Weston. He laughed loudly, and his smile was continuous throughout the conversation. When the shop started to close, she noticed the time to be after midnight. "Oh, I hadn't realized the time; I have an early flight and need to pack."

She rose and went to put her coat on as he stood to help her. His hands ran over her arm and down to her hand. "My lady, thank you for this. It's been quite a while since I have been in the company of such a beautiful lady." She looked into his deep-blue eyes for what seemed like a long time and smiled; he took the hand he was holding and raised it to his lips and kissed it. Emily left without looking back, went to the elevator, and entered her room.

The lights were off so she noticed the red button on the phone. When she called the front desk, she found that Robert's doctor had left a message that Robert was comfortable at home. Exhausted from the evening, she fell asleep quickly. In what seemed like a few minutes, she was awakened by a call from the front desk. Her time was limited as she quickly packed the clothes she brought and the ones she purchased the day before. As she checked in with the airlines, she had but ten minutes before leaving. Copenhagen was not a place she would forget, nor was he.

Emily arrived in London just after noon to a rainy, wind-blowing day. When she left Copenhagen, she was wearing her new outfit she purchased the day before. The dress was a pale-pink coat dress with large, black buttons; it had a matching black coat trimmed in pink. Emily also purchased a new hat to match her outfit, along with a pair of thin heeled shoes. "Surely, I can walk in these better today than last night," she mumbled to herself.

She was surprised to see Robert's doctor waiting for her as she entered the terminal. "I've been trying to get in touch with you, madame. I am leaving later today but wanted to go over your husband's situation." They went to the coffee shop and she sat down to hear about what was to be her duty in life. She remembered her father saying that it was her duty to make her marriage work. The word duty had been fixed in her brain from the time she was a small child, whether it was seeing to her bedridden mother or her conduct in society. Emily found out that Robert was paralyzed from the lower waist down. He would never walk again and would not be able to control his bodily functions either. The young doctor had made arrangements for his care. Robert hired a male nurse to see to his needs. The young man would live in the servant's quarters and be at Robert's aid. Emily did not have any idea of the detailed care that Robert would need. She had taken care of the children when they were sick as youngsters, but that was with the help of the servants and a visiting nurse. Anger still welled in her when she thought about being left in Copenhagen. There was no concern for her wellbeing, but she smiled to herself as she thought about the tall, blue-eyed man.

After leaving the terminal, she noticed a driver holding a sign with her name on it. "Lady Weston, my name is Gifford, and I am here to carry you back to Weston. May I take your bag?" Emily thought to herself, *well, at least he did not leave me stranded again.*

When they arrived at Weston, her lady's maid and butler were waiting outside for them as they drove up. She was glad to get home and was anxious to see Robert. After acknowledging those waiting for her, she ran upstairs to Robert's room. As soon as she entered, she noticed the bed was gone along with the other furniture. She ran back to the stairs. "Sir Robert has moved to a room on the bottom floor, my Lady," said Stubbs. She followed him to the room behind Robert's library.

He was sitting up in the bed, dressed in a fresh nightshirt with a young man standing next to the bed. "Emily, let me introduce Edmund Fellows. Edmund, this is Lady Weston." Emily nodded her head as he bowed his head slightly. He was a stern-looking young man with a rather pointed nose, long face, and close-set eyes. His hair was nearly shaved and he smelled of soap. "Emily, I believe you met our new driver, Gifford. Please check with me before you take him away from Weston."

Emily felt that his tone was one of ordering her and such a conversation should be in private. "Please excuse us, Mr. Fellows." He looked at Robert as if to get permission. Emily turned so as to hide her distraught facial appearance. The young man walked out of the room but not before stopping and nodding at Emily. "Robert, I don't think you should speak to me in such a condescending manner," she said. Before he could answer her, she started to explain to him that she was here for him, as she always had been. "I realize you may not think so after leaving me to fend for myself but I am here to help you," she stated loudly, without yelling. She was still furious about Copenhagen.

The first weeks after Robert came home, he lapsed into a deep depression. He remained in his room only associated with his aid, Mr. Fellows. The servants were instructed to leave his trays outside the room. He remained in bed and asked to be left alone. The doctor from the village attended to his needs, and when Emily would try to visit him, he simply turned his head away, or she was told he was asleep and not to be disturbed. The weather outside was as dreary as the inside. Charles was able to cheer him up a little by reporting on the profits being made from the sale of some of the properties Robert had invested in, but Charles now stayed in London. There were times when Mr. Fellows tended to his own needs and spent time in the village, away from Weston. It was one of those times when Emily heard Robert sobbing one night. At first, she awoke from the wind howling outside and decided to check the house. Emily's room was upstairs, away from Robert's, who stayed downstairs. As she walked down the staircase, she could hear him crying. She walked over his room and noticed Mr. Fellows sitting in a chair outside his room. Emily put her finger over her mouth as not to embarrass Robert. She moved her hand so that Mr. Fellows would follow her down to the kitchen. "Please sit, Mr. Fellows, I will put on the kettle." He quickly asked if he should call the cook. "No, no, I am perfectly able to fix us a cup of tea." Emily stated she knew of Robert's condition with coping with his recent illness. She stated she was planning on visiting the doctor as soon as the weather cleared. If he had no resolve, she would make an appointment in London. She told Mr. Fellows to get some rest and she would stay by Robert's door until the sounds stopped. Emily waited for a while before slowly opening the door to Robert's room. She walked over to him as quietly as she could, without disturbing him. He was sound asleep on his back with his nightshirt open. His breathing was heavy and he moaned unclear words in his sleep. There was enough light from the moon for Emily to notice his chest, and she almost gasped as she looked down at him. There were scars across his chest as if he had been whipped; the scars were wide in size and clearly erratically placed. Since his return from the POW camp, their relationship became closer than before the war, but their intimacy was guarded; she never saw him without a shirt on. The lights were always off and the covers were always up. Emily stood, staring at her husband, realizing what he went through those years in Germany. She felt sheltered and naïve. She turned and walked out of the room. She prayed to God for more compassion and understanding. The anger she had toward him after being left in a strange country left her, and she vowed to help him as much as she could.

The next day, she went to the village to speak to his doctor. She told him of Robert's night of restlessness and sobbing. Dr. Wellborne, being a country doctor, said he was perplexed as to giving her an answer, but he would make an appointment for her in London to speak with a specialist. After she left his office, she felt more confused than before. Dr. Wellborne did tell her that the doctor she was going to see specialized in Robert's condition. He helped many war victims from those who lost limbs to those completely paralyzed from the neck down. "At least Robert can move his arms, we should see about him using a wheelchair," he said.

The next week, Emily went to London to see a doctor by the name of Dr. Coats. She was escorted into his office and told that he would be in—promptly. He came barreling into the office some 30 minutes later. The older doctor was a large man with white hair and a mustache that curled on each end. He sat down in his rolling wooden chair and pushed himself closer to his desk with such an effort that he bounced back as his stomach hit the desk, after which he had to push himself closer again. Emily was about to laugh but thought his first impression of her would be compromised. "Lady Weston, I presume?" She smiled and told him that he was correct. Along with the appointment, Robert's medical records were sent to Dr. Coats. The doctor's plan was to get Robert as mobile as he could. “There’s absolutely no reason at all for your husband to not lead a fairly normal life. We will get him wheelchair-bound and he will be able to do most things. His attitude will be better once he gets out and gets back to doing the things he likes.” He told Emily, of course, he would never walk again but he would certainly get back to going to his office and working again. He knew of Robert’s business ventures. He suggested that Robert stay at his facility for a week as soon as the arrangement could be made. Dr. Coats would get in touch with Dr. Wellborne and together, they would approach Robert.

In the weeks that followed, Dr. Wellborne informed Robert that some more tests were needed, and he would need to spend some time in London. When he approached Emily, he simply said that he had to go to London for some test and Mr. Fellows would be accompanying him. Emily was hoping that he would ask her to go with him but as she went to speak, she remembered Robert that night she saw the scars on his chest, and she reminded herself of her prayers that night.

When Robert came back to Weston, he seemed so different. He called when he reached the train station in Canterbury and said he was on his way back to Weston. He asked Emily not to have the servants there to meet him. She instructed everyone about his arrival and asked that they honor his request. Emily changed her dress and readied herself to meet Robert when he arrived. As she stood outside waiting, she marveled at the beauty of Weston. The stables were rebuilt as soon as Robert returned from the war, and Weston was restored to its former beauty. The estate was now a working one. The changes Emily made during the war went on and kept on producing a profit. As the car approached, Mr. Fellows exited from the other side of the car first and walked away from the auto. Robert opened the car door, pulled out the wheelchair, and opened it; he then placed his hands on the arms rails, swung himself around, and sat in the chair. After positioning himself, he turned it around and faced Emily. She clapped her hands in delight and he returned a broad smile.

For now, Emily let the young Mr. Fellows attend to Robert and his needs. Whenever she saw him, he was in his wheelchair, dressed and shaved. He was in the dining room for breakfast every morning and in his library working daily. Charles was now finished with university and Robert brought him into the family business. He attended meetings with his father when it came to the property Robert had purchased after the war. The rebuilding of London after the war began slowly but seemed to be moving quickly now. The investments Robert made were paying off nicely; some he sold and some he leased. Charles—being a graduate of business school—was able to give his father advice and most, he listened to. When Robert had meetings in London, the preparation began several days ahead of time. The meetings were set in offices that accommodated wheelchairs. To Emily, he was getting his life back to normal the best he could. Life seemed to be getting back to normal. Young George was getting ready for graduation from University soon. Not being the student Charles was, George seemed to prosper more socially than Charles. Emily's two sons were so different with Charles being just like his father, stern and somewhat cold, and George being more like Emily. George was certainly the more sensitive of the two; he also seemed the more outgoing.

Emily planned a party for George's homecoming. The timing seemed right for Weston to get back to what it had once been. "Well, my dear, what a grand idea," Robert remarked. The day would begin with a hunt before noon, followed by a lunch of game and foul. It had been years since they used the hunting lodge, so Emily had the repairs made and cleaned for the upcoming event. The guests were to stay for the weekend and a formal dinner was later that night. Rooms that were closed down were opened and refreshed for the incoming guests. George had several friends coming from school, with friends and family coming in for the event. Emily busied herself with every task. She was able to delegate everything, down to the smallest detail.

The night before everyone was to arrive, George came home with several friends. As George and his young friends came into Weston Hall, Robert went up to greet them. It was evident George had not explained to his young friends about his father being in a wheelchair. With the stress from Robert's internment and accident, Robert looked years older than he was. When he came home, his blonde hair turned to a light gray and his face was drawn. "Gentlemen, I would like to introduce my father—Sir Robert Weston," George said with pride.

For a moment, the boys stood there without a word, before walking over to shake Robert's hand. It wasn't very long but enough for Robert to notice. He graciously welcomed them and asked that their bags be carried to their rooms. It was an embarrassing moment for Robert and as he turned to go into his library, Emily came running down the stairs, apologizing that she was sorry she had not been there to greet Robert's friends. "My dear, you need to start acting like the title you've been given by marrying me," Robert snapped. The excitement of the weekend slowly went from her. As a child, Emily remembered Robert insulting those around him. When he would be in a situation, like not being the best at what he was doing, he would throw out insults to those that exceeded more than him. Emily had not observed the stares of George's friends that cut into Robert and would not have realized the scope of his low self-esteem after his accident.

Dinner was to be served that evening with those arriving early that day. It was to be less formal than the dinner planned the next evening. Emily chose the menu herself and had the cook prepare George's favorite dishes. The young men George invited were well-mannered and a welcome change to Weston. To Emily, it was good to have youth around. After dinner, the gentlemen went into the library while Emily attended to the needs of the festivities of the next day. Before retiring that evening, she decided to check on Robert. As she went down, she heard the boys still in the library so she knocked softly and entered. They quickly rose to greet her as George walked over to her. "Hello mother," he said, as he kissed her on the cheek. To Emily, they clearly had many drinks as she noticed George swaying in his posture. "Father excused himself some time ago," George replied. Emily left them and went over to Robert's room. She knocked softly and opened the door, and she noticed his eyes closed. She knew that he was not asleep but his actions indicated that he did not want to be disturbed. His mood was foul and she hoped that his attitude would be better tomorrow.

The next morning was clear and warmer than normal. Emily thought she could not have wished for better weather. Robert was up before George and his friends so Emily joined him for breakfast. After asking him several questions, he sharply said he was not in the mood for small talk. She wondered what she had done but dismissed his mood to his inabilities. When the idea of the weekend festivities came up, he seemed excited about the prospects but now he seemed indifferent. He would be able to hunt with the help of Mr. Fellows. Robert had been an advent hunter from an early age. His father taught him well and Robert followed through with teaching the boys before the war. Charles was expected back from London for the weekend. Most of his time was spent in London of late since he was able to stay at the flat that the Weston family owned. Emily was happy to have her boys home. She dismissed Robert's mood and went about her preparations. The guests arrived early morning as car after car approached Weston's main entrance. The servants were busy carrying their bags to the appropriate rooms as the guests gathered in the main gallery. Most went to their rooms, prepared for the afternoon, and then took their leave to the lodge. Those who did not want to make the journey by foot were escorted by car. Bird hunting was usually successful on Weston; there were ample pheasant, grouse, and partridge. Robert positioned himself to greet the guests as they arrived. For some, it was the first time they had seen Robert since his accident. Emily could tell as they whispered to each other. Her heart went out to her husband; she could tell how hard this was for him. Robert's upper body was strong but his legs were thin and frail.

As everyone went to their appointed area, Emily joined Robert in the small truck. Mr. Fellows had a chair installed in the rear bed so that Robert could sit and shoot. He was fine with the shoot and even successful with twelve birds. When he came into the lodge, the men praise him for his success. George and Charles were even teasing each other as they had in years past. Being so very different in personality, Emily was pleased they got along so well, but for all those years during wartime when all they had was each other. The main hall of the lodge featured a table as long as the room. The room was filled with past trophies and game from all over the world. Wood paneling covered the walls along with wood planks on the floor. To Emily, it was a perfect room for such an occasion. As the supper ended, the men went out to smoke their cigars while the ladies retreated back to Weston for an afternoon nap.

Emily cautioned George about his drinking. The evening before, he was loud and stayed up until the morning hours. His eyes appeared red and swollen, still, and she reminded him to mind his manners. Charles's actions were not of concern for Emily—being so much like his father, he was always in control. After one last check with the head cook and walk through the house, Emily retreated to her room upstairs. The main dining table held 30 people when fully extended and tonight, every chair would be filled. The cook made a cake for George in celebration of his graduation, and Emily planned for his favorite foods to be served. The dress for dinner was formal, so she purchased a new dress for the evening. Robert returned before the others from the lodge. He was taken in from the back hall and went directly to his room. Emily knew he was adamant that no one sees him being carried from the car to the wheelchair. Mr. Fellows knew of his wishes and followed them through.

The evening started off with a gathering in the main room of Weston. In previous times, the main hall of Weston was used as a ballroom. The room was the largest in the manor house with ceilings 25 feet tall, with ornate sculptures encased in framed squares. The staircase was made of a heavy wood with each post being carved animals that inhabited the estate. Emily noticed that George did not come down yet; she summoned one of the maids to find him. It was not until dinner was ready to be served that he appeared. Emily was devastated at the appearance of George. He looked like he got dressed and went to bed and came downstairs without putting a comb through his hair. His clothes were wrinkled and his tie was crooked. He walked into the room with a drink in his hand. Charles excused himself, went over to George and spoke to him, who laughed and left the room. Emily thought the best way to handle the situation was to ignore it. She went about her business, speaking to everyone as she went around the room. She was almost giddy until she noticed Robert's angry face. Emily turned and started walking the other way.

When dinner was announced, Emily joined her guests and proceeded to the dining room. She knew if she went over to Robert, he would raise his voice to the point of everyone hearing him. The days had passed when he would handle a problem like this quietly; lately, he seemed mad at the world. Emily's attempts to help him were dismissed and after repeated attempts, she gave up trying. Guilt would consume her and she would again try to get back the closeness they once had but the effort would be short-lived. Robert was her cousin, her childhood friend, and she hoped, her loving husband but even though she loved him, at times she did not like him. Emily asked that the dinner be served, even though George and Charles had not returned. It would be an embarrassment for her to leave and check on them. Emily watched the door, hoping Charles would bring George back but their chairs remained empty.

Weston Manor house had a total of 117 rooms which included several dining rooms, three cook rooms, and 56 bedrooms for family and staff. Even with the house being so large, everyone could hear the rumble going on upstairs. Speech stopped, eyes went to the ceiling, until a loud thump bought Robert's hand slamming down on the table. Emily rose and went out of the room to the stairs. Her heels could be heard, running up the stairs and down the hall. Robert rolled his chair to the bottom of the staircase and waited for an explanation. The guests stayed at the dining table, perplexed as to what to do next.

When Emily entered George's room, both boys were on the floor. Charles was in the corner, sitting on the floor, holding a handkerchief over his eye, while George was lying head down on the floor. Emily went to George first; as she tried to move him, he turned and looked at her. With his mouth bleeding and his hands skinned, he smiled, "See, the little brother can still beat big brother. Charles, you are a weakling." Charles got up on his feet, came after George and started to hit him until Emily started yelling at them. She stopped suddenly, realizing her guests, and then she started to cry. The boys stopped and went to her, putting their arms around her. Crying was something Emily rarely did; her father would say it was a sign of weakness. The boys had never seen her so upset. George asked her to sit down as Charles went for a glass of water.

"You boys straighten yourselves and come downstairs," Emily stated. She went to the room and washed her face with a cold wet cloth, fixed her hair and put some color on her lips and cheeks. As she was getting ready to go downstairs to her guests, she experienced a sharp pain in her stomach. The pain was so sharp, that she held on tightly to the bedpost. It nearly took her breath away. As quickly as it came, the pain seized. Catching her breath, she started downstairs.

As she went downstairs, Lady Barkley came running up past her. Emily turned to say something to her when she noticed another guest right behind her. It was Randall, Robert's brother. He was holding his mouth while running to his room. Emily could hear that he did not make it to where he needed to go. When she made it to the room where all were gathered, two more ran out of the room. As she looked at Robert, she could see that his face was pale in color; he was patting his forehead as he was perspiring profusely He was unable to feel or control the results of the coli poisoning he had. The witnesses to his embarrassment were the people he had known since childhood and business associates. To Robert, it would be a night that he would never forget.

Before the evening was over, nearly everyone in attendance was ill including Emily. Somehow, the servant was not, nor was George while all his friends were ill. The doctor was called and came within the hour. Unable to take care of Roberts, Mr. Fellow was confined to his bed along with Emily. George was the one to help his father. After witnessing his father's illness, he quickly wheeled him to his room and helped him get ready for bed. Robert protested the entire time but George pursued. He removed his father's clothes, washed him, and picked him to put him in bed. George stayed with his father throughout the night and followed the doctor's instructions as to his care. "My God, how can I live with this," Robert said. George heard him and got up to go to him, but he noticed the tears running down his face. He knew the night had been hard enough on his father, so he sat quietly in his chair in order not to let his father know he was in the room. Later, as George looked at his father, he felt that if it had not been for him, his father would have avoided all that happened that night. The guilt overwhelmed him; George felt he was the cause of all who fell ill that night. Two of the guests were taken to the hospital, and the rest left Weston as fast as they could. The doctor concluded that the illness was caused by the salad greens consumed at dinner. George and the servants did not eat any greens. Mr. Fellows resigned and George stayed to care for his father, but not without his father's protest.

Days at Weston were quiet and uneventful. As fall turned to winter, the darkness of the outdoors seemed to move into the hall of Weston. Emily went about her usual daily activities. Correspondence rarely needed answering, since invitations seemed to seize—most times, George was the only one Emily had tea with. Emily would ride out to the estate's farms and keep in touch with those on the estate but she was no longer in charge of any business with the farmers, as she was during the war. When Robert returned, he took over all the business and now Charles had taken over. Charles's visits were few except when needing his father's signature. Robert was still the Earl of Weston and the head of the business of Weston, but as far as the decisions being made,

Robert wanted no part of it. Weston was now a working estate and was far better off than some of the older estates of England. Many were sold after the war, mainly because the families could no longer maintain them. Some even opened their houses to tourists for viewing or staying for periods of time for holidays. Having the farms around, using the land for livestock or crops kept funds coming into Weston; it was a win situation for both the Weston Family and the farmers. Emily kept in contact with everyone, even though she was no longer in charge of what they did. When Robert came back from the war, he was eager for the challenge and seemed to relish making money. When she looked at him now, she felt sorry for him; he was pale and frail and never seemed to smile at anything. The change was apparent since the graduation party for George. But George was the one who saw to his needs. He changed from the drinking young adult he was, to a loyal son who was Robert's only comfort. At times, Emily was jealous of the attention that Robert would give George, but she was thankful to have George home, attending to his father.

George and Robert were constantly discussing history and world events. He read the newspaper daily to Robert and they talked about the changing world around them. George would go down to the village and purchase books and records for his father to listen to. On days when the weather cooperated, they would sit in the east garden and George would read to him. Robert started suffering from severe headaches which came on now and then. At first, the pain would start on one side of his face and rotate to the top of his head. The village doctor said they were migraines and gave him medication but after taking the medication for a few weeks, the pains grew worse and more frequent. Emily tried to stay with him during these episodes until he stated he wanted George to see to his needs. She was so used to Robert's rejection that it hardly fazed her. After his pain grew to the point that he would cry out, she summoned the doctor from London, even though it was against Robert's will. The doctor wanted to move him to a hospital in London for tests. "I will let you know when I am ready to go to London, sir," he answered him.

The next morning, Robert asked George to get the wheelchair for him. He wanted to go to his library to work on some business. Both Emily and George saw the request as a hope that maybe he was feeling better. "I'd like to write some letters I have been meaning to, I'll ring my bell if I need help," he said. As they left the room, he asked them to close the door. Both Emily and George were puzzled by his request. After several hours went by, Emily heard the bell, "My dear, why don't we have tea together in the morning room?" She wheeled him into the room at the back of the house that overlooked the main garden. The sun was shining through the large windows and the garden was in full bloom. "This is my favorite room in the entire house. It always seemed so bright and cheerful." The kitchen-maid brought in the silver tray with a fresh pot of tea and sweet biscuits. She poured Robert's tea and fixed his napkin on his lap.

Conversation lagged at first until Robert stated he wanted to speak with her about matters. "Robert, you're scaring me; please tell me what matters we need to discuss?"

His lips pressed together, and he started to speak, "I know, Emily, being married to me has not been easy. I was such a pompous young man and had no concern for anyone but myself. Then, I came back bitter from my internment during the war and now look at me. This can't have been easy for you. We were playmates as children—cousins, for God's sake. It wasn't that we fell in love and married like most people today." Emily knew he was right but had always hoped they would become closer through the years. "I do care about you, Emily, but if anything were to happen to me, I want you to go on with your life. I don't want you becoming some old countess, withering away." Emily smiled at him and told him he was not going anywhere.

Two days later, the headaches started again—this time, the doctor was called in to give Robert a shot of pain medication. That evening, he was finally able to sleep through the night. Emily went to check on him and found him sleeping soundly. She also checked on George's room next to Robert's, to see him fast asleep too. As she walked up the main staircase to her room, she noticed lightning in the distance and hoped it would not wake Robert. Exhausted from the day's events, she went fast to sleep until she woke with a loud sound of thunder. Lightning was flashing behind the curtains as she turned away from the windows. The thunder was loud and seemed to be rumbling on, but between the thunders, she could hear someone crying. She put on her robe and went downstairs, noticing the light on in Robert's room and a sobbing sound coming from the room. As Emily opened the room, she saw George leaning over the bed, sobbing and rocking back and forth. As she went closer, she saw blood spattered on the head of the bed. Her slow walk increased to a run to get closer—nearly falling onto George—but her hand caught the post as she stopped, seeing Robert oozing blood. "Oh, George, no, no, what has he done!" She tried to pull George away but he would not let go. He was covered in the blood that continued to pulse out of Robert's head. Emily looked around the bed when she smelled the familiar odor of gunpowder until she saw the gun on the floor.

"George, please let go; please, son, let him go." George put his father's body down. Emily did not realize the horror of it all. The top of Robert's head was gone and beside the blood, there was gray matter spattered everywhere. It brought back the memory of the bombing she witnessed in Canterbury, a sight she would never forget. Emily told George to sit in a chair over by the window, picked up a large quilt and placed it over Robert's body. As she stood rubbing her hands together, she watched George sitting and staring at the floor. She went over and pulled up a chair next to him. "Listen to me, George; I am going to call the doctor and I want you to go and clean yourself up. Put your clothes in a bag, take them out to the disposal, make sure no one sees you."

He looked up at her with a puzzled face, "Mother, he's dead—I don't think the doctor will help him."

Emily wiped the tears away from his face and said, "Your father was a good man, we will never understand what he went through during the war. Nor will we understand how hard it's been for him since his accident. I won't let this follow our family; the doctor will take care of this. Now go get cleaned up, and remember what I said about your clothes. I don't want the servants to know about this." Emily told George to use the washroom closest to the room. The servant quarters were on the other side of the house. Emily quickly removed the soiled linens and washed the headboard of the bed. She gathered the linens and took them downstairs to dispose of them.

Charles was called the next morning and was to arrive on the evening train. The paper was notified that Lord Weston died from natural causes. Emily drove to the station to meet Charles; she wanted to tell him before arriving home. The first thing he noticed when he got off the train was his mother's appearance. Her eyes were bloodshot with dark circles under them, and she appeared frailer than the time before. He knew the past few months had been difficult for her but had not realized the extent of how much so. She patted his cheek and looked into his eyes, "Take care, son, this is going to be a difficult week." He followed her to the car and started to ask for the keys, "I'll drive Charles." As they left the station, she went off the way down a dirt road that led to their hunting lodge. When he was about to ask where they were going, she stopped and turned the car off, "I need to tell you about your father's death." Charles said he was wondering why she did not tell him on the phone exactly what he died from. "Charles, your father committed suicide with your grandfather's pistol. Poor George found him. I asked the doctor to put that on the death certificate. Besides the doctor, you, George, and I are the only ones that know the truth. I want it to stay that way. I want your father's memory not to be muddied by this or the rest of the family. I trust this will stay between us."

Charles felt bad for his father—had he known how unhappy he was, he would have given up the business to help him. Instead, it was George who was with him. "I will keep your secret, mother."

The funeral was the following Saturday, and once again, the house was filled. Relatives came from all over England and some from Scotland. Robert was buried in the family plot alongside his father. As Emily stood, looking down at the graveside, she couldn't help but notice the place where she was to lie below Robert's grave and next to Robert's mother. She smiled to herself; even in death, the women of Weston were below the men. Following the funeral, a light lunch was served in the main dining room. It was the first time since the horrible weekend of the graduation party. The cook had been instructed not to be serving any salad greens and to make sure everything was cooked thoroughly. Even so, Emily noticed how everyone picked at their food.

When all had gone and the house was back to normal, it was time for the reading of Robert's will. Without any question, the title would now go to Charles, being the oldest male, along with the estate of Weston and all it included. There wasn't any surprise to that, but Robert had not forgotten about George. He changed his will only weeks before he died. Emily was to remain in the main house as long as she lived and would run the house until Charles chose to marry. George was to have equal partnership in the investment business in London, which made Charles leave the room in a rage. He was able to remain at Weston for as long as he chose, or live at the manor house his parents shared when they were first married. The house would remain George's for as long as he lived. There were funds set up for running the household as well as personal funds for Emily. Emily was surprised that Robert gave George an equal share of the company. The only advantage Charles received from his father's death was the title. He would now be known as Lord Robert Weston.

When all was read, there were provisions for Robert's brother, his nieces and nephews, and even the house staff. Robert set up a small educational fund for Smithy's son, who was Robert's blacksmith and childhood friend. Emily rose and acknowledged all present for the reading of the will and excused herself quickly. The others in the room felt she was emotional, having lost her husband and dismissed her actions as such, but Emily wanted to go to Charles before George did. She vowed to herself that there would not be another commotion as there was during the graduation party. To Emily, Robert had stated his intentions and all must abide by his wishes, without question. She went up the stairs faster than usual but not as to cause notice. After knocking softly on George's door, she heard George walking toward the door, saying, "Ok Charles, let's get it over with." Sheer surprise met him as Emily stood there. "Mother, I am sorry—I expected Charles to pay me a visit," he said as he opened the door.

"I'd like to speak with you, George. Please let's sit; over there by the window would be nice." Emily walked over and moved two of the chairs so that they would be facing the window.

George went on talking as Emily closed her mind to what he was saying; instead, she saw the smoldering fire in the distance. She knew instantly what was burning. Emily asked Mr. Pace—whom she trusted to look over the property—to take the bed Robert died in and burn it. This was after she washed all indications of how he died from the bed. The last thing she wanted was for the servants to spread the word of Robert's suicide. To Emily, it was a sign of weakness and would be a disgrace for the family. "What are you looking at, mother? Where's the smoke coming from over there, should we call someone about it?" George said, as he turned and looked at his mother.

"I had the bed burned. That night after they took his body, I washed any trace of blood from that bed, and then I had it burned," Emily said. The trance she was in seemed to break, as George touched her shoulder. "Yes, yes, let's sit down and talk. I have something to say to you, George."

Emily went on asking him to consider what his father had left him. He was equal with Charles in a prosperous business and should take advantage of it, but as she went on about the opportunity he had before him, he stopped Emily from going any further. "Mother, please, I am not interested in the business. I don't want to travel to London and hobnob with a bunch of spoiled brats. I did that all through school. I want to stay here on Weston. If there's any chance I can oversee the estate, I would like to do that, but again I run into working with Charles."

She smiled to herself and said, "Let me deal with Charles."

During the reading of the will, Charles had stormed off. When Emily went to his room, he was nowhere to be found. "Stubbs, do you know where Charles has gone?" she asked.

"From what I know, Sir Charles went out for a ride. I saw him riding his horse toward the old Chapel, my Lady." It was the first time she heard Charles referred to as "Sir Charles." The title was bestowed upon him when his father passed, and now it was his until his death. Emily knew that the old Chapel on the east side of Weston was one of his favorite places. There were times when he would go there and sit for hours. He later referred to it as the place where he felt peace of heart. Emily went to her room, dressed in her riding clothes, and left for the stables. As she headed down the main stairs, she noticed Robert's dog lying on the floor. It was the dog that she had given Robert when he returned from the camp—a small white West Hyland Terrier who was faithful to Robert and no one else. She walked into Robert's room, bent down some feet away from him and patted her hand on the floor, hoping he would come to her—but instead, he just stayed there. "Alright Cotton I will give you some time."

The day was bright and sunny and warmer than the past week. On the day of Robert's funeral, it rained as if the sky had opened. Emily felt it was an omen of God washing away Robert's sins. Her stance on his suicide was clear; she thanked God that only she, the doctor, George, and Charles knew about it. As she rode up the hill, she noticed Charles's horse tied to an old gate. The chapel was the third church built on Weston. The first had been destroyed over 500 years ago by a fire while the old one here was abandoned because of the small size. As the estate grew and the tenants attended the same as the family, there became a need to build a large church on the grounds. As Emily went into the small chapel, she noticed Charles kneeling in a pew with his head in his hands. Emily walked up to the pew and sat next to him. He turned, looked at her, and put his head back down. "I am going to miss him so much, mother. I hope I can fill his shoes, but what if I can't?"

Emily rubbed her hand across his back, "Charles, I have every faith that you will make your father proud. You are so much like him and we both have always been so proud of you."

He leaned over to her and put his arm on her shoulder. "Thank you, mother," he said, as he walked to the door. He stopped before going out and turned to her, "Why did you burn the bed, mother? That bed was over two hundred years old."

Not knowing how to answer him, she stated, "The memory of the way your father's died is hard for me to bare,"

The boys had a meeting with Robert's solicitor to work out any problems between the business in London and the overseeing of the estate. Emily's business during the war had prospered to the point that Weston was a working estate. Cattle were raised along with sheep and other small farm animals. On the far end of Weston in the lower valley, farming produced an abundance of crops. If it had not been for Emily's ingenuity, Weston would not stand as it had in the past. It was with this extra income that Robert was able to invest in real estate after the war, and the investment had paid off.

Robert's suicide had brought back painful memories to Emily. Some years after her marriage, her mother had committed suicide. Her father had the papers say that she died from a long-time illness. The funeral was only attended by close family. Her father who lived in London had remarried shortly after. When he visited Emily before his upcoming marriage, he brought the woman with him to Weston. It was quite a surprise that she accompanied him. As Emily walked into the library that day to see her father, she was not only surprised by her father bringing the lady, but by the fact that she knew her. She had been married to her father's partner in his business in London. It wasn't until after the marriage, that she found out that her husband had died of questionable circumstances. It was the last time she saw her father, who died several years later.

Still, even after working out the business aspect of Weston between the boys, there was a tension between Charles and George. Charles returned to his flat in London the next day and George took to his new duties. His excitement was evident and he seemed happier than ever before. Emily worried that Robert's suicide would affect him. The image of Robert haunted Emily's dreams for some time. Her nights were filled with restless sleep. One afternoon, she visited Dr. Wellborn about her sleeping problems. He listened to her intently and then prescribed her medication. "That's the same medication my mother took, I'll think I will pass," Emily said, having left out that it was the same medication she took to commit suicide.

"Well, I suggest you get out more, exercise, keep your mind on other things and your body strong. The only other thing is to get away from Weston—go on a vacation. You deserve it!"

She knew he was right, a vacation was the one thing she had not had. Her recent correspondence from her cousin Clara mentioned visiting her in Ireland. She married a nobleman after the war and was living in Northern Ireland on a large estate in Tyrone County. The estate was just outside of the city of Dungannon. It would be a great change of scenery and Clara was always entertaining. George was able to run the house while she was gone, so she called Clara that evening and made arrangements to leave the next week. She seemed excited about her visit and told her that her eldest daughter was announcing her engagement soon. She asked Emily to plan on staying for at least a month, for the parties. Emily thought she would stop over in London to do some shopping and then proceed to Dungannon the next day. Charles decided not to stay in the flat owned by the family; instead, he used one of the apartments in a building the business owned. He wanted to be closer to his office and a larger space.

Emily took the 6 am train out of Canterbury to Victoria station. The train was nearly full with those going to London for work. While it seemed like a long ride to get to work, many people preferred living in smaller towns and worked in London. Just getting away rose her spirits, and she loved the hustle and bustle of London. She knew she should have called Charles the evening before but thought that she would surprise him instead. She did call the housekeeping service in time, to take care of the flat before she arrived. At the station, she paid a valet to take her bags to the taxi station, thinking it would be best to get settled this morning before going to Harrods for a buying trip.

Emily laughed when the attendant picked up her empty suitcase, not realizing it was so light. "Sorry, sir, I should have told you about the empty case, but I plan on filling it today," she said as she laughed.

The flat was musty from having been closed so long even though it was cleaned the day before. The first thing she did was to open some windows to get fresh air moving. She noticed some furniture missing and thought Charles possibly took some items for his new space. There were so many reminders of Robert around—pictures from his childhood and a large oil painting of him around the age of three was hanging over one of the fireplaces. Of Emily's two sons, George favored his father most. Her stomach growled from hunger so she decided to have a late breakfast on the way to Harrods. She knew of several tearooms on the way to the store but decided to stop in one of the store's tearooms instead. Dr. Wellborn suggested exercise so she decided to walk. The day was clear, and there was a slight chill in the air. Knowing the temperature would be colder in Ireland, a new coat would be in order.

The streets were busy with everyone going someplace in a hurry. Emily went up to the third-floor café and ordered a pastry with a cup of coffee. The table she chose was in direct view of the elevator. A woman offered the morning paper to her as she was leaving. Settled in the seat, she started reading the news and enjoying her coffee, when she felt a presence near her. When she looked up over the paper, she saw him smiling down at her. It was the gentleman from Copenhagen, Michael Callahan. "It's nice to see you, Lady Weston; may I join you?"

At first, Emily thought him rude, but she decided to say yes. As he sat across from her, she was again mesmerized by those blue eyes. He asked her how she was and it took a while for her to answer. "I lost my husband several months ago after a long illness." His face changed expression, telling her he had heard and was sorry about her loss.

After drinking his tea, he started to tell her about his life. "I come to London frequently for business. During the war, I worked with the US government in shipping, and I work in that same area, but I now own my own company." He went on and told her about all his travels. Emily told him she was going to be visiting her cousin in Belfast and had stopped for some shopping in London beforehand. She said she needed to excuse herself and needed to hurry since she was meeting her son.

On her usual trips to Harrods, she was fitted by the seamstress for each outfit but since time was short, she purchased clothes sized for her, forgoing the fittings like before. Apparently, this was the new way of doing this. Emily was to meet Charles for dinner that evening. He asked Emily about bringing a close associate. Emily thought maybe it was someone from his office, which was odd. She preferred to be with Charles alone. It never occurred to her that this would be someone special to Charles.

Emily dressed for dinner and was directed to a table, somewhat away from the dining room. As she looked up from her table, she saw Charles and a young lady coming toward her. "Good evening, mother; this is Louisa May Baxter; Louisa, this is my mother, Lady Emily Weston." Emily extended her hand to which Louisa responded. Charles did most of the talking as Louisa either smiled or nodded her head. She was a physician practicing psychiatry and mostly working with those injured in the war. When speaking, she seemed very intelligent and very poised but she would not fit with Charles, being a commoner. Emily hoped their relationship would pass.

Louisa excused herself earlier than Charles, because of an early commitment the next day, and Charles rode back with Emily to the flat. "Charles, she seemed like a nice young lady. I am sure you realize that friendship should be all between you both. You must remember who you are and the position you have, which will not allow you to marry a commoner."

Charles remained silent, walked Emily to the door, and said, "I am in love with Louisa and plan to marry her. I know my position, mother, but I want a happy marriage!" He turned and left. Deeply hurt by what Charles said, she hardly got any sleep. But when Emily thought about her past years with Robert, there were really not that many good memories—most were stressful times.

Emily took the train to Liverpool in order to take the ferry over to Belfast. She was booked in a separate compartment on the train which catered to the upper class. Her bags were numerous, and she noticed the porter mumbling about carrying them. From there, she took a car that was previously arranged, to the port of departure. Never before had she endured such sickness. The weather outside was rainy and windy; she dared not go out on the deck as the waves washed water over the boat. The sickness came early and lasted throughout the voyage. Looking completely disheveled, she made her way to the waiting car and Clara's smiling face. As usual, Clara was her bubbly self; she talked the entire way to her new husband's estate—some two hours away. Emily did not have the strength to answer, and when she tried, Clara would interrupt her. Finally, when reaching the large manor house, she looked in amazement at the estate. She had never seen such beauty. The grass seemed to be greener than any other Emily had seen with the shrubbery neatly cut and exquisite gardens as far as you can see.

"Let's get you a nice, hot bath and I have a lady's maid to help you arrange your clothes. We will be having dinner in the morning room, and you will get to meet my Morris. Emily heard from friends that Clara's husband was quite a bit older than her. Someone even used the word ancient to describe him. His land was acquired from his brother who was in the House of Commons. As she walked into the main hall, she noticed the mounted heads of game animals from hunts on the property. Emily surmised there were several hundred. As her lady's maid escorted her to her room, she spoke incessantly like Clara but faster. All Emily could think of was getting soaked in that warm water and resting her eyes.

She woke up to see Mary in her room, opening up the curtains to the bright sun. Emily instructed her of her choice of dress and accessories. After getting dressed, Mary showed her to the morning room. As she walked in, she noticed the table is ready, but there was not anyone to meet her. Emily walked over to the large lead windows and stared at the beauty in front of her. In a way, she missed Weston but she promised herself to relax as the doctor said. As if in a dream looking at the estate, she felt a hand touch her shoulder. "Who are you?" Morris said.

Clara was entering the room at the time. "Oh, Morris, I told you Emily will be staying with us for a while." Emily turned and looked at the elderly gentleman. "Emily, come sit by me," Clara patted her sofa. Morris was still standing and Emily noticed that Morris had been tall at one time, his thinning hair was pure white and his eyes were a grayish-blue. He walked back to his seat, and Clara ran over to help him sit. The estate was larger than Weston, with half of it being forest. Clara was getting ready to have an engagement party for her daughter. Clara's daughter, Elizabeth, was working in London as a bank loan officer, where she met her fiancé who was the vice president. Clara said he was somewhat older than Elizabeth and had been married before. "Thank goodness there are no children involved," Clara said. The party was to be the next weekend. There were people coming and people going out, prior to the party—Clara spared no expense. Elizabeth was Clara's only child; when she was married before, they told her she was unable to have children, which was a hardship for her marriage. Her husband was notorious for having affairs, three of which Clara knew about. As soon as they entered an event, Clara could see ladies' hands covering their mouths, talking about him. It got to the point that Clara stopped attending events with him, but that did not stop her—she tagged along with her friends. A few times, she saw him with other women, so she asked him to let her know where he would be in order to avoid embarrassment. Clara became a widow at 38 and married Morris the next year. The pregnancy was a surprise to her as much as Morris, but he was thrilled at having a child.

The last time Emily saw Elizabeth was over 10 years ago. She was always off at boarding school or vacationing with some family friends. When she walked into the room, everyone turned to look. She was certainly a beauty, tall with long, blonde hair and her father's eyes—she was stunning. When Clara and Elizabeth were together, no one else could get a word in; both would ask a question and answer their own question. If you were included in the conversation, you never got to answer. Morris would sit in his chair and fall asleep.

The evening before the party, Emily met Elizabeth's fiancé, Morgan Fairchild. He was a tall, good-looking young man, who was very personable and easy to talk to. His parents were coming as well as his close relatives. Clara had a full house. Dinner that night was in the main dining room, with Emily sitting next to Clara. She felt bad for Clara since Morris fell asleep before being served. Clara asked his attendant to let him have his dinner in his room. "It's the only way he will eat if someone feeds him." The men moved to the library for cocktails and cards, while the ladies excused themselves to the music room. The next day, there was a dove hunt for which several women went along. Emily excused herself, but Clara was eager to go. She had been on many hunts with Morris, but when he shot one of the dogs, Clara put a stop to it. Emily dressed in a blue evening gown that accented her eyes. The gown was set on her shoulder with small cap sleeves; she added a set of three-strand pearls accented by a diamond pendant that her mother gave her. She was truly one of the prettiest women there. Clara wanted her to be in the receiving line, greeting the guests. A strand of her hair fell down her forward blocking her sight for a while and when she went to put it back, Michael Callahan appeared in front of her. "I was hoping I would see you again," he said. There was no verbal response—she just extended her hand to him—after a short time, he moved on. She thought herself to be ridiculous. For most of the evening, she tried to stay away from him but he followed her to each room she went in. "Are you avoiding me, Lady Emily?" he asked.

Feeling like a silly schoolgirl, she started to laugh, "You're quite right, sir!" She asked him to call her Emily and agreed to the next dance with him. The party went on until the early morning and Emily stayed the whole time. Michael had been to Dungannon before and was a longtime friend of Morris, both being in the shipping business. He frequently hunted on the estate and showed Emily some of his conquests hanging on the wall. Clara had asked him to stay.

Emily asked to have a plate from the kitchen. The evening was too much for her, so she took a long, hot bath and decided to go for a ride afterward. Mary got her bath ready and Emily slid down into the hot water and almost fell asleep. "Lady Weston, you better be careful; that water is very hot. Look at you, you are all red! I'll be putting some towels for you—just ring the bell when you want me to help you," said Rose.

The peace and quiet felt wonderful as she relaxed even more. "Who are you?" a man's voice said. She woke up to see Morris standing over her.

She let out a scream, and as he was walking out as fast as he could, he ran right into Rose. Rose fell on the floor and Clara came running, helped Rose to get up, and told Morris to go back to his bed. "I am so sorry, Emily. I think I am at the point that I need to hire a full-time attendant; he seems to be roaming a good bit."

Rose helped Emily out of the tub and gave her a robe. "I am fine, he just startled me," Emily said and both the women started to laugh.

"You know, Emily, he's blind as a bat." They laughed so much that they had tears running down their cheeks.

Emily asked the stable boy to saddle a horse for her. He pulled out an old mare. "I need something more spirited, please," she asked. So he bought out a black stallion. "He looks perfect!" She rode over the meadows surrounding the main house and reached one of the hunting lodges on the estate.

There was someone's horse outside, so she started to leave; when she turned around, she heard someone call her, so she turned around to see Michael standing there. He was in his tailored riding coat with a pair of brown riding boots. "Lady Emily, I am so glad to see you after your mishap this morning!" Emily started to laugh and got down from her horse. "My goodness, you picked out one of the best horses they have, and you're able to ride so well?" She told him she had been riding since she was a child. "Let me show you this beautiful lodge," so they went in. All Emily could do was to stare at the many animals on the wall and floor. The entire lodge was decorated from a safari in Africa which Morris attended. There were zebra rugs, leopard skin hanging on the wall, and a full-sized crocodile on the floor. She had never seen anything like it. They walked from room to room, talking the whole time. It wasn't until they stopped in the main front room. She turned around to Michael to say something but stopped—he took her in his arms and kissed her hard. When he pulled away, she kissed him again until she stopped and looked straight into those blue eyes and was helpless.

When they arrived at the house, Clara said she was worried about them, with a crooked smile on her face. "Excuse me, I'll go up and dress for dinner," Emily said.

The next week, Michael and Emily spent almost every day together. Clara found someone to attend to Morris, so she and Elizabeth went to London for a few days to get Elizabeth fitted for her wedding dress. "Emily, we will back on Wednesday and I believe Michael said he wanted to do some hunting, so I told him to use the lodge as long as he wants to," Clara said while raising her eyes. Emily could hear her laughing as she was leaving. Michael and Emily spent their days between the two houses. During the day, they would ride, have picnics near the river, and dinner near the lodge's fireplace. Emily asked that they keep it discreet, to the point that they never spent the night together. As each day went by, she found herself more in love and feeling so differently than she felt for Robert. Her love for Robert was more of a duty than love. As her years had gone by with Robert, she had hoped it would change but it never did. When she went to the lodge, he would be outside, waiting for her. There were times when she barely could get off her horse; oftentimes, he would carry her to his bed. She felt that she could never get enough of him, which in a way scared her.

Clara stayed in London longer than she expected, which gave them more time together. Emily knew this could not last because their lives were so different. He was to leave the next day, so they planned to dine at a small Inn in Belfast. "When will I see you again, Emily?" he asked.

She really did not know how to answer him. "I'll have to let you know," she answered. Emily explained how she felt about Charles's plans to marry someone Emily thought unsuitable. Michael was quiet the whole ride back; when he walked her to the door, he kissed her and left. She stayed awake all night; she thought about things and decided to get up at dawn to see him. She noticed first his auto was not there, and when she went in, all his belongings were gone. She went to her knees and cried.

Clara was coming home that day and Emily did not want to face her—not so much of any shame, but Clara was not exactly someone to have a serious talk with. So, Emily asked for her meals to be served in her room. She told her lady's maid, Mary, to deliver a note to Clara when she arrived home. She told Clara that she was not feeling well and wanted to rest. Emily knew she could hide in her room for long; the next morning, Clara was knocking on her bedroom door. "Oh, Emily, are you feeling any better? I know Michael left yesterday and is that why you are upset?" That was all it took Emily to burst out into tears and she started to tell Clara about everything that happened.

Emily said she could not think of what she did to cause such a change in Michael's behavior. "What were you both talking about beforehand?" Clara asked. Emily said she was telling him about Charles's relationship with Louise and how she was against their engagement. "Well, Emily, he probably thought you felt the same about him!" Clara said. "You're upset with Charles because you think he's marrying below himself but think about it—he thinks you feel the same about him."

Emily said she loved Michael and would do anything for him. "I need to get in touch with him but don't know how to do so. At least, I can explain how

I do feel. You know how to find him, don't you?" The only address Clara had was Michael's company's address.

Emily wrote a note to Michael about how sorry she was and how she felt. She had Clara read it. "Emily, did he tell you he loved you?" With all their time, he never told her he loved her; she took Clara's advice and left the strong emotional feeling out of the letter. When she handed it to be posted, she thought that maybe this wasn't what she thought it was.

Morris was having trouble getting along with his attendant, so Clara suggested going to Dublin so she would be able to get another attendant. She had a good friend that worked in that field and wanted to find someone who qualified for the post. When Morris started to forget himself, she started with nurses to take care of him, but Morris would try to touch them in certain places—as they put it—so they would walk out. When she had younger men doing the job, Morris would constantly yell at them so she needed someone with experience. "We can stay for a night or two and do some shopping if you would like to?" Both Emily and Clara thought the trip would do them some good.

After a long train ride, they had the porter call a car for them and they checked into the Castle Hotel. Clara's appointment was that afternoon at 2 pm, so Emily was on her own for the afternoon. "Emily, promise me you won't get lost," Clara said as she kissed her on the cheek. As she walked down the street, she found a tearoom and sat by the window to watch the people walking by. After finishing, she continued the walk down through the city streets, looking in windows until she came to one where she saw the bed. Emily stayed outside, looking through the large glass to see the beautiful large bed. It had four large posts, each one carved with vines and flowers; the head post had larger flowers intermingled with different farm animals, all of which came together to a grand piece of furniture. Emily had never seen anything like it. She walked down and went into the main entrance.

As she was walking around the separate rooms looking, a gentleman from the other side of the store came walking toward her. "May I help you, madame?" he asked as he extended his hand to her.

"Yes, I would like to see the bed you have in the front window." He asked her to follow him, and they walked down a hall into the room where the bed was. "This bed was made by a local furniture maker. Is it not one of the grandness pieces of furniture you have ever seen?"

As he was describing the bed, her thoughts went to Robert's bed and the horrible night of his death. The bed she had burned. "Yes, sir, if we can come to a suitable price, I would like to purchase the bed," she said. He explained that the furniture maker may be still in town and he would see if he could get in touch with him and call her at her hotel. It may not be today, it may be tomorrow. Emily walked back to the hotel and told the desk that she was expecting a call from the store.

Clara came back several hours later. They decided to have dinner in the hotel since they were tired from their trip. Emily told her about her outing and the purchase of the bed. "Well, you have a house full of beds; why would you buy another one?" So, she told her about Robert's death in that bed and that she had it burned. That night, the two women poured their hearts out about Clara's first husband and his infidelity, and Emily's days with Michael. By the time they went to sleep, they had had two bottles of wine delivered and it was two in the morning.

Both women were holding their heads, complaining to each other about who had the worse headache. A bellboy knocked on the door, saying he had a note, which he slipped under the door. The note said that the furniture maker, Paddy Finnerty, is there to meet Lady Weston at 1 pm that afternoon. Emily and Clara decided to go down to get breakfast before their meetings. Clara was going back to interview some attendants for Morris. After a large breakfast and several cups of coffee, Emily walked down to meet Mr. Paddy Finnerty. When she walked by the window she noticed a young girl in the room with her arms wrapped around one of the posts, as if to hug the bed. She started to wipe the tears from her eyes. When Emily walked in, the girl looked surprised and said, "Are you going to be buying my mother's bed?"

Just then, the salesman walked in with a middle-aged man. The girl stood up straight and apologized to Emily. "My dear, that's ok. Was this your mother's bed?" The father told her to excuse herself and turned to extend his hand to Emily. When Emily shook his hand, she noticed how rough his hands were.

"This is Lady Weston; Lady Weston, this is Paddy Finnerty!"

Paddy went on to apologize for his rash behavior. He explained the flowers on the bed along with the story that is told about the animals and forest on the bed. He pointed out the animals on the headboard, passing through the forest. As Emily looked at the headboard closely, she could see what he was telling her. Then, he went down to the footboard and explained the footboard animals, coming out of the forest with their little ones. Paddy explained that the bed was like a puzzle and needed to be put together like a puzzle. He would need to do that for her. "I do have a question, Mr. Finnerty; did your wife die in that bed?" Emily was not superstitious, but she wanted to know. He told her that his wife was murdered and killed in their barn while he was not at home. He decided to sell the bed since it brought back so many memories of her, and it was hard on his children. "I am from an estate outside of Canterbury. I will pay for the shipping of the bed and you setting it up in my home." They decided on a date of shipment and passage for Paddy along with passage home.

"My lady, may I request that my daughter accompany me? She is familiar with the bed and can help me," he asked.

"Certainly, that would be fine," Emily remarked.

Emily was to leave for London the next day. After taking a short train ride to Belfast, she would board a ferry for Liverpool, then take another train to London. She was planning on staying at the flat for a while before going home to Weston. She hoped she could have dinner with Charles, but his business kept him traveling, so it was hard for him to make time. Emily called ahead to notify the service that she was going to be staying at the flat. After her note to Michael, she was hoping to hear from him, acting like a schoolgirl waiting for a note from him. She tried her best not to worry about it. Finally, she heard from Charles; he was to meet her at the flat so they could go to dinner together. When he arrived, they talked for a while without mentioning Louisa. Emily hoped he had forgotten about her. The restaurant was down a block from the flat. It was small but served very good food. Charles ordered a bottle of wine and ordered for his mother. When the wine was served, he said, "Mother, I have something to tell you. I have given Louisa an engagement ring, the one grandmama left me. I hope you will embrace this. I love her and plan to marry her in the spring."

Emily was getting ready to say she was disappointed by his decision, but she remembered him saying that his parents' marriage was a loveless marriage. He was right, and then she thought about Michael. "Charles, I will support you, I promise."

Before she left Clara's, she was handed a note with Michael's address on it. Undecided, she thought about not going to see him, but she felt she should apologize in person for being so insensitive. That morning, she went to the salon she used before, had her hair cut, makeup done, and got a new outfit. She decided to walk instead of using a cabbie. As she walked down the street, she noticed a sprinkle or two, then the whole sky opened. After forgetting her umbrella, she was soaked, her hair was frizzy, and her makeup was washed down to her new clothes. She stood under a store entrance and almost cried. When she wiped her eyes, her hands were black from the makeup. Trying to find another handkerchief while digging in her purse, she heard someone say, "Can I help you?" Blinking her eyes, she realized it was Michael.

He took a cloth and wiped her eyes the best he could. "Come with me, Emily, let's get you cleaned up. I don't live too far from here and the rain is letting up," Michael said. "I saw you—from my office—walking down the street, then the rain started, so I thought I would come and rescue you," as he started to laugh. His apartment was on the top floor with large windows in every room. It was extremely modern but tastefully done. "If you want, I can have your clothes cleaned. I can have some clothes delivered if you tell me about your size? But first, you can dry off in the room down there and I will get you a cup of tea," he said. Emily wanted to clean up as soon as she could. She went to the room he was talking about which included a large tub, a shower, and a built-in sink with mirrors around the entire room. She had purchased a new dress and coat that matched the dress and shoes that matched it all. Her coat had protected the dress somewhat, but the shoes were ruined. She tried to brush her pair, but the weather made it difficult to get a brush through it. She washed all her makeup off, put on some lipstick she had in her purse, and took off her stockings. When she walked out, she was barefoot with her hair curled around her face. "Emily, you're beautiful!"

They sat as she sipped her tea. He said he received her note but did not know if she wanted to be contacted or not. She told him about Charles and their recent conversation and about purchasing the bed, but she also included that she had it burned. "Why did you burn the bed?" he asked. Hesitating to explain, she told him about Robert and how he took his life in front of his son, George. She did not want that to get out because of the children. Michael put his hand on hers, "You've not had an easy life, have you?" he asked. Michael ordered a change of clothes for her from a shop across the street. After the clothes were delivered, he suggested they go out to dinner. A limo was waiting for them downstairs, that dropped them off at a waterfront restaurant. They talked through dinner until the hour was getting late and the place was closing. "I'll see you home, Emily," disappointed, but knowing he was right. When they got into the auto, "I have something to ask you, Emily. I have to go out of town to Italy next week and would like you to join me if you could." She accepted right away. He would take care of all the travel arrangements and send them to her next week. As soon as she walked into the flat, Charles was on the phone, looking for her.

The next day, her clothes were delivered and she packed to leave on the next train. So excited about her travel coming up, her mind would not stop thinking about it, until she finally fell asleep from exhaustion. She wished she had time to shop some more for her trip until she remembered that the bed was being delivered the next day. She asked Mary to make sure that the staff had two rooms ready for Mr. Finnerty and his daughter. The next afternoon, she saw the truck coming down the main road. She decided that the bed be brought in through the main gallery because of its large posts. It took three men to carry one post and four to move the headboard. Paddy's daughter came with him and watched as they started putting everything together. "Maureen, why don't you come with me for a cup of tea?" Emily asked.

They went to the morning room on the other side of the house. Winter was almost going into spring and the sky was sunny that day. Emily asked for tea and some sweet biscuits to be set on the round table near the large, leaded window. Maureen was dressed in a pretty dress that accented her auburn hair. As Emily looked at her, she noticed how pretty she was with clear beautiful skin. "How old are you, Maureen?" Emily asked."

"I am 17, my Lady." She said she had completed her schooling, but she was now helping her father since her mother's death.

She wanted to learn to be a lady's maid but felt bad for her father. "Maybe I can speak to your father if you would like?" Emily said. As they were getting ready to go back to the room to check if the crew was finished, George came into the room. "Excuse me, mother, I wanted to tell you that the bed is fully assembled." When talking with them, George's eyes stayed on Maureen.

Maureen and her father stayed the night and were to leave early the next morning, but Emily asked to meet with Paddy before he left. When he came to the main floor, he was shown into the library where Emily was waiting for him. "Please sit, Mr. Finnerty." Emily could tell he was nervous. "I had a cup of tea with your daughter yesterday while the bed was set up. She indicated that she had completed her schooling and wanted to train as a lady's maid. I would like to give her that opportunity if I had your permission."

Paddy looked startled at first. "I do not know of this, she has not told me," he said. "But if that's what she wants and she will get training here, so be it," he concluded. Emily thought him to be angry as he went to leave, but then he turned and thanked her. When Emily went into her room, she was so pleased—it was as if the bed belonged there. Excited about her purchase and knowing that that room would be hers, she started planning the rest of her room. Charles's marriage would mean that they would occupy the main bedroom upstairs.

In a week, she would be in Italy with Michael. She thought she should tell Charles and George about her plans, but Charles was going to be in the US for a week or more. She planned on telling George, but only that she was going on a trip again. Even though she told Charles that she was fine with his upcoming marriage, she still harbored the wish that Charles would change his mind. She asked Mary to look after Maureen and teach her what would be expected of her. Emily thought about going to London for the day to shop for her trip but thought she would just buy clothes when she got there. Michael called and told her he was having the tickets sent to her; he said he wished he would be with her on the flight but would be over earlier for business. Without her saying anything, he said he had reservations for several rooms—they were all adjoining. She was worried about her children finding out so the more discreet, the better.

She asked George over for dinner that night—even though he was living within a few miles from the main house, he was busy with overseeing things. That night, they dined in the library so they could talk. George had grown into a handsome young man that she was so proud of because he did what he wanted to do. If he had worked with Charles, he would have been unhappy. When she told him she was going on a vacation, all he asked was where she was going and to keep in touch. Charles would have asked more questions and wanted a complete itinerary.

A car arrived at the expected time that took Emily to the train to Victoria Station, where a gentleman was waiting with a sign that had her name on it. The bags were carried to a waiting limo and they drove past the terminal to a private boarding on Michael's company plane. When she followed the attendant up to the entrance, she was expecting other people on the plane but to her surprise, Michael was the only one. She went to him as fast as she could as his arms wrapped around her. "I had no idea that you were so wealthy!" she said.

"I had no idea that you were so royal!" he said.

After a full dinner, they arrived in Rome where again, a limo took them to a beautiful villa. "I thought we were staying in a hotel?" she asked.

"I rented the two top floors of the villa so that we would have plenty of room," he said. The next two days, they explored the city. The art was amazing along with the beautiful building. They would stop to eat and drink and then continue on their travels. That evening, they ate out on the villa balcony and talked the entire evening. Emily told him about her marriage and Robert's time in the prison camp. Michael told her about his marriage, with his wife dying shortly after of cancer. He said he poured himself into his work. They made love like never before with closeness she had never felt before. The next morning, he had a meeting at his office there and she went shopping. The weather there was getting warmer and she wanted something that fit with the locals. She bought a diverse number of outfits—from the local, long, full skirts to tailored dresses for the evening. Michael insisted she has the clerk send the bills to his office. She laughed at herself; she was now a kept woman. From a never-been-kissed child bride to this. There was so much to see in Rome, that she thought it would that a month to see it all. During the next week, Emily did not call home; she knew if she called, she would be wanted home.

Michael told her he got tickets for an Opera along with reservations for dinner that night, so she went to one of the shops she had been to before. After trying on a new dress, she went out to the mirror to see what the saleslady thought. While looking in the mirror, she noticed that the lady coming in was Doctor Wellborn's wife from Canterbury. She quickly walked back into the dressing room. The saleslady came running after her. "Can you please tell me if that lady that just came in is still here, and if so, please let me know when she leaves," Emily said.

"Oh, yes mam, I understand," the saleslady replied. Emily thought things like this must happen all the time. It wasn't before long that she purchased her dress along with a large hat to leave. She dared not look around, in case she would make eye contact.

"Michael, I don't want to run into her again." But he assured her that the Opera has been sold out for months and the cost was something even a doctor's wife couldn't afford. He said their restaurant was secluded and their seats were in a separate room. Mrs. Wellborn had been known to gossip and to add a little to the story. When Robert died and Dr. Wellborn attended to him, she told people it was questionable the way he died. Emily was sure Dr. Wellborn did not tell her about Robert committing suicide. Emily had attended Operas in the past in London but this was so powerful. Even though she knew very little Italian, she felt so many extremes of emotion watching this. Their dinner which was after the performance was one of the best she had in Italy. Michael had a list of the guests so he assured Emily she would be good the rest of the evening.

"I have looked into getting a house in Tuscany and wanted to check with you. It is off the beaten path of the usual tourist spots." Michael asked. Emily felt so relieved and agreed they could leave in the morning. The house in Tuscany was high on a hill, separated from the city below. The view of the Mediterranean was breathtaking. The house was furnished with antiques, some hundreds of years old. There were frescos on the ceiling and walls. "I know you are trying to protect my reputation, and you have been so sweet to be doing so, but I don't want to hide how I feel about you so don't worry about it. I love being with you, and I don't care what anyone thinks."

Their days were spent exploring the surrounding areas. The countryside was known for the many wines it produced. The wines were celebrated all over the world. Michael and Emily enjoyed sitting next to the water, enjoying different kinds of wines. Vendors had daily tasting along with many types of bread with different olive oils. They took tours of several vineyards in the area; some invited them to their homes. The harvest was coming up and Michael asked if they could help in any way; he learned how to correctly cut the grapes off the vine as Emily joined in on the smashing of the grapes. "Look, Michael, my feet are purple," she joked. From the first day there, she shopped at the local shops, she adopted the local way of dress. Her skirts were full and long while her blouses were large with puffy sleeves. At times, she would even wear sandals like the other women in the area. Michael would comment on how well she looked, and she felt so relaxed and happy. The tension seemed to lift out of her and she was enjoying each day.

"I only have the house until the end of the week since it was a last-minute rental. I'd like to take you to Venice next week, during their yearly festival called Venice Carnival. There are Grand Balls, daily parades, and celebrations in the streets. We will need to have several customs along with masks. Does that sound good to you?" Emily had heard about the festivals during Lent from her father, who went every year, mostly by himself. She told Michael that it sounded lovely and was looking forward to it. When they were getting ready to leave, she went out to look at the sea one more time. Michael came out to join her and brought a bottle of wine with two glasses. "We're going to miss it here, even though it was for such a short time. I promise I will bring you back, Emily."

When they arrived in Venice, it looked like the celebrations had already started. It was in the evening and people were dressed in costumes, some wearing masks. As soon as their bags were delivered, they went out to join the celebration. They found a small café and enjoyed a meal of meats, fish, and cheese. They went back to the villa they were staying in and fell fast asleep. The next day, they went custom hunting and then found masks that went with their clothing. As Emily and Michael were walking down an alleyway to the villa, they ran right into Lucy Wellborn. "Well, well, Lady Emily and?" Finally, Emily introduced Michael to her. "What, pray tell, Emily are you in Venice for?" she was asking while looking at Michael the entire time with raised eyes.

"We're here for the Venice Carnival! It was nice seeing you, Mrs. Wellborn. Please excuse us!" Emily started walking away as Michael hesitated and caught up with her.

"Emily, are you alright?"

Instead of answering him, she just started to laugh. "You know, that felt so good." The next day, there was a note waiting for them at the desk. They were invited to one of the largest balls in Venice. Michael ran into one of his friends from Copenhagen the night before.

The next several days, Michael and Emily were busy going from one party to the next. One of the rooms was filled with several costumes. There wasn't any hiding that Emily was there and it was only two days before the phone rang, with Charles on the phone. "What are you doing, Mother, running away from home?" She laughed and said yes. "I need you to come home, I am getting married soon and we need your help. I need your help!" She knew the time was coming to go home. Michael was in the shower; she put down the receiver and dropped her robe and joined him. With the shower coming down on her face, he could not see the tears coming down her cheeks. The girl that was so modest, to the lady who was playing her role in life, who was now a woman, who gave her everything to this man.

The next morning, she got up from a restless night to watch the sun come over the horizon. Michael knew she had a bad night and stood there, watching her from a distance. Not knowing what, he went out and sat next to her. "Emily, you have something on your mind, I can tell," he said. She looked at him with sad eyes. "You have to go home, don't you?" He picked her up, put his arms around her, and held her tight.

"I don't want this to end," she said.

"It's not over, I promise."

The next day, she got a plane out of Venice to London. Michael said he had to stay to finish up some business and would be flying back to Rome to tie up some loose ends. Emily rested her eyes while on the flight. When she arrived, Charles was at the gate, waiting for her. She did not know what to expect when she saw him; he was so much like his father, he would probably start off scolding her. But after giving her a kiss and saying he was glad to see her, he simply started talking about the wedding. He said he was going back the next day and had reserved a cabin for them on the train. She asked if she could go to the flat since she was extremely tired. So that night, she fixed a bath, lingered until it turned cool, put on a robe, and fell asleep quickly. The phone rang early the next morning with Charles reminding her about the time. She quickly got up, dressed, packed only one bag with the clothes she brought with her and went out the door.

She sat for a while in a small café down from the flat, until she saw Charles's car go by; she paid the bill and went out. Charles was knocking on the door of the flat. "I'm here, Charles!" There was hardly a word spoken on the train; he told her he was worried about her because she looked tired. Emily felt as if the happiness of the past month had left her. When she arrived at the house, the servants were there to greet her. Charles was only home for a few days. He said Weeza would be coming the following week to go over plans. The couple passed on having an engagement party for the announcement—instead, it was announced in the local paper and all the London papers. Weeza's parents were deceased and the only immediate relative was her sister, Eleanor, who was several years older than Weeza. To Emily, the engagement had so many aspects that were not fitting with the customary protocol.

Charles mentioned that he thought they should have a small wedding with only immediate family and close friends. They wanted to get married in the chapel on the Weston Estate and have the reception at the house. He asked Emily to help guide Weeza but keep in mind that it was her wedding. "Charles, I intend to let her do what she wants to do," Emily answered. The following week, Weeza came home with Charles for a few days to prepare for the event. Emily went over every aspect with her and to her surprise, she was very easy to please. Emily even recommended a bridal house in London to make her dress. Together, they picked out invitations, colors for the flowers, and food for the dinner afterward. The day she left Weston, the entire wedding was planned.

Whereas the length from an engagement to the ceremony itself was usually several months, sometimes even a year, for Charles and Weeza it was only four months. There were several parties given by relatives and family friends beforehand. During this time, Emily did not hear from Michael; there was only a note saying he was glad she got home safe. Charles did not ask his mother about her time in Italy, the subject never came up… Weeza asked her sister Eleanor to come early the week before. Weeza said she was older than her and was married to a US ambassador. Eleanor and Emily somehow seemed like old friends. Weeza attributed their ages being close as the reason. Eleanor was very prim and proper as she had to be with her husband, being in his position, but she was very easy to be around. She would easily give her opinions as to the ceremony and to everyone's surprise, Emily agreed with her.

The wedding was a success after all of Emily's worries. Family and friends seemed to approve of Charles's choice; only a few seemed to have a problem with marrying a commoner. Weeza was a beautiful bride and Emily could tell by her actions that she truly loved Charles. Eleanor vowed to come back and visit soon; she even asked Emily to come to stay with them. Eleanor's husband was older than Eleanor but was a very kind and gracious man. After the many people staying at Weston and the house staff being so busy, it was nice for Emily to get back to a quiet time. She was glad to get back to her bed and rest. Emily let most of the staff off for a few days except for the cook and her lady's maid.

She seemed to sleep for hours—when she woke up it was after 12 pm. As she reached up for the pull to summon Mary, a sharp pain caught her on her right side. She stayed still until the pain subsided, thinking it was just the way she moved around, having to twist her. Emily sat on the side of the bed to reach for it again but only had a little ache. She wanted to call George to ask him to come for dinner that evening. When she went downstairs, she was surprised to see him there. "Our two minds are thinking alike, George." He said he came by to ask her to come over that evening; he wanted to speak with her about something. She agreed and he left without even sitting down. Perplexed, she wondered why he was so serious about his agenda.

When she saw Stubbs, she asked him to summon Maureen since she wanted to see how she was doing with her new position. “Sorry, my lady, she is not here today.” Feeling that odd for such a devout worker as she was, she simply passed it off as being ill.

George had spoken with Emily’s driver about her going to Brighton House that evening. When she came down, he was waiting for her. George was at the door when she exited the auto and led her into his study. She was surprised to see Maureen sitting in a chair next to the fire, folding her hands as if she were worried about something. When Emily came in, Maureen stayed seated without looking up. “George, please tell me what’s going on with you and why is my maid here?”

“Mother, I ask one thing. I am going to speak to you and I would like you to listen first, please. I guess the easiest way to say this is to tell you I am in love with Maureen and plan to marry her as soon as possible.” As Emily went to speak, George stopped and put his finger up, as if he was telling her to let him finish what he was going to say. “I wanted to tell you that we are having a child. I am going to do this, no matter what anyone else thinks!” At that point, Maureen started to cry.

“This will not be the first time that a member of a prominent household gets a maid pregnant,” Emily said.

George stood up, “She is going to be my wife, and I am going to take care of my child. I think you are missing the point, Mother; I love her deeply. I don’t think you know what love really is since your marriage was arranged when you were a child.” Emily’s mind went to Michael, and then she remembered when Charles said almost the same thing to her about his marriage to Weeza.

It was decided that George was to get married in the small chapel on the estate, with the new pastor agreeing to marry them. Maureen was several months pregnant with the birth being around Christmas. Charles and Weeza returned from their honeymoon after George and Maureen’s wedding. Charles’s first reaction was very much like his father would react. He claimed George had ruined the family name. Emily was hoping Charles would come around to accept his brother, no matter what. Weeza arranged for the doctor to see her in London and to make sure everything was going on schedule. Emily was glad Dr. Wellborn was retired and there was a new doctor in Canterbury—Dr. Gibbs was young and was trained in the latest medicine of the time. Maureen was nervous when Emily was around and was always so quiet, so Emily decided she should have her over for tea. She instructed the staff about this and told them she did not want to see one sour face in front of Maureen. After she walked away from telling them that, she could hear the laughter so she went back into the room, put her fist on the table, looking at each of them and walked away without saying a word.

When Maureen came that afternoon, she was dressed like a lady with a lovely hat. George had taken her to London for new clothes. Emily grabbed her hand and walked with her to the east room facing the garden. When a servant came in to serve them, she behaved as if she was serving a lady. Emily smiled at her and thanked her. "I have been afraid to see everyone I worked with," she said.

"Don't worry; if anyone treats you unkindly, please let me know. When you here when your father delivered the bed, you were a child—that's why I wanted to use this room for our tea. You have moved your stature to a lady." That evening, Emily felt better about the situation and was happy to have a grandchild coming. Charles was distant at first but seemed to be getting used to the circumstances.

Michael was constantly on Emily's mind and she was upset that she had not heard from him since their trip to Italy. She decided to go to London for a few days; she was planning on going by his office to see if she could catch him. After she arrived at the flat, she went to Harrods's salon for a cut. Her hair was always so thick and wavy, but of late, she had noticed a few gray hairs so she wanted their opinion. The girl told her she had so few, she would give her a cut that the grays were blended into the style. When she left, she had her makeup done by one of their artists and her hair styled. She went downstairs to shop and ran into Clara. "Oh, I was going to give you a ring; come, let's have tea, I'm staying in London tonight at Elizabeth's."

Emily noticed that Clara was not her chatty self; she wondered if she was alright. Clara asked for a table in the back and as they walked there, Emily said, "Clara, what's wrong?"

She said she called Michael's office and was told he was in a plane crash on his flight from Italy and was seriously hurt. Emily started to cry silently. "They said he was going to be fine, but she said he did not want any visitors. Emily, calm down—at least he is going to be ok."

When Emily went back to the flat, she felt exhausted from her day out. It was only late afternoon, and she wanted to go to bed. She decided to take a long bath and go to bed early. She ran the water in the tub and let it fill to almost the top. When she got in, she slid down, closed her eyes, trying to relax until she felt the water up to her chin—she was startled and sat up. As she looked down into the water, she noticed she was bleeding from below. The blood was bright red and she knew her time had long past thinking something else was going on. She rose from the tub and put on the robe hanging near, but when she went to climb into bed, the sharp pain she had before came back to a point that she went to her knees. It was a while before she could get up, and when she did, she was still bleeding. Her first thought was to go back home, but she wasn't sure she could make it, so she called Weeza. When she told Weeza about what was going on, Weeza told her to stay there—she would come to her. She asked her to stay off her feet and raise her legs up. Weeza took the next train in, which was faster than driving. During the next two hours, Emily's pain came back; each time it did, she would pull her knees up to her chest until it subsided. When Weeza arrived, she said she had made an appointment with a doctor who would see her this evening. "He's a friend of mine and will be glad to see you as soon as possible." Weeza helped her get dressed, combed her hair, and even help Emily put her shoes on.

"Weeza, what do you think it is? Do you think it is my appendix?" She told her that they needed to wait until the doctor examined her.

The doctor's office was in the lower part of the hospital. The walls were painted white as was the doctor's office. He was waiting for them when they walked in. "Lady Weston, so glad to see you," he said to Emily. She held her hand out and told him that Weeza was Lady Weston—she was now referred to as Dowager Emily Weston. He turned and walked into his office and sat down behind a large, sterile-looking metal desk, asking her to follow him to the examination room and put on a gown that was open in the back. Emily was clearly embarrassed with Weeza helping her, but she could not do it herself. The pain had lingered on to a constant ache but was not as bad as it once was. When she was flat on the table, the doctor came in and pulled the gown up to her waist. He began feeling all around her stomach and stopped at one point when she gasped as the pain hit again. "Ok, I'm sorry if I hurt you. I am going to send you up to have an x-ray and I want you to stay here tonight until we see what's going on," he said.

She protested and said she had never been in a hospital before. She had her children at home. He seemed not to care and was sure she would be fine. She was to stay on the gurney while they wheeled her upstairs. The x-ray room was a large room with large machines, that moved around to take the pictures the doctor was talking about. After moving around for several pictures, they brought her up to the third floor to a private room that Weeza had requested. "I'm sorry, Weeza; I know you would like to be home with Charles," Emily said.

Weeza told her not to worry, she was going to be staying tonight at the flat and Charles was coming in on a later train to be with her. "He's so worried about you, Emily." She kept the tears from her eyes. Charles was so much like his father, never showing any emotion—she felt that Weeza must have changed him.

Her night started out being a sleepless one, due to worrying about what was wrong, but the nurse came in and gave her a liquid to drink, and she was fast asleep within minutes. When she woke up, Charles, Weeza, and George were standing by her bed. Charles spoke up, "Mother, the doctor is going to come in and go over the results from the x-rays. We just wanted to make sure we were all here for you." Weeza helped her by putting the bed in an upright position and arranging her pillow.

Before she could say anything, Dr. Martin came into the room. Nodding his head to everyone, he said, "Lady Emily, as revealed in your films, you have a large mass on your left side that needs to be removed as soon as possible. I don't know if the mass is malignant or not, but it is blocking your intestines. The intestines are not fully blocked but will be if not removed. I have set up an operating room at 11 am today to do the surgery."

Emily felt that could not be happening, he must be wrong. "Are you sure, doctor?" she asked.

Charles was holding her hand, but George left the room. "Mother, I can get George for you," Charles asked. Emily shook her head no and told the doctor to proceed. After what seemed like a short time later, they came to wheel her to the operating room, and before she realized it, she fell sound asleep.

Her memory left her until two days after the surgery. The only aspect of those two days was the pain. When finally awake, she told Weeza she wanted to see her stomach. Weeza lifted part of the bandage and showed Emily. "I am cut from top to bottom, aren't I?" she asked.

Weeza told her that it was a large tumor and the doctor did what he had to do. "Emily, I will be there for anything you need, and I promise I will get you through this."

Here was someone she was so against for so long, and she promised she would be there to help her. "Thank God for you, Weeza!"

Emily was in the hospital for almost two weeks before letting her go back to Weston. Her recovery was without problems, except for her mental state—she was deeply depressed. Weeza was true to her word; she dotted after her and tried to keep her busy with walks around the gardens. But it was George that helped her through it most. He would come by in the late afternoon, before going back to Brighton to Maureen. They would talk about the past and about what they hoped for in the future. Emily would talk about Michael and things she never told Charles, or anyone else. George told her he loved Maureen the minute he saw her. When he came in to check on the house while Emily was on her vacation, he found Maureen standing by her mother's bed—she had been crying. After that, he came by to see her in the evenings. "I know you don't think that this was right for me, but I love her so very deeply." At times, Weeza could hear her laugh. Slowly, Emily gained back her spirits, mostly for the help of her family, but also she vowed not to be like her mother. It was hard for Emily to understand how her mother could take to her bed for the rest of her life. When she mentioned it one time to Clara, she said she thought it to be more related to Emily's father's behavior than just depression.

Emily was due to a doctor's visit to London, so Weeza went with her to the doctor's office. Dr. Martin said he felt he had gotten it all, but in telling Emily about her illness, he never mentioned the word cancer. Her visit was short—he examined her abdomen and asked her some questions. After examining Emily, Dr. Martin went out to speak with Weeza. "This was a very fast-growing cancer—if you could keep an eye out for any pain and if so, please bring her back. The tumor had grown from her ovary and started to invade her bowel." To Weeza, Dr. Martin did not sound too positive.

With the tree changing to fall color, Emily started riding again. Slowly at first to be careful and get her strength back, but then she was riding like she used to. As she came back one afternoon, she noticed that an auto was coming down the drive to the main house. She did not recognize the auto but decided to go back to the stable, in any case. As she was dismounting, she heard Weeza's voice. "Emily, there's someone here to see you. It's a gentleman, Michael Callahan. Do you want to see him?" Weeza asked.

She told Weeza to have him come out to the stables. As Michael walked in, she couldn't believe the difference. He was thin and his hair was now gray, but the thing that struck her was that he was wearing a jacket, that on one side was sitting on his shoulder. Emily knew he had been in a plane crash, but she did not know the details. "Michael, it's good to see you," she said as she walked up to kiss him on his cheek. They walked out of the stables back toward the main house but stopped in the east garden to sit on a bench.

Emily learned Michael was severely injured to the point of losing his left arm. He was in the hospital for months and received therapy for several months after that. He said he sold his company and was living in London right now. "I know I promised you I would see you again, Emily. I was trying to get back to you," he said. His voice quivered as he was talking. She stopped him and told him she was planning on going by his office when she was in London but got sick and had to have surgery. He looked surprised; she thought Clara would have certainly told him. She asked him to come into the house, but he said he needed to get back to London. Michael told her he did not feel easy about getting out as much, but he had to come to see her. When he was leaving, he kissed her softly and said he would be in touch.

One evening, the telephone rang and it was George, calling to tell her Maureen had had a baby girl; Charles answered the phone at first. As George told him about it, Charles put the receiver down and said Emily had a call. After Emily put the phone down, she asked Charles if George told him. Charles looked at her and shook his head. As he walked away, he muttered, "What have we come to?" Emily was beside herself with anger. Weeza was standing in the next room and heard his remark. After Emily left, she remarked to him that their circumstances were not that much different. She hoped he would change his feelings.

The following week, Emily asked if she could see the baby and was to go to Brighton that afternoon. She was surprised to see Maureen up and dressed. George said, "Come, Mother let's go see my beautiful daughter." He was so happy, smiling and enjoying the occasion, The couple stood over the cradle, holding hands and gazing at their little one. "Mother, we want to ask you something," and as Emily nodded George asked, "Would you mind if we named our daughter Emily?" Tears welled in Emily's eyes as she felt so blessed. Her full name was to be Emily Catherine Weston and she was baptized two weeks after that. Her father came to the ceremony along with two of Maureen's sisters. At first, Paddy Finnerty felt out of place and somewhat embarrassed but after a few cocktails, he seemed to enjoy the occasion.

As soon as spring arrived and the weather turned somewhat warm, Emily Cate was outside with her Grandmama. Emily enjoyed every minute they were together. She was getting ready to turn a year old and was walking a few steps. Emily bought a pram at Harrods along with outfits for the next few years. Charles had come around, somewhat, with George but Emily suspected that maybe he was jealous of his brother. She hoped both having children of their own would bring them closer. Weeza's sister, Eleanor, came to Weston to stay in between her husband moving to a new embassy. Eleanor and Emily acted like they knew each other for a lifetime. It was during the time of Eleanor's visit that Weeza announced she was pregnant. Emily was so happy to hear that—she would have two grandchildren. She thought surely it should bring the two brothers closer. While she was sitting watching Emily Cate, Eleanor walked out to sit with her. The child was playing with the acorns from the oak tree as she tripped and fell down. Emily got up and went to pick her up. As she bent down to pick her up, a sharp pain grabbed her and she had to put her down before she went down too. The pain was one she remembered, the same as before. Eleanor ran over to her and asked her what she could do. Emily Cate started crying from the excitement around her. When Emily got her breath, she told her to take the baby in and tell Weeza. "I don't think I can walk without help." Weeza came running out along with Charles to help her get to the house.

"Emily, I am calling an ambulance."

"Maybe I will be alright, get me to my bed." They put her in her bad and still called. They called Dr. Martin, who said they needed to get her to London. Charles made arrangements for a private train car for Emily with Weeza staying by her side. They gave Emily some medication to help with the pain until she arrived in London. There was an ambulance waiting for her at the station and before she could wake up, Dr. Martin had scheduled her surgery. X-rays revealed her cancer was back and had spread to her spinal cord. The pain was coming from a blockage in her intestines that he hoped could be relieved by a dissection. The operation would relieve some of the pain but it was only a matter of time after that.

Emily's pain did subside for a while, but now when she had her granddaughter over to the main house, she asked one of the maids to help her. One afternoon, shortly after George dropped the baby off, he came back to tell her that Maureen's dad was taken ill and was not expected to live much longer. Maureen felt she should go at once. "Mother, I'm sorry, but I feel that I should go with Maureen. I need to speak with Weeza—is she here?" he asked.

"I'm here, George, I saw you come in and you looked like something was on your mind." George explained to Weeza about Paddy Finnerty being ill and Maureen wanting to go as soon as possible. "I will have the child's Nanny come here also."

Emily was about to speak up but realized she was no longer in charge. "Don't worry about it, George, we would love to have her stay. I think we can manage." He thanked them all, took the baby and said he would bring her back as soon as he booked passage. The train to London would be easy, but then they had to go to Liverpool and take the ferry. Emily was relieved they were leaving the baby home. She remembered her trip and the sickness she had on the ferry.

George arrived with the baby and Maureen, the driver was waiting outside to take them to the train station. As Maureen kissed her child, she had tears running down her cheeks. She was dealing with not only her father being so ill, but also leaving her little girl for a length of time. Emily had a small nursery step up on the same floor as her bedroom. There were times when the cell would take a nap when Emily was watching her. The room next to the nursery was for the nanny, in case she woke during the night. Emily put the child down for the night, checked with the nanny, and took one of her pills for the nagging back pain she suffered from. She fell asleep quickly until someone was shaking her to wake her. She woke up, startled, and realized it was Weeza. Her first thought was Emily Cate, but Weeza asked her to put on her robe—Charles wanted to speak with her. She helped her up and went to the library where

Charles was sitting, wringing his hands, looking down. "What's wrong, son? Please tell me! Charles!"

She noticed he had tears in his eyes when he looked up at her. "Mother, there's been an accident. The ferry George and Maureen were on collided with another ship. Apparently, there was a good amount of fog. They said there are no survivors." After the realization hit Emily, she got up from the chair walked to the baby's room, and sat next to the child's crib. Falling asleep in the chair, Emily Cate woke up and put her little hand out between the rails and started patted Emily. When she first woke up completely, Emily felt like she had a bad dream. She picked the baby up and held her close.

The British Navy was called out to help look for any survivors; when none were found, they looked for bodies instead. George and Maureen's bodies were never found. After waiting for four days, they were declared lost at sea. There was a memorial service in the large church on the estate. Everyone from near and far attended the service. Maureen's family did not attend the service due to Paddy's illness. Emily said she wanted to have her plates brought to her room until further notice. She felt she had given in to illness like her mother before her. One evening, as she sat by the large, leaded glass window, she heard the door open. "Mother, it's Charles; I came to check on you. I'm sorry it's taken me so long to get here." He turned and pulled a chair over to her, "I have been extremely upset and wanted to tell you I am sorry for my behavior," stopping to hold back his tears, "My behavior to George. I know I wasn't fair to him, I miss him terribly. I really loved him."

Emily took his hand and lightly stroked his hair back. "He knew you loved him, Charles and like all those who went before us, we will see them again."

Emily's pain was getting worse but she did not complain. Weeza noticed the difficulty she was having just moving around. In the morning, Weeza would check on her and bathe her. Some days, Emily would feel like getting dressed and others, she could hardly move. Weeza increased her pain medicine to injections so it would relieve faster. "Weeza, you take such good care of me, after the bad time I gave Charles about marrying you. I am truly sorry for that, please forgive me."

Weeza answered, "There's nothing to forgive."

As Weeza was leaving the room, Emily said, "I don't think I will be here to see my new grandchild."

Weeza turned and said, "Of course, you will."

Eleanor decided to stay awhile with her sister. To her, the family needed help with Charles being too upset about George and Weeza being pregnant. Eleanor would take Emily Cate out to the oak tree as her grandmother did. She would sit and rock her to sleep. The child's future had not been decided yet.

Eleanor worried getting too close to the little girl for fear she would have trouble leaving her. As she got up from the wicker rocking chair under the tree, she felt an odd sense that someone was around—she turned, looked around, and saw no one. That evening, she visited Emily in her room and prayed with her. She noticed how much better Emily looked; her eyes were clear and bright, she seemed calm and peaceful.

The house was quiet that night—not a peep from anywhere. The usual cracking and groaning of a house as old as Weston was somehow silent that night. When the door opened, there was no sound; when the massive door to the garden opened, there was no wind blowing in, and so moved the small feet across the graveled driveway to the lush green grass, down to the meadow below. The chair did not creek but simply rocked back and forth.

The next morning when Weeza came to check on Emily, she was not there. She went to the lavatory to see if she was there. Unable to find her, she told the staff to search the house, and she was nowhere to be seen. It wasn't until the groundsman came in yelling—she was in the chair under the tree. Everyone went running outside, trying to see if she was there. Emily sat in her rocking chair with her hands holding her mother's Bible. She looked as if she was sleeping—her head was tilted to the side against the old chair and she was dressed in a white linen gown. "She looks so peaceful, Charles," Weeza said.

"Yes, she does," he replied.

Emily was buried next to her husband Robert in the family plot. The family and close relatives gathered afterward. During the ceremony, Weeza noticed the man that came to visit her in the back of the church, so she went over to him after the service and introduced herself. "Your name is Michael Callahan. Thank you for coming. You meant a great deal to Emily, she loved you deeply." His eyes welled up and he nodded his head. He turned and walked away. Weeza knew how much Emily loved him from the talks they had before she died. She told her of their travels and time together. He was the love of her life.

Eleanor asked Weeza several times about Emily Cate. With everything happening, the fate of the child had not been decided. Weeza said she and Charles would raise her. One afternoon, Eleanor told her she needed to discuss a matter with her before she left. Weeza assumed she had something to discuss about her moving back to the states. So, they both sat down in the library to have tea one afternoon. She noticed Eleanor was nervous at first. "Eleanor, I'm the one always fretting about something; what is it?"

Eleanor put her cup down, tightened her lips, "Ok, I'm just going to come out and say it. I want to adopt Emily Cate! There, I said it." Weeza was without words, she never thought about Eleanor wanting to take the child. "That way she will be still with family—well, in a way."

Weeza told her she had no idea she was thinking about adoption. "I'll have to bring this up with Charles," she said.

"What will you have to bring to Charles?" he said as he entered the room. Eleanor was very convincing as she spoke with Charles. "I don't know if maybe Maureen's family would want to raise the child. I would rather her have the opportunity you or I could give her. Let me speak with my solicitor about this. I'll have him handle this." Eleanor thanked him and called her husband about it. Eleanor's husband was 10 years older than her but seemed excited about the idea. After a few calls were made and the papers were drawn up, the solicitor called Maureen's family and spoke with one of her sisters. He learned that Paddy Finnerty died the day after he heard about Maureen's death and they had just come back from the burial. The family wanted to know who was going to be adopting Emily Cate. She agreed to the adoption, providing Emily Cate knew who her parents were. When Charles got off the telephone, he told Eleanor the conditions she would have to agree to. Her husband was to arrive that evening and she felt that he would be fine with the family's request.

Phillip Abbot arrived at Weston around half-past eight that evening. Eleanor and Weeza were waiting for him. Eleanor was beside herself with the anticipation of adopting little Emily Cate. The next day, they signed the adoption papers and two days later, they were to leave for America. Phillip's new assignment was in Washington DC, but he was more anxious to get back to his beloved city of Charleston SC. The afternoon before they left, Weeza said she had something they were forgetting. She took them to Emily's room and told them of the history of the bed. Paddy left plans for the dismantling of the four-poster bed and instructions to the assembly. Phillip was so impressed by the craftsmanship, he said he planned to buy a home in Charleston and he would make sure the home had a room to accommodate the bed. Weeza said the bed was made by the child's grandfather for his wife, Cate.

The next morning, Emily Cate started her new journey with Eleanor and Phillip. Her clothes were packed for shipment and she was dressed in her rose-colored coat, matching hat and Mary Jane shoes. She was walking now, and as Eleanor put her down, she started to point over to the large oak tree. Everyone was surprised to hear her say "rock."

"She remembers Emily rocking her in the chair. Eleanor, I will have the chair shipped to you," said Weeza.